KARMAYOGINI

KARMAYOGINI

VIJAYA JAHAGIRDAR

Translated by

SANGITA SOMAN

Mehta Publishing House

✆ +91 020-24476924 / 24460313 / Mob. No. 9545000513

Email : production@mehtapublishinghouse.com

Website : www.mehtapublishinghouse.com

KARMAYOGINI by VIJAYA JAHAGIRDAR

Translated in English Language by Sangita Soman

Email : author@mehtapublishinghouse.com

Publisher : Mehta Publishing House
1941, Sadashiv Peth, Madiwale Colony,
Pune 411030. INDIA

Printer : TRINITY ACADEMY FOR CORPORATE TRAINING LTD.

Cover Design : Mehta Publishing House

Price : ₹ 350.00

Publishing Date : March, 2017

P Book ISBN 9789386342560
E Book ISBN 9789386175267
E Books available on : amazonkindle Apple Books Google Play Books

This story, of a luminous personality
Dedicated to
The sunshine of my life…
My girls…Ketaki -Mihika
& Anagha
Mohana, Sharvari and Ashwini

Undoubtedly … ***Aaji's*** legacy will continue…

Preface

All through my growing up years in school, in Maharashtra, and even until much later…whenever anyone asked me if my mother was a working woman or a home maker, I would say, "She is a writer". People then would be ever so curious to know her name and the mention of 'Mrs. Vijaya Jahagirdar' would make them exclaim in awe! "Oh! She is your mother?"…they would ask me wide-eyed…and I would say a simple yes and move on…not understanding the excitement of all those Marathi literature enthusiasts!

As I stepped into my thirties, I slowly began to fathom the work to her credit. She had published more than 25 books by then [now over 50!]…she edited a weekly…wrote short stories…novels…poetry…puzzles & brain teasers for children…and so much more! She dabbled each time in a different genre and fashioned commendable work. But for me…she was my mother…that's all…a mother, who writes in all the free time available to her. In fact, I remember, every day when I returned from school …she would wait for me to have my snack and freshen up. Then, she would swish out this piece of paper with a flourish and look at me. I would instantly know, that it was her 'literary creation' for the day!

She always wanted to read out her writings to me and seek my first reactions and suggestions! I could still wriggle out of the short stories and novels...citing overwhelming homework! Poems were much shorter and quicker to deal with! For the puzzles though, I would hide under the bed! But she was not a lady who would give up easily...she would find me under the bed. I remember solving a few of those with her looking upside down at me with a sense of triumph as I cracked the riddles!

Many years later, after I became a mother myself, I realised that I never gave her the appreciation that a mother looks for, from her daughter. We were all, no doubt, very proud of her literary prowess and encouraged her in every way. In fact, my father was her most ardent fan but a mother always wants something extra from her children... and one day, I decided to give her that little extra appreciation.

I had seen her work very hard, researching the life and times of Ahilyabai Holkar...scanning every detail available in every library, accessible to her. Those were not the days of the internet. She had to physically visit Indore and other places where Ahilyabai's existence was etched as a golden period in our history.

This translation of one of my mother's favourite works, is my way of appreciating, her remarkable achievements in her literary journey of life. An inspiring tale of Ahilyabai Holkar, a lady, known to be deeply religious and exceedingly philanthropic. But what needs to reach people, is the story of her courage...her determination and vision...her sense of justice...her diplomacy in the times of war...her security systems...her self-confidence...her statesmanship ...her loyalty to the Peshwas and her integrity...her love for her subjects...the improvement in the water systems and growth of trade and commerce...the list is truly interminable!

In my own humble way, I join hands with my mother in her endeavour, to carry the inspiring tale of an extra ordinary lady, who was well ahead of her times...A lady who weathered a stormy and tragic personal life with grit and pluck. The untimely death of her husband, Khanderao...the loss of her 22 year old son, Malerao...the death of her grandson, Nathoba. While grappling with the sorrow of these demises, she still tussled to save eighteen women of her family from the wicked tradition of Sati...including her own daughter Mukta, whose husband fought a losing battle with Chlolera.A life fraught with personal tragedies was hers to bear...

In the era she lived in...it was not just tough, but unheard of, for a woman, to make a mark in the male dominated political set-up of our country...Read on to know more about an extra ordinary life...the life of Karmayogini- Ahilyabai Holkar...

Some significant people / relatives in the life of Ahilyabai Holkar.

Subhedar Malharrao Holkar: Ahilyabai's Father-in-law

Gautamabai alias Baiji: Mother-in-law

Dwarka and Bana : Other wives of Malharrao Holkar

Harkuaai alias Harkunwar : Malharrao's 'wife'-Khaandarani: A woman who marries the sword and is thereby referred to as the person's wife. Though she was in effect, Ahilyabai's (step) mother in law, she was only four years older than Ahilyabai.

Khanderao Holkar: Malharrao's son and Ahilyabai's husband.

Oodabai and Sitabai: Malharrao's daughters. (Ahilyabai's sisters-in-law)

Malerao Holkar: Ahilyabai and Khanderao's son and the heir of Holkars

Mukta : Ahilyabai and Khanderao's daughter. She was married to Yashwantrao Phanse.

Yashwantrao Phanse: Ahilyabai's son in law.

Nathoba Phanse: Mukta's son, Ahilyabai's grandson.

Maina and Peerta : Ahilyabai's daughters-in-law; Wives of her son Malerao.

Balabai and Gauri : Wives of her grandson, Nathoba.

Mahadji and Shahaji Chaundikar: Ahilyabai's brothers.

Ranoji Chaundikar (Shinde) : Ahilyabai's brother

Shahaji's son. Her nephew.

Anu : Ahilyabai's brother's granddaughter.

Tukoji Holkar: He is supposedly said, by some historians, to have been sired by Malharrao Holkar. There is no evidence of any adoption. We consider him as one of the Holkars. After the death of her son, Malerao, Ahilyabai protected the rights of the Subhedari by declaring Tukoji as the heir. She had established a mother –son relationship with Tukoji.

Santaji Holkar: Tukoji's brother.

Bharmaldada Holkar: Malharrao's 'daasiputra' (Son from a daasi) [Daasi is a lady employed as domestic help in the palace]

Rukhmabai Holkar: Tukoji's wife

Kashirao and Malhar: Tukoji's sons.

Radhi : Tukoji's concubine

Yashwant Holkar: Son of Tukoji and Radhi.

Bapu Holkar: Tukoji's nephew (Son of Tukoji's brother)

Jayappa Shinde and Dattaji Shinde (Scindias) : Sons of Ranoji Shinde who was Malharrao's friend and ally.

Janakoji Shinde: Jayappa Shinde's son

Office Bearers:

1. Gangadhar alias Gangobatatya
2. Anyaba Palshikar
3. Mukund Hari
4. Raamaji Yadav
5. Ganesh Vitthal
6. Sharifbhai
7. Paarashar dadaji
8. Appaji Jagdev
9. Raajaaram Ranchhod
10. Raoji Mahadev
11. Visaaji Shaamraj
12. Keso Bhikaji
13. Govindpant
14. Naro Ganesh...and a few more

The Peshwa Lineage during the time of Ahilyabai Holkar:

1. Bajirao Peshwa: (1700-1740)
2. Nanasaheb Peshwa: (1720-1761) : Son of Bajirao and Kashibai
3. Madhavrao Peshwa: (1745-1772): Son of Nanasaheb Peshwa
4. Narayanrao Peshwa: (1755-1773): Narayanrao was the third son of Nanasaheb. His elder brother Vishwasrao died in the third battle of Panipat. His second brother Madhavrao succeeded the throne after his father's death. (Bajirao's brother Chimaji appa's son Sadashivrao bhau was also killed in the third battle of Panipat). Narayanrao's murder is known to have been plotted by Raghunathrao and his wife Anandibai.
5. Sawai Madhavrao Peshwa: (1774-1795/96) : Son of Narayanrao born posthumously (Ahilyabai passed away during his reign)
6. Raghunathrao Peshwa – He was Nanasaheb's younger brother, Madhavrao's Uncle. The infamous family feud between him and Madhavrao Peshwa is an unfortunate page in history.

PART I

1734

It was early one morning. The soft rays of the rising sun diffused an orange glow. The dark silhouettes were receding, gradually defining something extraordinary. The palace of the Holkars was lit up with hundreds of oil lamps...the aroma of exotic perfumes drifting through the palace decorated with fresh flower trimmings. Golden yellow flowers in intricate frills on the ceiling, soft red petals carpeting the hallways, large pillars detailed with elaborate, colored glass patterns, and amidst all this, in the centre of the palace was little Ahilya, expertly negotiating the gathers of her dress and deftly creating rangoli [1] designs on the ground…the mud settled by spraying perfumed water, lending a canvas for her to showcase her art. Not too far away from her, Oodabai and Sitabai were observing their sister-in-law, effortlessly create magical rangoli designs.

"Vahinisaheb!" [2] exclaimed Sitabai, "when did you ever learn to make such delicate, pretty designs?"

"Oh! You are always very generous in your praises, Taisaheb", [3] replied little Ahilya demurely.

"Not in the least! Father always says...Ahilya is our lucky charm...It is her good providence that has brought us this Subhedari [4]…"

An embarrassed Ahilya smiled and said, "Now ...now… that's an exaggeration! My father-in-law is far too courageous and capable to ever need any lucky charms! Taisaheb, he showed Syed Ali Hussein his place, put Muhammad Shah under siege…He apparently ensured that Dawood Khan, Daya Bahadur, Muhammad Bangash and their armies bite the dust!" Oodabai looked at Sitabai …

"Ohhh ...How do you know all this…our parents seem to indulge their daughter-in-law…share stories with her…nothing with us…." Though Oodabai said this in jest, Ahilyabai sensed that she had made them feel unimportant. She quickly moved in to mend the situation.

"Not at all!! But when Mamanji, [5], describes war stories, I just get so fascinated by them that I forget everything and just listen… riveted to my seat…captivated by the electric atmosphere…I too want to ride a horse…fight a battle… valiantly like my father-in-law…I believe his dedication and valor is being recognized today…The Bajirao Peshwa has bestowed this Subhedari on him…

Oodabai and Sitabai exchanged disinterested glances and hurriedly pushed to change the topic!

"Let's go", said Sitabai… "what we need to worry about is putting up the decorations..!" They all nodded in agreement and hastily resumed their work…there was indeed a lot to accomplish.

All the doors of the palace were curtained with fresh flower garlands…huge drapes stretched from one pillar to the other…soft velvet carpets were spread lavishly on the floor…beautiful chandeliers, the typical clear and colored glass lamps, hanging from the roof, created kaleidoscopic sprays on the walls…the plain, fresh, silk sheets, of the Indian seating on the floor were complemented by embellished crisp bolsters….the preparations were in full sway!

In the sanctum sanctorum of the palace temple, the royal

priests, Raghodas and Antoshastri, were chanting prayers rhythmically…everyone was busy...

Little Ahilya was focusing on the banana leaf decoration…tying one stem of the leaf to each of the legs of the traditional low table, the 'chaurang' which was barely 10 inches high…the altar of all auspicious rituals.

Little Ahilya was distressed that she could not tie the stems right. Sitabai saw her struggling with it. "It is only a banana leaf stem, Vahinisaheb…Do not expect it to bond straight…" But Ahilya was unhappy. She said that she believed in doing things right…doing them well.

"Well…in that case, Vahinisaheb, ensure you take good care of our brother, the young subhedar too!" …said Sitabai ,rather mockingly.

Ahilyabai looked at Sitabai wondering… 'take good care?? What does that mean? What was I expected to do? I do not even see him anywhere…who do I ask, about my own husband??Baiji, Mamanji,? Where is my 'husband'?'...She kept wondering.

"Sitabai…do not be unkind to the little girl! Mother and Father are capable of taking care of our brother…she is such a young girl herself...lets go now…" Oodabai turned lovingly to Ahilya and said," He must be in his quarters. Do not worry". She rushed Sitabai from there, leaving Ahilya perplexed about her husband.

'There is such hectic activity...but no sign of her husband'…she thought… 'why is he not included in these celebrations…yesterday she heard someone talk of some potion…what potion could it be…' Ahilya, in her mind, was trying to find her way through the crowded observations …stumbling on some…navigating others…

A loving, masculine voice snapped her out of her thoughts… "Excellent…! Beautiful decorations…I must say!" She turned around. It was Mamanji, her father-in-law…followed by Baiji, her mother-in-law. He looked at his wife and gave an approving nod about their daughter-in-law's aesthetic sense and talent. Ahilya was elated at being appreciated! He continued. "Baiji, you may now request the priests to commence the Puja. Also, may I suggest that you take personal interest in these rituals? The lawyer from the office of the Peshwa will arrive any moment. I have assigned Ranoji Shinde, Anand Pawar and Jivaji to welcome him. But I would be happy if you keep a keen eye on the details…and yes! I want Ahilyabai to accompany me when I receive the Subhedari papers."

Ahilya was embarrassed. "Me?"…she thought… "Why me..?" Why not the young Subhedar...my husband?...a girl sitting amidst the men folk…in the Diwankhana??"She was more confused than embarrassed now…Baiji gave her no time to think or talk. She was whisked away into Baiji s chambers and Baiji helped her drape a rich silk lemon yellow outfit with a striking gold and lush green border…

The colors transported Ahilya back to her village…Chaundi gaon… the thick greenery…the clear stream…and the Shiva temple on its banks…A smile spread on Ahilya's face as she reminisced that day…not too long ago… playing by the riverside with her friends…making sculptures out of sand and mud…giggling…bantering …oblivious to the horses, from a nearby army camp, galloping crazily…unsettling the dust…hurtling towards them. Suddenly there was chaos. The sound of the hooves and dust curtains, closed in on them. Her friends ran for cover. But, little Ahilya threw her arms protectively around their sand and mud creations, and stayed put. The horses screeched to a halt inches away from her.

A mildly reprimanding voice said, "You…little girl…what is the matter with you? Your friends ran to safety …and you sit here? Guarding these mud sculptures? You could have been crushed!"

Little Ahilya looked up fearlessly, she said… "I was taught

that if you create something then you must protect it, even if, at the cost of your life"

The man on the horse, Bajirao Peshwa, who was in his early thirties, was stunned. He looked at his forty year old companion, smiled, and said, "What conviction! What courage! Malharrao, I think, this girl is just perfect to become your daughter-in-law!"

The setting sun of that day brought her straight into this palace from her village...to begin her life, as the wife of Khanderao Holkar, son of the great Malharrao Holkar...

It had barely been a year, in this palace...but the thought of Khanderao disturbed Ahilya...Where was he? How could someone sleep through these celebrations, in his quarters? She pondered... "Wear your anklets, Ahilya...Ahilya...the waist band...Ahilya...Baiji's distant calls tugged Ahilya's wandering thoughts back into the present. Ahilya encased smart femininity in her outfit as she dressed up for the celebrations. She was now to be beckoned, by the people, as Ahilyabai, the young Subhedar's wife.

"Perfect! Now let me make a delicate crescent moon shaped kumkum with the red powder on your forehead." Just as Baiji etched out the crescent, the sound of the bugles filled the air. Conches were being blown ... signaling the arrival of the guests. Baiji hurried towards the Diwankhana. It was packed with people spilling over each other, right upto the main entrance .Baiji could hear the crowds milling around even outside the main entrance. Ranoji Shinde and Anand Pawar welcomed the guests and ushered them inside with great dignity and honor. A few feet down the path, Banaai [6] and Dwarkaai, the two other wives of Malharao performed the traditional welcome ritual, with oil lamps. For just a moment, Baiji felt a pang of jealousy, as the beauty of the two women pierced her heart. Harkuaai was a co-wife too. But surprisingly, Baiji was very fond of her. Harkuaai showered love and affection on Baiji, never competed for

Malharao's attention and certainly never used the fire of her youth and beauty to singe relationships.

'Well', thought Baiji, 'I still hold the title of being Subhedar Malharrao's wife! The other women are mere numbers.' Almost instantly, the thought instilled a sense of pride in Baiji. Ignoring the two beauties, she adjusted her sparkling nose ring, assured the glorious ear danglers and walked briskly to join her husband and pronounce her importance.

Malharrao Holkar looked handsome in the silk and gold outfit. The red silk head gear, the strings of pearl necklaces, the emerald brooch and the symbolic gilded knife, completed his masculine charm. Everybody took their seats.

The ceremony was set to begin. The lawyer bowed respectfully to Malharrao Holkar...looked around, paused and went on to applaud the achievements of the Subhedar…his victories and valor. The wealth and his work for his villagers was unparalleled. Finally, he announced what each one was eager to hear…that Shreemant Bajirao Peshwa has bestowed on Malharrao Holkar, the Subhedari of the Malwa region, along with all the rights to collect taxes as well as access to all the Mahals, [22] in recognition of his dedication and loyalty to the throne of Pune.

Saying so, he handed over the official papers to Malharrao Holkar.

The crowds erupted spontaneously in his praise."Long live Malharrao Holkar!!…Victory be to Malharrao Holkar!!"

He too, responded by respectfully placing his head gear and the family flag on the throne, signifying appreciation of the inheritance from his maternal uncle…and suggesting that, he was merely at the service of the throne…and his people…not above them in any way. He glanced at Baiji…next to Baiji was eight year old, doe eyed Ahilya, watching the ceremony intently. Malharrao walked up to her, held her little finger...turned around, taking her with him. There was stunned silence, as she stepped on the red velvet carpet with him…walking tenderly beside him… her anklets jingled, as if resonating of the success stories that the future held…her waist band exultantly sashaying the accolades that she was to bring to the Holkar dynasty…her earrings shone…as though giving a glimpse of her brilliance…the sound of her bangles were to drown the clang of many a swords…She was to have a strong grip on the administration like her stiff straight bracelet with a definite design…destiny's design.

As the little girl hurried down with her small steps trying to keep pace with her father-in-law's strides…the gathers of her dress, flying behind her…as if foretelling, that she was to unfurl the Holkar flag beyond the expanse of Mawal skies…this girl was, to come to be reckoned as 'Lokmata', mother of the people…the true altruist…Karmayogini! Her green and gold dress ...a harbinger of prosperity and dazzling accolades …

Unknown to what lay in store for her, little Ahilya was enjoying the moment…feeling special… for what she did not know! She followed Malharrao to the platform. Malharrao took the gold tray carrying the authorized Subhedari papers worth three lakhs and ceremoniously handed it over to Ahilya. Everyone present, had mild smiles on their faces…some amused...some appreciative…some disapproving…Ahilya was intrigued. Clueless, as to what she should say or do… She looked up innocently at Malharrao and asked, "What do I do with this? Should I take it away?"

A wave of laughter broke out in the darbar!! The lawyer endearingly mocked Ahilya and said… "Yes! Do take it away…and take very good care of it!"

Everyone gathered there burst into a loud applause…not knowing…that it was indeed a prediction …made unwittingly.

The rest of the day was spent normally, playing around the palace with Oodabai…Sitabai…but her husband, thought

Ahilya...was nowhere to be seen...all through the preparations...the ceremony...nowhere...

Finally at sunset, she asked Oodabai... "Where is my husband??Everybody says he takes some potion and sleeps...what potion?...why?

Oodabai pretended to tease Ahilya for asking about her husband, and then said... "Oh! Look! Baiji is calling out to you. Go! Looks like something important!"

As Ahilya turned to go, Oodabai was relieved that she had managed to squirm out of answering the question. She did not want to be the one, to break the bad news to her...

Ahilya ran to Baiji s chambers. She saw all the ladies there. Dwaarkaai, Banaai, Baiji, helping each other untangle their hair decorations.

"Baiji...did you send for me?" Baiji shook her head...

"You were playing my child...but now that you are here, sit with us for a moment" said Banaai and continued as she unhooked her waistband. "Baiji, I suggest you perform your ritual of driving away the evil eye with chillies and salt...this little girl was looking rather pretty today!" Ahilya felt mighty important and pleased. But she did not forget to call Oodabai and Sitabai to join her in the ritual!

Baiji held salt and red dried chillies in her open palms. It was believed, that, drawing imaginary clockwise and anticlockwise circles in the air, around the girls, with salt and chillies in open palms, cleared the negative aura of human beings...driving away 'evil eye' cast by anyone...

The young girls enjoyed the attention and the importance... suddenly making them feel energized! The older women were contented at accomplishing the task, of protecting their little girls, against any 'evil eye'.

It was dark now. Dinner was over. Little Ahilya was tired. Dwarkaai was putting Ahilya to bed with a lullaby. Ahilya's eyes too, were heavy with sleep .Flashes of the day were going through her head. On the edge of sleep Ahilya was fighting something that seemed to nag her…Oodabai…avoided answering her question…where was her husband? What was that potion everyone was talking about… Ahilya was drifting into sleep…still searching for the answers to her questions….

****

The construction work of a bigger and more majestic palace had been on for the last six years. By 1740 , It was nearing completion. So was Ahilya's education.

Malharrao had made absolutely no distinction between Ahilyabai and the two other sons he had sired, Tukoji and Bharmal. The three of them were given exceptional training in accounting, finances, justice procedures, history, statesmanship, war strategies, swordsmanship, horse riding, self defense, attack… Ahilyabai was brilliant. Her dedication and commitment, remarkable! The 15 year old Ahilyabai was like parched earth, impatiently soaking in every drop of knowledge.

She would occasionally spot Bharmaldada [7] and Tukoji during horse riding sessions. But,never Khanderao. Even within the palace, she could add up on her fingertips, the number of times she had had a chance to converse with Khanderao, in the last six years. But today, it was rumored, that Khanderao was to attend the horse riding class. Ahilya's heart was beating fast… she was excited to catch a glimpse of Khanderao …eager to get charmed by his horse riding …she had resolved that she would not let go of this opportunity to talk to him.

Ahilya reached the ground. She spotted Bharmaldada riding her horse. As soon as he saw Ahilya approaching, he got off the horse and started walking towards her…the horse in tow. He handed the reigns over to her. "I can't wait for today's lesson to begin! How to leap on and off a galloping horse!!That's going to be thrilling!" said Bharmaldada."Come! Let me call out to our Guruji."

"Wait" said Ahilya hastily as Bharmaldada set out to call their teacher. "No…wait…please…I hear Khanderao is expected too? Will you do me a good turn? Will you please convey my message to him? Tell him, I need to have a word with him."

"…Err ..yes..uh..most certainly" … a hesitant Bharmaldada promised tentatively.

In one swift move, Ahilya got astride the horse…seized the reigns and progressed into her practice rounds… galloping… holding back…tightening and loosening the reigns with grace …impeding and stirring up the horse's pace…displaying her adeptness to her Guru but hoping to somewhere impress Khanderao, if he indeed did arrive. Ahilya had been fantasizing their meeting…deliberating the lines she intended to say to him…living and reliving their imminent meeting in her mind…reveling in it…

And from the corner of her eye, she spotted him. She noticed Bharmaldada talking to Khanderao...conveying her message to him…as he looked in her direction. Her heart started beating even faster with the anticipation of meeting Khanderao. But the very next moment, she heard Khanderao crack his whip. She noticed his horse take a few steps back, turn right around and gallop away in the opposite direction. Bharmaldada shook his head and lightly shrugged his shoulders.

Khanderao had turned down her request. This time she felt more insulted than embarrassed. She did not want to face Bharmaldada. She too stirred up the horse and galloped hard towards the palace… the wind blowing across her face, failing to calm her burning ears and stinging tears…

****

The next two months just breezed past. The Holkars moved to their new, stately residence. A majestic palace, that was beautifully lit up, by the best chandeliers and sparkling brass oil lamps. The corridors reflected their shimmering flush in the bejeweled mirrors lining them. The pillars had impressive wooden carvings. Velvet-soft silk carpets, adorned the floor. Ornate four post beds, decked with elegant silk rushes nestled in every room, gave the private chambers a very warm feel. Yet there was just something missing…Khanderao…He was never to be seen anywhere…

"Where was Khanderao after all? Why was he never around?" An awkward, teenaged, Ahilya would not know who to put this question to… Malharrao? He was in his darbar or at his desk, overwhelmed by the burning issues of war, crystallizing peace time alliances or attending to more critical demands. Baiji, was loving …but there was still a distance… Oodabai and Sitabai, she had noticed, avoided the question …

Ahilya tried hard to overlook these niggling questions when one day, something unusual stared at her. She panicked!

Ahilya had crossed the threshold of adolescence and stepped into womanhood. But Ahilya did not know what was happening to her…" Had she hurt herself while riding…" she wondered…She rushed to Oodabai…told her that something grave had probably happened to her…

To her utter surprise, instead of worrying, Oodabai was overjoyed! She hugged Ahilya tight…told her "this was not unusual…but the most normal cycle of nature!" She left the baffled Ahilya there and ran to break this good news to Baiji!

As soon as Baiji received the news, there was as though, a surge of energy within her! She burst into hectic activity! The first message was sent to the glass bangle shop. Within no time, the owner himself came to the palace with decorative baskets full of, colorful, glossy glass bangles for all the women of the palace!

Ahilya was told to sit aside…not touch anything other than her own things. Ahilya now had faint flashes of recollection…her mother too would occasionally sit aside like this…Is this what used to happen to her too…? She was devoured by suspicions.

But no one had the time to answer her questions!

Baiji announced a Puja and celebrations to be held at an auspicious time, twenty days later. Gifts and sweets were being distributed…Invitations for the Puja were being sent to friends and family. A personal message from Baiji was sent to Ahilya's parents and they were invited with utmost respect and pomp.

This was getting too overwhelming for Ahilya…finally she managed to accost Oodabai… "Oodabai…. …what is…all this…?"

"You have been asking about Khanderao all these years…it is time now to meet him…" and she laughed naughtily… disappearing before Ahilya could even complete her sentence…

Ahilya froze. She was reminded of the silhouette of Khanderao galloping away from her…a slight hint of unpleasantness resurfaced. But before it could find strength in her heart, Harkubai arrived there. She sent Oodabai away on an errand and turned to Ahilya…very affectionately...she hugged her…held her face in her palms…looked into Ahilya's bewildered eyes...and said, "You are a woman now. Leaving your childhood behind, you enter the youth of life…the beginning of your marital life. You now carry the enormous responsibility of giving an heir, to the House of Holkars…give us a grandson…bear a son."

Ahilya listened, wide eyed but clueless … "Am I supposed to give you all this…but how? I do not know how to have a son..." Harkubai smiled. "Your mother is coming for the celebrations. Ask her all these questions. She will tell you." Saying so …Harkubai left.

Ahilyabai was thrilled to hear that her mother was arriving! She wanted to see her mother…show her the new palace…more importantly, she wanted to show off, with great pride, all that she had learnt in the last few years…horse riding, accounts, Modi script writing, shlokas, mantras, sword fighting, archery… everything…and so much more. She wanted her mother to meet the courageous Malharrao Holkar, a loving Baiji, friendly and vivacious Oodabai...her enthusiasm dampened when she thought of Khanderao... 'I have nothing to tell my mother about him...', she thought..."But I have many questions to ask my mother ... I am most certainly going to ask about this potion that people drink and sleep all day...why do they do it...? And yes...How does one have a son!!??'

...and her mother arrived.

Locked in many heart to heart chats with her...Ahilya began to make sense of the man-woman relationship...the unification of Shiva and Shakti- the God and the Goddess...as her mother explained to her...the beginning of creation...a divine relationship...a long lasting bond called marriage.

Ahilya was quiet. Serious. Looking away from her mother...towards the corner of the ceiling...intently looking but not seeing anything. She was numbed. It was too much information...she could not fathom. The prospect of entering into conjugal relations with a man she had barely met...hardly ever spoken with...in fact sleeping with a man she did not know at all? If at all, the only introduction of him was the rejection of the request to even have a word with her...

How could this feel even close to anything her mother had described...

Ahilya took a deep breath and nodded. Her mother's words were ringing in her head...The one thing she clearly understood was that, this was the only way to give an heir to the Holkar dynasty...it was her responsibility ...and she had to fulfill it.

She smiled and hugged her mother for a long time...she bent down to touch her feet and seek her blessings. Ahilya's mother tenderly put her hand on Ahilya's head...her eyes moist...a lump in her throat... She shut her eyes tight hoping there was marital happiness in store for her daughter, on the other side of these celebrations. She held Ahilya's hand. Her eyes showering her with love, they were just settling down cozily…when, without warning, Khanderao, unexpectedly, entered their room…looking rather regal in a blue brocade outfit… brooch on the headgear …the pearl necklaces... This was a different look! She had never seen him like this before. She was indeed taken aback…and therefore, after a moment of hiatus…She steadied herself and rose to greet him.

"I do not wish to disturb the Holkar's favorite daughter-in-law! There is absolutely no need to take the trouble of standing up!" …saying so, he forced a mild smile…sought the blessings of his mother-in-law, by touching her feet briefly. Before either of the women could react, Khanderao was out of the room!

Ahilya could not understand why her blood was rushing …her face was flushed…her heart was beating in her throat…

****

2

The Puja started. The Puja was being performed by Khanderao .Ahilya took her seat next to her husband. All through the rituals ,Ahilya had to join hands with Khanderao…This was the first time she had felt his body so close to her's…the touch sending incomprehensible warm tremors of excitement through her. In her mind, she kept going over all that her mother had described to her. The unfamiliar thought of bearing a son was now acquainting itself with Ahilya…

Not for a moment, since the celebrations began a couple of hours ago, had Khanderao left Ahilya's side. He had to hold her hand…touch her forehead…bend down together…turn around each other…come close face to face …as they performed a myriad rituals around the small holy fire…their bodies lightly brushed against each other's… She was beginning to melt in this warm togetherness…

Her heart was racing even as they sat down next to each other at the lavish lunch...served regally to all guests...silver plates and bowls...fresh flower rangolis framing the silverware...oil lamps...incense sticks...rose petals decorations...delectable sweets...

The atmosphere was charged with enthusiasm and laughter...the guests alternating between food and chatter. Everyone having had hearty servings of both...they trickled out of the dining area slowly... feeling heavy and contented...barely being able to walk towards the family room...where the traditional betel leaf wraps were served to all. A beautiful heart shaped green leaf, with a filling of sweet rose petal preserve, folded artistically and tucked in place with a clove.

As a mark of respect, every guest was presented with a shawl. After all, the wives of all the sardars too had flooded the room with gifts...presents...good wishes. The women's quarters , overflowing with light hearted banter ...with naughty subtleties...sexual nuances...all of them teasing Ahilya, who was drifting about, with her senses overloaded, numbing her...barely registering the details...the melee around her just a blur.

The invitees started departing one by one...leaving just the family members sitting around. That was when Baiji brought out the special gifts...a distinguished ruby pink, silk Paithani[8] sari and a strikingly deep green, emerald necklace and bangles to contrast it. But the most attractive of them all was a pair of exquisite armlets. Ahilya was mesmerized by them. She could not take her eyes off them...but when she did, what she saw stunned her further! Her jaw dropped when she saw what her parents had mustered up for her...a heavy gold necklace-earring set and a rich silk sari for Ahilya...an expensive, brocade suit, a decorative brooch and a pearl necklace for her husband. Suitably impressive were the gifts for her parents-in-law, Oodabai, Sitabai...no one was left out.

Ahilya's heart sank. She looked into her mother's eyes...as

if, to question her. Her modest parents were no match for the affluent Holkars... 'How did they manage this...'she wondered... Realizing, that these gifts must have dragged her father deep in debt, the heavy gold set began to weigh on Ahilya's mind...

But Ahilya's mother merely smiled. At the first opportunity to talk to her daughter in privacy, she calmed her down. She put her hands on Ahilya's shoulders and said, "Have faith in the Lord. Don't worry about how we will repay this debt...all this is material wealth, perishable. But what I want you to give me in return is something everlasting. A promise, that your noble deeds be such, that they shall dazzle brighter than this blinding wealth...that the fame of the house of Holkars shines down through the ages. You will endeavor to ensure that the name of this family carves a warm place in the hearts of the people." Ahilya bent down and touched her mother's feet. "May all your blessings come true, mother. May the Lord give me the strength to bear this responsibility..."

Just then Baiji sent for her. Ahilya's walk had changed. There was a lot of weight on her shoulders now.

She entered Baiji's room. She was aghast to see the countless open boxes, containing gold ornaments, displayed on the bed. Each one better and bigger than the other! Ahilya could not focus. She did not know if she should look at Baiji or the boxes...

"Ahilya...I want you to choose one of these for Sushilabai, your mother, as a return gift"

Ahilya instantly understood...this was Baiji's way, in all fairness, to compensate her parents for all that they may have spent on these celebrations. Baiji's gesture warmed Ahilya's heart, but she hesitated. "Baiji..."she said, "I do not understand this. Why don't you decide?"

"Ahilya, you are growing up now. You must understand things ...Quick! Choose!"

Ahilya stood there...confused. ..hesitating...embarrassed to make a choice…debating if she would look greedy if she chose the crescent moon long necklace…or if she would not end up compensating her parents enough, if she chose the leaner ones…

Baiji stepped closer to Ahilya and said a little firmly, "Ahilya, you have to be able to decide…and decide quickly"…Ahilya received a lesson more valuable than all her gifts… as Baiji continued, "Making the right choices and carrying them out quickly is the cornerstone of good administration. Remember you have to imbibe all this now."

Ahilya nodded and went on to dutifully choose one of the ornaments. Baiji smiled. "We are, after all, indeed indebted to your parents for giving away their bright daughter in marriage to our son."

What Baiji said after that made Ahilya restless…

****

It was late in the afternoon. Everyone was resting after lunch. As she lay quietly on the bed in her room, Baiji's words were whirring in her ears. "…Ahilya…you are about to begin a new life with a man , Khanderao… my son. I know you have many questions about him…I have seen them in your eyes many a times. But I have no answers my child. You have to discover them yourself. As a mother, I have been incapable of keeping him away from addiction… to those intoxicant potions that he consumes…Needless to say, all our hopes now rest on you…and the heir that we hope you will bestow upon us…the honor of carrying not just the name of the Holkars forward but even the legacy of this Subhedari now rides on you. It's a lot of responsibility for your young shoulders at this tender age…"She had looked into Ahilya's eyes…held her hands and tightly squeezed them…But Baiji was not smiling…Her eyes were moist..

With every passing moment a new perspective of what Baiji

had said was becoming clear to Ahilya…and each realization was drawing her deeper into thought…every consideration clocking an unknown heaviness inside her…an anonymous apprehension…

The die had been cast…she had to play her best shot with the cards, that destiny had dealt out to her…to come out a winner.

She was staring at the ceiling for a long time…trying to make sense of the thoughts floating around her head…like standalone notes of music…with just one chord out of tune. Every time, any which way she arranged the notes, that one chord seemed to ruin, the otherwise perfectly harmonious piece of music…killing the melody…so jarring to her ears that she would shut her eyes tight…put a pillow on her ears…until she could not hear her own feelings anymore…

Finally after many attempts…drifting in exhaustion…she was drowning into sleep, away from the cacophony in her head.

****

Ahilya woke up with a start to the sounds of the bugles and the dholak…She dragged herself out of bed, peeped out of the window which overlooked the courtyard. She could see the wives of all the sardars, entering the palace, dressed in their fineries…laughing …chatting, with baskets full of fresh flowers… making their way up to Khanderao's quarters…to decorate the conjugal bed. Ahilya's heart sank. She felt a pit in her stomach…

Just then Baiji sent for her. She steadied herself, took a deep breath, freshened up …and charted her path right to the center of the courtyard… drawing from determination and inner strength as she took each step.

As soon as the women noticed Ahilya, they hurried towards her, bringing her gently amidst them...made her sit on an engraved silver chair with silky velvet cushions. Everybody milled around her ...busy beautifying her. Bowls of wet freshly ground henna ...chandan paste...saffron milk were brought out. Baiji arrived with a tray brimming with ornaments and flower petals. Essential oils and perfumes were being poured in oil lamps. The vibrating sounds from the dholaks were diffusing the aromatic whiffs to all corners of the palace. A palace, looking beautiful...well lit...full of anticipation.

Harkuaai, who was earlier known as Harkunwar , merely 18 years old herself, had fallen in love with Malharrao Holkar three years ago when he was on a mission. She took the lead now and settled down with a dholak...rendering love songs. The rest of the women joined in, complementing the chorus ...clapping and swaying with the beats.

Ahilya's eyes were searching for her mother. She spotted her in the blur of a circle of dancing women. She saw how happy her mother was to know that her daughter was in the lap of luxury...better still, of loving in-laws. At every beat, when the dancers bent down, Ahilya focused on her mother... registering glimpses of her mother's facial expressions... happy... contented... smiling... proud... hopeful... relieved... assured.

Ahilya decided. She was not going to ruin this for her. She would not reveal Khanderao's dark secret to her. She wanted her to return to their village, happy and assured. Now, this was to be her journey...alone. She submitted herself back to the women who were dressing her up...

When Ahilya was finally ready, she looked resplendent in the ruby red Paithani...the striking contrast of the deep green emerald ornaments...she looked akin to Goddess Lakshmi.[9]

A traditional ritual of offering five fruits to Ahilya by five married women was done. Grains of rice...turmeric powder and kumkum were showered on Ahilya...symbolizing prosperity, fertility...fructification.

Just then, Baiji noticed Khanderao...with his friends entering the women's' quarters. His eyes red...walk unsteady. Baiji, was infuriated. She stood up and walking briskly towards Khanderao, confronted him. Baiji spewed muffled anger through her clenched teeth, ensuring no one else would hear her... "You should know that entering women's' quarters unannounced, is nothing short of violating the modesty code! I insist that you immediately apologize to the women present here...turn right back and leave. I will not accept any negotiation here."

Baiji's fiery reaction tamed Khanderao's expressions. He bowed to all present there with folded hands...lowered his eyes in an attempt to mend the damage... "I truly and deeply apologize for this breach. My friends... pushed me in here in harmless banter...I had no intention of disrespecting any of you...our esteemed guests. Please do forgive me and my friends."Saying so, he cast a sharp glance at Baiji and turned around to leave the area. Tension was palpable between the mother and son. Just then, one of the ladies flashed an accommodating smile and said loudly, "You are like a dear son to all of us here, young Subhedar! Today is your day! Some pranks by friends are in order...nothing dishonorable in that...Please accept the blessings from all of us gathered here!" A soft murmur of agreement emerged from the women gathered there...and the tension diffused.

Khanderao looked once again at Baiji, rather triumphantly, and said, "Trust, the most respected Baiji agrees with you! Else...everything I do, seems to displease her..."saying so Khanderao and his friends withdrew from there.

Baiji was relieved .She strained a smile and stepped back...knowing more than fully well, that it was only Khanderao's apology, that thawed the situation. Otherwise the disappointing glances of some women had not slipped Baiji's keen eye. Khanderao left feeling affronted but he left an initially aghast Ahilya feeling very differently...in fact, sparking hope in her. 'Apologizing is never easy...' she thought to herself. '...and if Khanderao could do that, then it was nothing but a hint of righteousness in a person.' Her heart felt reassured. In a very strange way, this distasteful episode left behind a hopeful Ahilya...After all he had saved the honor of the Holkars. He did care....

****

The function concluded. People retired to their chambers. Baiji handed a silver glass full of warm saffron milk to Ahilya. "Offer this glass to the young Subhedar...and begin your married life with the blessings of us all! I truly wish, that you both have a long and happy married life...that this etches a new chapter in your life as well as the young Subhedar's...May you bear a son...an heir to the Holkars ...May God be with you always."

Ahilya never felt so tentative about anything in her life before. Her first meeting with Khanderao in privacy...her first night. Her head was a big muddle of feelings...she was panning her thoughts vigorously...she still hoped to cull a few specks of gold dust at least... She knew she was not walking down the rainbow path to find a pot of gold at the end...

She nodded to Baiji, turned around and made her way to Khanderao's chambers.

"Welcome! Lady Subhedar! Welcome!"

Ahilya's heart warmed...the moment she heard the word welcome!

"How lucky am I! The supremely talented daughter-in-law of the Holkars has graced my chambers!"

Ahilya looked up. An ornate four post bed with a gold and purple silk canopy was decorated with a floral umbrella of delicate jasmine flowers...the subtle fragrant whiffs filling up the room as she stepped in. In a fleeting glance, Ahilya saw that the oil lamps were giving out soft aromatic light. Garlands of fresh flowers from the ceiling embraced the pillars right down to the floor. Kaleidoscopic rays from the chandeliers above, beamed colorful glimpses around the room. Small side tables were dotted with filigreed silver bowls brimming with dry fruits…sweets…fruits. And then she noticed something that made a pit in her stomach…a decanter full of alcohol…and a glass carelessly toppled over, by its side.

"Please do enter…Lady Subhedar" Khanderao repeated.

"Please call me Ahilya…you are my lord…" Khanderao roared out laughing before Ahilya could complete her sentence, and retorted, "Me? Lord? This evening did you not witness how I was made to apologize?"

Ahilya sensed bitterness and wanted to steer their first conversation away from it. "May I offer you this warm saffron milk?"

"I have had my fill…of insult in the evening…in front of all the guests. I now have no appetite for anything else. My image is discolored…already…the saffron will not help. What will help the situation is…."…and Khanderao pointed to the decanter of alcohol. "I don't drink milk…I need this..." He took the glass and looked at Ahilya through it. "Let things be transparent between us…" Ahilya missed a heartbeat. "I need alcohol…I am more than certain, that wicked stories about me must have reached your ear…No wonder you never bothered to befriend me.."

"Please do not say that…I had requested an audience with you on the horse riding ground…" Khanderao cut her short. "Yes! To parrot out words of wisdom? Advise me on how I should be more regular with my instruction classes of archery, accounts, Modi script writing…I am fed up of Baiji and father insisting on it every waking moment…and this does not interest me one bit"

Khanderao was evidently troubled, Ahilya tried to soothe him…calm him. She put down the glass of milk and said "Then what interests you? Tell me…maybe I can …"

"I like to play dice, go hunting…drink wine…"

Ahilya was shaking inside. But she tried to maintain a calm

exterior, responding as best as a fifteen/sixteen year old could. "Alright, I will be your partner in the game of dice…go hunting with you…" Khanderao looked at Ahilya with raised eyebrows. "Then …could you please pour me a glass of wine?"

"Yes, but not too much please" said Ahilya and poured half a glass of wine. Khanderao gulped it down before she could even blink. Ahilya was taken aback. This happened thrice. Ahilya was now nervous…her eyes now burning as she tried to fight back tears while pouring the fourth glass. Khanderao stood up…barely…embraced Ahilya …wiped her tears…It was heartening for Ahilya to sense that he was not totally bereft of emotions for her. She wanted to believe that there was a fine young man trapped in the negativity beneath that intoxicated exterior. Ahilya wanted to somehow convey to him that despite what others said…she did not hate him. She was making a feeble attempt to speak but was unable to even whisper. Before she could weave her feelings into a sentence, Khanderao started faltering. He was drunk now. Khanderao fell awkwardly on the bed. Ahilya tried to steady him…only to be thrown off balance by Khanderao's inaudible mumbling… "Shabnam, where are you…come …who are you scared of? Come…fear no one."

Ahilya froze. She was trying to shake Kanderao into consciousness, tears now streaming down, saying, "I am Ahilya…your wife…not Shabnam…who is Shabnam..."

"W..h.o?" fumbled Khanderao. "She is my favorite…my love. You, are Ahilya, the great , the glorious , talented Holkar daughter-in-law! Not like me…the drunk , wasted son…So, Go away!"

Saying so he struggled to open a drawer by the bedside, took out a black tablet…Ahilya was now horrified. "What is that tablet?" she asked fearfully…hesitant to hear the answer…

"Don't you know...I am devoured …by this habit? Of intoxicants? Has nobody told you yet??" murmured a smiling Khanderao sarcastically.

Ahilya was now cowering to a corner…crying in spurts, but no sound coming out…as she saw Khanderao swaying around the room. Not knowing what to do she watched him cautiously until he lost his balance and collapsed on the bed…toppling the glass of milk…now stone cold…unapologetically staining her ruby red sari.

The smell of alcohol had crushed the aroma of saffron. 'Where was that… 'union of body and soul' that mother had told me about…' she thought. She wanted to run out of the room that very moment…She felt claustrophobic in that large room…But she knew she could not run away from this. She had to face this and that she would .She spent so much energy persuading herself… that she could face this daunting situation… that she finally felt drained. She sank into the chair…staring at the ceiling for a very long time until the heaving in her heart weighed her eyelids down…

****

The bugles and the drums started beating at dawn. Ahilya opened her eyes. The early morning gentle sun rays were drizzling in through the carved openings in the walls. On the other side, Khanderao was spread in an unshapely harsh way, on the bed. Her heart started thumping louder than the drums.

She looked at her sari. The part where the milk had spilt last night was shriveled and crusted. She poured water over it and numbly watched, as the saffron milk ran out of the sari. The room looked ransacked. She shut the drawers…put the decanter and glass on the table…the leftover milk in the glass, soured overnight, was stuck to the base of the glass. She looked at it…cleared it out …like her soured hope…

She started collecting her emerald jewellery which she had put on the table next to the chair, carefully replacing it in the velvet case…and her heart missed a beat! The armlets were missing!

She searched everywhere…frantically…under the bed, on the mattress, in the drawer…table…What would she tell Baiji? Lost in thought, Ahilya walked to the dressing room. She freshened up, changed…steadied herself and came down to the family room. She greeted everyone, touched the feet of the elders and sought their blessings. Ahilya reached her mother. Her mother tried to look into Ahilya's eyes…Ahilya wanted to avoid eye contact. She hugged her mother and pasted a broad smile on her face as she gave her a knowing, happy look.

Sushilabai felt relieved at this seemingly good beginning of her daughter's wedded life. She immediately glanced at Baiji and conveyed the message through her eyes. Baiji, in turn, looked up at the sky as if to thank the Lord and hope that Ahilya could reform her son.

Everyone was crowding around Ahilya…teasing her about the night…Ahilya nonchalantly retaining the façade…sometimes smiling…at times avoiding…and most times being cryptic.

Just then Khanderao appeared and all the girls disappeared instantly! Ahilya moved forward to greet him respectfully and whispered... Khanderao looked surprised! "You are greeting a man like me?"

"What do you mean 'a man like me'? No one is perfect…and with the exception of your addiction, I would believe you have the makings of a great man too."

Khanderao was pleasantly surprised! "I had only heard about your greatness…today I am experiencing it…I apologize for last night…deeply and truly apologize"

"I have not breathed a word about last night to anyone…"

Khanderao thanked her impatiently. "I will remain indebted to you forever, for this…had you told Baiji, she would have stripped me of the little respect that is left…How do I repay you for this favor?"

"If you really mean this," Ahilya paused and looked into his eyes… "then I sincerely urge you to free yourself of this addiction, please…" Khanderao nodded. "You deserve better. I am not good enough for you. I promise I will make all efforts. The next time we meet, I will not touch alcohol…meet you, only then" Saying so he patted Ahilya's hand, smiled and left towards the bath area. Ahilya smiled back and was just about savoring the moment when she noticed Baiji rushing towards her, visibly disturbed. She had the velvet ornament case in her hand…

Ahilya knew what was coming. "The armlets, Ahilya, …are missing! Have you misplaced them?"

Ahilya sensed that Baiji was struggling to choose what she should make of it…

Ahilya had been dreading this moment. She felt small, and guilty, that she had been careless about the family heirloom jewellery. Ahilya, as it is, had been traversing a path that made her emotions fragile at every turn …As soon as Baiji questioned her about the armlets… crumbling in embarrassment… Ahilya broke down... apologizing and crying …assuring Baiji she had looked high and low …but had not found them…

Baiji Stiffened. Her face hardened. It was as if something had dawned on her. She patted Ahilya's shoulder…dismissed the servants in the vicinity…and headed straight for the bath area. Khanderao was just stepping out of the bath…dressed up…and reaching for his jacket. Baiji blocked his way. Looking her son straight in the eye…she warned him, "You have squandered immeasurable wealth on your vices. Be warned … never ever touch Ahilya's ornaments …ever."

Khanderao was furious at the allegations made by his mother. "You have demeaned me enough since last evening in front of Ahilya. The only thing now is to strip me and whip me. It would then be complete." Saying so Khanderao stormed out. Baiji stood rooted to the ground. Her angry look, escorting him, right out of the room.

Ahilya's heart was thumping in head…ears…throat…all at once. She never expected the whole issue to escalate in this direction. She followed Khanderao…a safe distance from Baiji's wrath. She called out to him in an attempt to douse the tension… "Are you going out? Can you spend some time with me…?" Khanderao was upset but appreciated her sentiments. "If you want to spend time with me, you are welcome to the other palace. I cannot stay here." Saying so…he left.

Ahilya stood there for a while in the shadow of what happened. She thought to herself… 'Every disgraceful word hurtled at Khanderao was sinking the odds of him ever improving. His respect in this house had to be reinstated…'She had to work on this. Ahilya was serious …lost in contemplation. She turned around…and was startled!

A whole bunch of girls were waiting to surround her…tease her…hear stories of her first night! Ahilya strained to smile …this hide-n-seek of emotions was draining her. She calmly melted into the crowded laughter…

****

3

One morning, a messenger arrived with a scroll… announcing the return of Malharrao after four years. A flourish of enthusiasm raced through the palace…transforming every nook and corner. The palace looked and felt different. Decorations…drums…flower petals…oil lamps….The roads were lined with people waiting to welcome Malharrao and his army.

The flag of the Holkars was now flying high atop the palace…signifying the arrival of Malharrao at the palace.

A constant trickle of visitors kept Malharrao and everyone else busy through the day…files…meetings…papers…

But post lunch, was family time. He made an effort to sit with everyone assembled around him…narrating war stories and updating political developments...sharing wisdom and experiences. "I have fought many battles...Dawood Khan, Nizam, war of Bhopal, Aurangabad, Bundelkhand... Palkhed...Fighting alongside Bajirao has always been a learning expedition. Stretching the limits of courage...pushing the boundaries of determination...His leadership has given rise to many emergent leaders and sardars like Pawar, his brother Chimajiappa, Jadhav, Shindes, Patwardhan, Kadambande... the list is endless. They are the gems in the crown of the Peshwas. Unfortunately, the lackluster administration of Shahuji disappoints me...It is in fact, Bajirao Peshwa who has inherited the legacy of Shivaji Maharaj in the real sense...a visionary and a shrewd strategist."

Malharrao described how he had received a scroll from Bajirao Peshwa describing a threat from Nadir shah of Iran... who was plotting an attack on Dilli [Delhi]. It read... "An imminent attack by Nadir Shah of Iran endangers the very existence of us all...Individually we will fall one by one...but together under one flag we can repeal the attack...United we stand, Divided we fall ! "Vayam panchadhikam shantam" You did study this in the epic Mahabharata...correct? Nadir Shah ultimately retreated." He looked at Ahilya... ...

Ahilya nodded. She was engrossed in listening... fascinated by these stories. She hesitated... "Maamanji, it would be an honor to receive an audience with the Peshwa sometime...Go to the battlefield... Isn't it Baiji? Have you ever been on the battlefield?" Ahilya's eyes were wide with excitement.

"I had been once...to Aurangabad..."said Baiji. But before she could continue, Ahilya rushed her attention back to Malharrao... "Please be kind enough and take me with you...once..."

"Of course!! Why not? Absolutely Yes!" Malharrao responded with tremendous pleasure! He was delighted that Ahilya expressed keen interest in matters of the state. He stood up. He could not contain his eagerness. "My earnest hope has always been to hand over the supervision of the artillery to you!" Ahilya could barely restrain her excitement!Now as she stood up too... Nothing missed Baiji's keen eye.

When Baiji was alone with Malharrao she looked at him…feigned jealousy…pretending to be upset with Malharrao… "Every time I asked you about your battles you have answered me in three sentences… 'We went…we fought…we conquered'…fewer details and even more sparing were the inspiring stories…But the daughter-in-law seems to be luckier!!!"

Malharrao turned serious. "Yes. All my hopes are pinned on Ahilya. About your son…well, the less said the better. She is the future Subhedar…a strong, intelligent, well trained chieftain. That is what I am coaching her to be. She will handle accounts and artillery…be a great statesman."

Baiji nodded. "Do not for a moment forget, that she is after all, a lady. Sometimes I worry…we may believe she is able and competent…but will others accept…" Malharrao cut her short.

"Do not doubt that ever. I have given her the best training…the best education…" saying so, in a bid to lighten the air, he stepped back and bowed to Baiji saying… "Trust me…trust your servant!"

"Stop teasing me…"said an amused Baiji…

"Not at all! I am serious. After all the Subhedari papers are in your name! What does that make me?" The couple laughed heartily to that…

After dinner that day,Baiji asked Malharrao… "So when do you intend to take Ahilya to meet Bajirao Peshwa?" Ahilya immediately looked at Malharrao eagerly. Malharrao sighed. "Not now…this is not the right time…He is very upset."

"Upset? Why would that be so ?" asked a surprised Baiji.

"The whole house …his own people, have turned against him…"

"And why would that be?" questioned Baiji.

"It's a long story…and in the eye of the storm, is a lady…Mastani…daughter of King Chhatrasaal, born out of wedlock, with a Muslim lady…all this goes back to, over ten years…"Malharrao continued, " Muhammad Shah Bangash not only defeated King Chhatrasaal's son , but also defeated King Chhatrasaal himself near Jaitpur. King Chhatrasaal dispatched a distress message to Bajirao Peshwa through his trusted messenger Durgadas. 'In deep trouble. Please come to my rescue'. I was myself with Bajirao, when we received the request. Under the cover of darkness, that very night we marched towards Muhammad Bangash's camp. He was caught unawares …we finished him right there. It was a resounding victory."

"From that moment on, King Chhtrasaal looked upon Bajirao with great fondness and reverence. He awarded one third of his kingdom, additional revenue of five lakhs and, his daughter Mastani, in marriage to Bajirao. This happened in the year 1729."

Bajirao and Mastani fell in love with each other...so deeply, that, Bajirao cannot live without her. He lives in her palace…conducts all official work from there…In fact, he now enjoys an occasional glass of wine and even food prohibited by the Hindu religion, with her…"

Ahilya was reminded of Shabnam…She wondered what could be so magical and special about love that it shrouds logic…defeats wisdom…and distracts people from all other attractions of life…

Ahilya was curious… "Have you seen her…?" She asked her father-in-law. She wanted to know more…

Malharrao said, as a matter of fact, "Ahilya…I say this with utmost respect, you have to see her to believe, that someone could be so delicately beautiful… extremely talented in dance and music…She is probably God's best creation…"

"The controversy is around the thread ceremony that the

Peshwa wants to perform, to initiate the son born to this Muslim wife , into the Hindu religion."

"The entire household is against this. His mother Radhabai, wife Kashibai…and even his son Nanasaheb ,do not support the father…the family members are aghast. The Brahmins in Pune are bitter over this sacrilege. The priests are contemplating a boycott of the event. But Bajirao is convinced that he wants to perform the ceremony. Nothing matters more to my dear friend Bajirao, than Mastani."

Everyone was quiet. Ahilya, one more time wondered about this divine man-woman love…a reiteration of the description her mother had given, before her first night…She thought, "What could be so overwhelming about this union of Shiva-Shakti that you are willing to fight the family…give up the world…" She hoped... she could experience it at least once in her lifetime…

About four to five months passed by…Naseerjung, the son of the Nizam, started playing political pranks. As soon as the intelligence reports of his movements and aspirations reached Malharrao, it whipped up a flurry of activities in and around Indore…recruitment into the army, messages to the sardars, strategies, alliances…infantry…cavalry…crisping up the act…and soon came the marching orders…to leave at dawn, the next day!

Baiji arrived at the main door of the palace to wish her husband good luck and success, the traditional way. She held a silver tray with an oil lamp in her left hand. With her right thumb, she made a vertical mark with red kumkum powder , halfway up Malharrao's forehead…sprinkled a handful of colored rice grains on him and then circled the tray with the oil lamp around his face thrice. The red mark of kumkum in the centre of the forehead was said to improve concentration…the flame of the oil lamp symbolized clarity and wisdom…the rice grains signified prosperity and success…

Just as Malharrao turned to go, Baiji said hesitantly … "Ahilya wishes to accompany you to the battlefield sometime…"

Malharrao looked pleased. He smiled, "Alright. When I think the time is right, I will certainly send for you. I also remember your wish to meet the Peshwa. In the meanwhile, it is time now for you to use all that has been imparted to you. You have to handle all the books of accounts. Keep a keen eye on finances. Be sure to separate personal and state expenses. A successful ruler is the one who knows how to manage the wealth that is earned by the state! That is indeed the fundamental rule to prosperity."

Ahilya pledged to do so with all her honesty and ability.

"You are the chief here now, when I am away… and very soon, even I will be taking my orders from you!" said Malharrao mockingly. Ahilya bent down to touch his feet and seek his blessings.

"Take good care of everything and everyone, my child…"

Malharrao had placed a lot more faith in Ahilya than responsibility. He smiled, got astride the horse and left on his mission.

****

Ahilya stood gazing out of the window…reviewing all that she had learnt in the last few months, under Malharrao's guidance. Being good at numbers and accounting… artillery…raw materials for the cannons…storing and cleaning of arms…payments…receivables…taxes. From sunrise to sunset Ahilya would be busy learning…acquainting herself with new facts ...data…information..

At night though …many a times her mind would drift to the Bajirao-Mastani love story. Khanderao had come to this palace merely twice in the last six months…met up with his father and left…almost as if they lived in two mutually exclusive worlds. She sighed, turned around…and stopped in her tracks. Khanderao was at the door. She greeted him and said… "Wish you had come a day earlier…father-in-law left just yesterday on his mission. He would have been happy to…"

"Well, had anybody thought of informing the son of this family…I would have most certainly come! But I forget that they have found a son in you! You are being trained to take over the Subhedari!"

Ahilya was taken aback! She quickly offered, "I will willingly and utmost gladly step back if you show interest in the work of this State. But you hardly even visit the palace, let alone the official quarters. You came just twice to the palace…and sadly did not even think of me…or wish to see me…"

"You seem to have forgotten my promise…about seeing you only when I don't touch alcohol"

"So have you been drinking…" asked a worried Ahilya…

"Well.., yes!" came the blatant reply…

Ahilya did not want to discuss this further. In a bid to steer the conversation onto a more pleasant note she said, "Now that you are here, let us meet Baiji. In the meanwhile I will arrange for some refreshments and fruit juices for you…"

"My drinks are different…" announced Khanderao audaciously. "So do not worry about that! If at all, worry about my funds. It may interest you to know that I was informed by the treasurer, that, from now on I will need your approval before drawing money on my account…by order from Malharrao Holkar!"

"Please do not embarrass me…All this is yours…not mine. Please inform Baiji and you are free to draw whatever you wish"

"Ohhh…" retorted Khanderao. "So you are not easily going to part with the money. You want me to plead a little more??"

"Please calm down, but I cannot draw money for personal use from state reserves without consulting Baiji."

Khanderao was furious. He stormed towards Baiji s chambers. Ahilya followed, close behind him… trying to keep pace with the stretched strides of an irate Khanderao…dreading an imminent confrontation…

Baiji was sitting at her personal place of worship …a small temple. As soon as she saw Khanderao…she said… "Once my husband leaves…I never know when he is going to return…months…days…years…" Baiji looked dejected as she continued… "He leads a miserably harsh life on the battle field while I am here, wrapped in lavish luxury…"

Khanderao did not know what to say. The moment either seemed inappropriate to discuss money…or maybe Ahilya's presence deterred him. He simply made small conversation with Baiji, enquired after her health and left.

Baiji looked at Ahilya and smiled… "I am so glad to see this small but pleasant change in Khanderao… He felt like visiting his mother…wife…A good beginning…May the lord grant you happiness and success!"

Ahilya nodded. She did not want to disappoint Baiji. Only she knew the real reason behind this visit.

****

The next day Ahilya sent for Khanderao's expense accounts. She was shocked to see that the entire year's allowance was expended in just two months! She knew... she would have to refuse Khanderao's request for more money. She dreaded that moment...it was not going to be easy…

The moment arrived earlier than expected. Khanderao went straight to the treasury. Gangoba Tatya, the trusted accountant, was scared stiff…not knowing what to say...but God was merciful on him as just then, Ahilya entered the room for her routine work. Gangoba Tatya breathed easy. She saw Khanderao…reddened, droopy eyes, spewing aggression, looking pointedly at Ahilya as he spoke "I need my money…just money. And…no advice please. I will not leave without my money."

Ahilya firmed herself. "I will be held accountable for every rupee that is spent in Mamanji's absence. I do not have the authority to sanction additional allowance, over and above the year's salary, which you have already drawn."

Gangoba Tatya did not expect such resolve from Ahilya.He looked at Ahilya in admiration, albeit, a bit fearful... of the consequence of such uprightness...He anticipated retaliation...and sure enough, without a warning, Khanderao snatched the book of accounts...whirled it away and shouted... "Do not try to teach me the rules of the book...and..."

But what was about to happen, was what Gangoba Tatya had not anticipated! Ahilya moved a step closer to Khanderao... looked only at Gangoba Tatya with determination and strongly pronounced a fine of 25 gold coins to the person who just showed utter disrespect towards the State and books of accounts! She gave Gangoba Tatya a couple of more routine instructions and left the office, leaving behind a shocked Khanderao!

Without wasting a moment Khanderao darted towards Baiji's chambers...demanding an explanation for the shabby treatment... "Your favorite daughter-in-law now dares to pronounce a fine, on me...her husband..."he crackled in anger.

"Is there a reason why she may have done that?" Baiji's response clearly reflected her trust in Ahilya...giving Khanderao ample indication of how the battle lines lay drawn...

Before Khanderao could say anything Ahilya entered the room...pleading to Khanderao... "Please forgive me...but if we disrespect the books of accounts, how can I ever inspire discipline? I have a duty to perform..." But before she could finish, Khanderao pushed Ahilya aside and snapped... "Who are you?? You are a no body. My parents are giving you too much importance ...else you are not worth even a dime..."Baiji raised her voice and intervened. "Khanderao, you may be used to women who come, dime a dozen. Remember, that Ahilya is not one of them. Never ever forget that you are talking to the daughter-in-law of the Holkars...and I will wait for the day when you prove your worth and deserve to hold some office in this Subhedari. I have had enough of this… You may leave."

It was heartening for Ahilya to receive Baiji's support … but it was more disheartening for her to realize the damage this would cause her relationship with Khanderao. Ahilya did not want the conversation to end like this. She moved forward in an effort to keep the conversation going… "Please try and understand…If I give you the money, I fail the State. If I do not give you the money, I still fail as a wife. In trying to protect the honor of the state , I am compelled to do this dishonorable act of fining my own husband. Please do not put me through this dilemma again…I have to put public duty over my personal obligation …" Saying so she turned to Baiji with folded hands… "I cannot dispense money from the state treasury…but the gifts that I have received at the Puja…" Ahilya looked away…and continued… "May I request you, if appropriate, to consider giving them to Khanderao? Please?" Baiji thought for a moment…went to the personal vault, took out a few velvet pouches with gold coins and handed them over to Khanderao with a forewarning, "I expect you to pay the fine from this and ensure this suffices for the rest of the year."Khanderao was pleased…Ahilya was relieved…and Baiji …assured.

****

Anyaba Palshikar had returned from Pune. He was the representative of the Holkars at the initiation ceremony of Bajirao-Mastani's son. He had carried gifts…sweets…blessings from the Holkar house to Pune.

So enamored was Ahilya of the Bajirao –Mastani love story, that she could hardly wait to hear of the stories from Pune. She wanted him to report every detail…

He gave sketchy details of the ceremony but the other details that Ahilya heard from him saddened her…in fact upset her…

Mastani, a princess in her own right, given in marriage to Bajirao Peshwa lawfully...embodiment of ethereal, delicate beauty...an ace horse rider...a trained swordsman...an accomplished singer and dancer...of exemplary character... follower of Hinduism...facing so much persecution at the hands of Bajirao's family...simply because she was born to a mother of a different religion... ignored by elders and disrespected by some...denied her rightful place...so much so that , Bajirao's son, Nansaheb, taking advantage of his father's absence, even tried to build inappropriate relations with Mastani. Anyaba had cautioned Ahilyabai that these were stories doing the rounds in the family but no evidence...such stories and even more...

But finally, what enraged Ahilya the most was getting to know that Mastani now, had been tricked into an arrest... Nobody knew where she was...house arrest...or... even...

Ahilya shuddered.

It was said, that, this had escalated to Shahu Maharaj, who had expressed his displeasure over the rumors of Mastani's house arrest. Everybody tacitly acknowledged that Shahu Maharaj's administration was rather weak...not a true legacy of Shivaji Maharaj. In fact, Shivaji Maharaj's inheritance, dazzled in the courage and strength of Bajirao Peshwa. On the one hand, Shahu Maharaj could not afford to displease Bajirao... and on the other Nanasaheb was his protégé...So it was unlikely that Shahu Maharaj would take any decisive action.

Mastani's plight secretly moved Ahilya to tears...What was her fault in all this? That she loved Bajirao...or then that she was a woman...and a strong woman at that...or that she shared a different religion... What good is religion if it persecutes true love? Love is the greatest religion, she thought to herself. Ahilya suspected that at the core of all this was the lust for money. All these detractors were using some pretext or the other to make sure they did not have to share their wealth with Mastani's son...

Ahilya was lost in the thoughts of Bajirao – Mastani pining

for each other…the son's initiation ceremony… Nanasaheb… property…politics…house arrest…Mastani's lonely struggle…

Her thoughts were suddenly startled by the sound of approaching hooves…

****

4

She was stunned to see her husband, Khanderao, crisply dressed in a soldier's outfit! It looked as if a lightening had passed through his spine and there was thunder in his words… "I am set to leave. If respect is about money, I will return when I have earned both."

Ahilya looked perplexed. Was this anger… immaturity… impulse…façade…Ahilya was trying hard to discern. "But…where are you going?"

"I am going to join my father."

"Well then…Why don't you take me along too? I wish to witness the swordsmanship of my husband…be taught battlefield strategies by Mamanji….and of course meet the great Bajirao Peshwa!"

"Not at all!"Replied Khanderao. "You have been awarded the responsibility of administering this palace…you stay right here…"

Hearing the commotion, Baiji arrived there…and was exhilarated to see Khanderao dressed as a soldier! She came to Ahilya and said, "I am beside myself with pride and happiness! He indeed feels like joining his father? Let him go…"

She called for the tray with the oil lamp…urged Ahilya to perform the traditional ritual and wish Khanderao success in his mission.

Baiji was thanking God silently…feeling grateful to Ahilya … 'it was probably the result of her appropriate treatment that inspired Khanderao'…she thought…

Ahilya took the tray in her hand…wishing all success to Khanderao…wondering if he would miss her the way Bajirao was known to miss Mastani…or…or…would he miss Shabnam…She immediately drove the real , dark thought away and hid behind the unreal hopes and expectations…lost in the surreal story of Bajirao-Mastani. It was as though she was possessed by that love story…

****

The curiosity to see Shabnam was insurmountable. More than that she wanted to discover, what men looked for, in women …grace…beauty…sensuality…

She did not have any illusions about herself. She knew she did not have extraordinary good looks…yet…What does Mastani have that ties Bajirao to her heart? Or Shabnam have…She had to find out. She wanted to meet the other women in Khanderao's palace…she needed to observe… learn… maybe improve …

She had a perfect excuse too. It was dusk …she could not wait. She turned to Baiji and said, "I think I must go to the other palace …inform the women there of Khanderao's expedition and assure them of care and support."

Baiji nodded and smiled. "Other women in our husbands' lives are a reality. Co-existing with them is a way of life. You cannot wish them away. Be secure in your position, Ahilya. Remember, they may have the choicest good looks but when it is about good choice, we all look at you. Be kind hearted…and you will do me proud."

Ahilya understood. She left. Ahilya stepped into the other palace. Jealousy pierced through her heart as she greeted the women there. But she remembered Baiji's words. She steadied her own emotions…looked around…observed…spent some time there... was polite in her conversation, as she assured them of care and assistance. When she was returning . . .she experienced an unusual sense of achievement and satisfaction…

****

1740

The summers were heating up. The palace ensured that huge earthen pots full of khus drinks, dotted the region in cool, quiet, spots to provide relief to workers, travelers and residents .Things were quiet…in fact too quiet. There was no news from Malharrao…no scroll…no message…no update of any kind. In fact Baiji was beginning to get anxious. This was unusual. Malharrao's birthday arrived and passed by quietly. Ahilya too was restless. She was eager to go to the battlefield…Malharrao was a man of his words. He had promised that he would send for her. She wanted to learn cannon firing …and then there was also the prospect of meeting Bajirao and his soul mate Mastani… This would be her chance to spend time with Khanderao…alone…Ahilya was pondering…there was no news from Khanderao either. Ahilya's anxiety was nibbling at her patience… just then a messenger arrived.

Ahilya was excited! She took the scroll and began to read it.

The news simply paralyzed her. Every word she read numbed her further. She took a deep breath as if to borrow strength from the Universe. She moved. Ahilya cancelled all her appointments and the entire schedule for the day. She ordered everyone from the administrative office to gather in the meeting hall. Ahilya could barely speak…She looked blankly at everyone…and announced "With deepest regret , I have to inform you all, that, our most respected and dearest Bajirao Peshwa has passed away on the banks of the Narmada…"

He was barely forty. A long saga, of courage and achievements, in a short life span. No wonder that his favorite horse and elephant too breathed their last with their master.

Ahilya was in shock. She managed to make her way back to the palace. She noticed Malharrao's horse outside. He had arrived. No bugles. No decorations. All quiet. Ahilya entered the family room. She had never seen her father-in-law so distraught. Every pore of his being, seemed to be invested in controlling his tears…yet they flowed boundlessly…as if no amount of resistance could stop them…He merely managed to stifle the sounds…Malharrao's body looked wilted as he wept and looked at Ahilya blankly…he was inconsolable.

Ahilya stood there, frozen. She could barely register what she saw. Her mind space was haunted by the thought of Mastani's pain…and her fate. Did Mastani even know? Would anyone tell her? What would happen to her…the night seemed to pass slowly before their eyes.

At daybreak, they received a scroll from Pune. The scroll was sent to acquaint Malharrao with the political developments and inform him that a formal invitation would follow…On 25th June 1740, Nanasaheb was to become the next Peshwa, against the wishes of many like Raghuji Bhosale, Baramatikar, Naik, Dabhade …There was furious politicking going on to stall the coronation of Nanasaheb. But he had the backing of Shahu Maharaj. It was the last bit of news that shook Ahilya …It said…Mastani collapsed the moment she heard the news of Bajirao's death. She did not survive her soul mate's death. Ahilya was stunned…to know that such love can be for real…she just stood there…unable to lock the tears inside her…Ahilya shut her eyes tight….yet…tears flowed down untouched by her efforts to prevent them…

****

Later in the day, suddenly, it struck Ahilya! Malharrao had returned...Bajirao was no more...So where was

Khanderao…which battle was he fighting!??Why had he not returned? ..and then, not too long after, Khanderao returned…preceded most naturally by some commotion. Ahilya rushed to the window to see what the uproar was all about. To her utter horror, she spotted Khanderao and his friends jubilantly carrying the carcasses of a deer and a tiger…back from a hunting expedition! Ahilya ran down the stairs to prevent a disaster. 'Khanderao probably was not aware of Bajirao's demise…'she thought to herself… hastened her steps to reach him. She very politely hushed the group up and informed Khanderao of the unfortunate event of Bajirao's death. He heard it disinterestedly and continued to look at Ahilya….as if expecting something…Ahilya was intrigued and she looked at him for a clue…

"Do you not have a single word of praise for my courage? I hunted a tiger! A tiger!?"

Ahilya fumbled for the right words … "Yes..err..oh yes…but this is not an appropriate time to talk about your courage. I truly wish you had been with Mamanji instead! You would have had the good luck and honor of meeting Bajirao Peshwa…" Saying so, she urged him to drop everything and proceed to condole with his father. Though his friends turned back disappointed that their wine and veal party was ruined, Khanderao willingly complied…

A young Ahilya, at tender 16 years of age looked forward to not just reforming Khanderao but also nurturing a love story like Bajirao-Mastani

****

The next day, a ceremony was organized for the peace of the departed soul. Malharrao maintained a brave front in public, but would break down in private…pour his heart out to Baiji and Ahilya…reminiscing…narrating anecdotes…reliving memories. Ahilya was listening…. "Never again in my life, will

I ever get to serve a master as great as Bajirao…A bond of friendship fostered by a shared vision…dedication to people and loyalty to the throne…"Malharrao cried till he almost got drowsy…and his words , mere whispers. Ahilya was still listening…

Everyone was around Malharrao …all day…sharing his pain…his loss. Only one person was missing. Today Ahilya was immensely embarrassed…to acknowledge…that wine, women and veal parties mattered to him…not the fact that his father was mourning the death of his dearest friend….

****

Nanasaheb donned the title of the Peshwa. Malharrao could not afford the luxury of being in mourning for long…There was political activity happening in the Karnataka region. Malwa-Prayag-Bengal areas were unstable. Malharrao's loyalty rested with Shahu Maharaj …and Shahu Maharaj had Nanasaheb under his wings…Consequently, the responsibility of bringing in stability lay with Malharrao.

Malharrao got busy in the North for 2-3 years. He would send scrolls, directing Ahilya. She would follow instructions with care and dedication. These scrolls were not mere instructions. They were lessons, grooming her for stronger roles…training her to strategize…understand regional politics…

Baiji immersed herself in piety…meditation. It had been four years now since Malharrao had stepped into Indore…

GangobaTatya would never forget that day in the treasury. After the death of Bajirao, many ceremonies and rituals were held at the palace in memory of the departed soul. Ahilya was scrutinizing the statements of expenses incurred on those events. She noticed that all the costs were debited to the State expenses. She questioned Gangoba Tatya on the same. "Well," replied Gangoba Tatya, "these were official events organized by the Subhedar for the Peshwa."

"I cannot fault you on that. But Bajirao was much more than just a Peshwa to the Subhedar. Their relationship went beyond that. I do not wish to slight their bond, describe these events as official and accept reimbursement for those expenses. Kindly debit the personal account for all the expenses incurred. Let us not disrespect their friendship."

Gangoba Tatya was proud that he was in the service of a sensitive, straightforward and honest lady. He was amazed at the clarity of her thoughts. He had now observed her for the last four years...seen her grow...Quick decision making and swift implementation was her dictum. Every scroll from Malharrao would be actioned upon at once... meetings...visits to the arms factory...maintaining good relations with all the sardars and Jahagirdars...the army too, always in a state of readiness. Ahilya had no forbearance for traitors nor any charity for negligence.

Malharrao had once written to her, "My strength is in a strong army and the army's strength depends on the might of the treasury. A strong treasury depends on the treasurer's might. So you are my strength! Ahilya never for a moment lost this lesson, ever.

****

1744

One morning, a barely 20 year old Ahilya was engaged in her routine work. All of a sudden, a widow breached the palace security and fell at her feet. Dressed in a frugal white sari, her destiny tattooed on her forehead, she pleaded with Ahilya to accept her entire wealth and property as donation to the State. She said, 'I am a childless widow...my estate has no heir. Therefore anybody and everybody, even remotely related to me, is harassing me to adopt their sons. All this, for the greed of money. It has become impossible for me to live... threat...

fights…plots…I now fear for my life. So I urge you to take away the root of this evil …money. Please allow me to give this all away in charity to the state.'

Gangoba Tatya was about to order the donation papers to be prepared. Ahilya stopped him. She said firmly, "No. never." Gangoba Tatya was taken aback. 'Why would we refuse a voluntary donation to the treasury', he wondered…

Ahilya stood up. She calmed the lady and said, "What is your wish? What do you want to do? Speak without fear. Do you want to adopt anybody? I do not appreciate that you want to donate your wealth simply because you think you are weak and vulnerable. You are not. Most certainly not, in the reign of Subhedar Malharrao."

The lady was in tears…looking down defeated…losing the fight against her own people.

Ahilya stiffened. In a firm voice she ordered the lady to stop crying at once. "Do not be weak. Be strong. Defend your own right. Fight for it. Speak up"

The lady said, hesitatingly… "I wish to adopt the child of my domestic help…my caretaker"

"Alright then. So be it." Ahilya ordered, that the lady be allowed the adoption and be given State protection. She also advised the lady to use her wealth, in her own right, in good discretion, for causes beyond herself.

Gangoba Tatya seemed to rue the loss to the treasury!

Ahilya believed that it is not what you do for your children but what you make them capable of doing themselves that is important. It was far better to support the widows and make them independent rather than make them dependant on the state after donating their wealth, that too a donation out of sheer exasperation. What she had added to the State was far more priceless: A fair and strong precedent that would herald a better society. She explained that she did not want to exploit the weakness of her subjects…she wanted to weaken the exploitation.

That evening as she reached her quarters, Baiji sent for her. Ahilya entered her room. Baiji glanced at Ahilya with overwhelming pride for the way she had handled the case of the childless widow. Baiji stepped forward and hugged Ahilya.

Ahilya looked very tired…something was weighing on her mind. Baiji advised her to retire early that night. Ahilya stepped back…smiled and left. Baiji's eyes followed her as she left. They had noticed something…Baiji sent for Khanderao next morning…

A week went by. Ahilya received a message from Khanderao. She picked up the scroll. Ahilya did not know she was rolling out a new chapter in her life…

The message said that as promised…he had not touched alcohol or meat for some time now and he invited her to spend a few days with him at the palace!

Ahilya was overjoyed! She ran to Baiji's chambers…and told her! Baiji had a smile on her face as if she was expecting Ahilya…

That evening Ahilya had a luxurious bath with sandalwood paste…milk and flower petals in the bath water…Anjana and Renu helped her dress up. A lovely blue sari, a neat hairdo with two delicate rose buds on the side, framing her attractive profile. Baiji saw the palanquin leave the palace…She folded her hands and prayed to the Lord…prayed hard for a grandchild…an heir to carry the dynasty forward…

****

Ahilya's visits to the other palace became more frequent…and Khanderao true to his word would not touch alcohol or meat, when he was with Ahilya. Everyone in the palace was encouraged by this promising change in Khanderao … 'after all', everyone reflected, 'Ahilya's righteousness was contagious.'

And righteousness, was indeed Ahilya's second name.

Negligence and Deceit were the most dreadful words in her tenets. Her administrative brilliance sparkled in the cases she handled. Her honesty resonated in the squeaky clean monetary transactions. Her commitment labored in her daily routine. Her razor sharp intelligence gleamed in her political skills. Malharrao's directive scrolls and Baiji's guidance, advice and wisdom helped Ahilya sail steady even in choppy waters and through unexpected stormy events.

Couple of months passed by. Lately Ahilya would feel a little drained especially in the mornings...Ahilya discussed this with Baiji and a very happy possibility dawned on the two women! Baiji called for the Vaidya and he confirmed the good news! Baiji was jubilant! She sent for Khanderao. Asked the couple to sit together and performed a small ritual to drive away the evil eye...with salt and chilies. Khanderao looked at Ahilya...the two barely shared some soft smiles and before they could realize...the whole palace was rejoicing...discussing what the baby should be named!

"I want a son", said Khanderao... "What if it is a girl?" teased Ahilya... "Oh! Even the Gods dare not deny you your wish", replied Khanderao smiling...

Someone suggested a name with letters from Khanderao's name....or Ahilya's ...or a combination of the grandparents' names...Malharrao and Gautama...and finally it was settled! One name for a girl and another if it were a boy...

Khanderao said to Ahilya that he did not want his influence on the newborn...not even letters from his name... "It's not me but the whole of Indore says...that you are a 'do-gooder' and me, a 'no-gooder'! Drinking, hunting, wine, women, addiction...

Ahilya put her hand on his shoulder and said, "I don't want to know what people say. For a woman, her husband's appreciation, love and attention are most precious. So that makes it two precious gifts for me today!!And why do you belittle yourself all the time? You have now started coming to work...you are trying to quit alcohol and addiction..."

Khanderao immediately quipped, "I am trying to quit it...but my dear, addiction won't quit me..."

****

That very evening, they received a message from Malharrao, informing them of how the battles were heating up and loyalties were melting in the political games. Malharrao ordered Ahilya to keep an army of 7000 people ready. He also gave her a very valuable lesson that day. 'In times of war, take utmost care of the people fighting for you. Battles are won on their strength. Do not cut corners. We are spending people to earn money. Do not hesitate to spend that earned money on people. Small things make a big difference.' He signed off saying that he was not unknown to the improvements in Khanderao's behavior and that he was very pleased with the same.

Ahilya finished reading the letter. Baiji looked disappointed. A message for more troops meant more months of separation. It also meant that his arrival would coincide probably with that of the grandchild. She wanted to convey this news personally to Malharrao!

"I will go myself and convey this news personally to father", declared Khanderao. Baiji felt lighter. She did not know if happiness made her feel light headed, or, it was as if, some weight was off her shoulders, to see Khanderao take on more responsibilities with every passing day...

Baiji issued instructions for the safe passage of Khanderao...acquainted him with the shifting political alliances of the region and cautioned him about the possible dangers. Ahilya looked admiringly at Baiji, appreciating her vision and planning skills. Ahilya knew, she had a lot to learn from Baiji...

Khanderao left the next day. Ahilya got back to her routine but now with some changes. She took frequent breaks, rested intermittently. She was now carrying another little life inside her. She managed her darbar, payments, receivables, court of justice...but not without assistance from her trusted people.

The baby had now started making vigorous movements inside Ahilya...It was a new experience. Outside too new developments were taking place in the Orchha region. The Marathas and the natives of Orchha had clashed. Ahilya received a message from Khanderao. 'The Marathas have defeated the residents of Orchha. I am holding fort here. You take care of self and the tiny life inside you. ..Will endeavor to be with you at childbirth...'

A soft soothing feeling warmed Ahilya's heart. She was proud that Khanderao was now taking interest in meetings...espionage loops...battles...Baiji looked at Ahilya and smiled with satisfaction. "I would not have blamed you, had you complained about Khanderao. But you did not do that. The entire credit of reforming him, undoubtedly, goes to you...your patience...I will remain indebted to you ever for this..."

****

1745

Months labored by...and finally the wait was over. The midwife and the Vaidya were on call. Ahilya started contracting mildly...and then the contractions gripped her with intensifying force and frequency...until she finally experienced the most gratifying wonder of nature...as she held her own baby to her bosom! That lone moment of joy miraculously erased all the pain she had suffered in delivering the baby!

Indore was jubilant...glittering like a bride! All homes were decorated .Drums and music filled the air...Elephants and horses donned their fineries and paraded the roads, distributing thousands of pounds of sweets. Malharrao and Khanderao were delighted! Khanderao took permission from his father and left for Indore to see his son.

The joy of seeing his son was indescribable! He saw Ahilya and their eyes met. They would have to wait for the 40 days rest and confinement period to pass before they could meet…

At an auspicious time, on the designated day of the naming ceremony, the baby was put into a beautifully decorated swinging crib and named Malerao. All the women of the nobility were invited. Ahilya was exhausted touching the feet of elders, seeking blessings, exchanging gifts…Baiji wound up the function and urged Ahilya to take her special post partum massage.

Traditionally, after childbirth, women were advised to take this massage lying on a charpai made of jute strings, without a mattress. A flat iron pot containing burning embers of medicinal wood, herbs, clarified butter was placed under the charpai. The medicinal warmth and the therapeutic oil massage strengthened the spine, helping women to recuperate and regain lost energy and vigor.

Not just Ahilya, but the entire palace now seemed to have acquired renewed vigor and energy…playing with little Malerao…crowding around him, vying with each other to look after the baby. More than one person would offer to run every errand associated with the baby! Discussions of what the baby should be fed... when... toys... clothes... playtime... sleep time…The palace woke up with Malerao every morning and retired with him at night!

1747

Malerao was two years now. Ahilya had to wean her attention away from Malerao. The throne of Jaipur was in the eye of the storm. Efforts were on, to settle the conflict, but a compromise eluded each time. The seed of this conflict was sown many years ago when Sawai Jaisingh married Chandrakunwar Sisodekar and she lay down two conditions for the marriage. One, she would always remain the official wife, the queen. Two, her son would be the heir to the Jaipur throne.

Now, her son Madhosingh, staked his claim to the throne. But Ishwarsingh, considered it his right, to the throne, by virtue of being the older son from Jaisingh's earlier wife. Ishwarsingh struck a compromise with the younger step brother, Madhosingh… promising to relinquish the throne in exchange for twenty four lakhs…but later reneged on his word…

Baiji hesitated…said, "I hear Jaisingh even tried to kill his own son…Madhosingh…" Malharrao cut a sharp glance across at Baiji. She instantly realized…they say even walls have ears…such insinuations are merely to be implied in politics…never spelt out…

"My dilemma is", continued Malharrao, "years ago, in one of our chance political meetings, Chandrakunwar had tied the thread of 'Rakhi' on my wrist, establishing the bond of a brother-sister relationship. Now, I am under pressure to honor that bond and ensure that Madhosingh is reinstated to the throne of Jaipur.

Ahilya was listening intently…with little Malerao on her lap…thinking to herself… 'God, let me not have another son. Two sons…their fights for the ascension to the throne…a daughter would be better' …she thought.

Khanderao was to leave the next morning. A gradual but definite change was apparent in him. Ahilya was happy... he was now sharing responsibilities…receiving some respect and recognition… She would pray every day for his well being and that of the State.

****

Finally a battle broke out at Raj Mahal. Unfortunately, the Holkar army was defeated. As soon as Ahilya heard that Khanderao had returned to the other palace she immediately wished to go there to offer words of encouragement …tell him that she was a wife who appreciated her husband's endeavors.

She did not want him to lose hope or interest…

She walked past the guards and went straight to Khanderao's room. Who would dare to prevent Ahilya from entering? She knocked on the door briefly and entered. What Ahilya saw stunned her. She was shocked. There were heaps of gold coins…gems…jewelry… all over the room. She looked at Khanderao, "So much loot? The news of defeat…? And why have you brought all this treasure here without informing anyone?" Ahilya was puzzled.

" Well…" said Khanderao with a smirk on his face. "You value honesty. So here it is…In fact, I had gone to war alone with the sole intention of collecting loot! Did you really think I enjoyed battles and a hard life at the camps? I like comforts…luxury…and I need money for that… which, it is obvious, is denied to me. I cannot beg nor give explanations on what I spend…how I spend…why I spend…hence, I have fulfilled my goal. And mind you, I have done it with great dedication and perseverance…"

Khanderao's unruffled answer was like a bolt out of the blue. Ahilya stood there, as if a lightening had struck her…all those fresh sprouts of hope turned completely ashen in it's flash…

She collected herself. " I suggest you deposit the prescribed percentage of the loot into the State treasury right away!"

Khanderao moved ahead and folded his hands…bowed down to her…and said, "Look…Oh goddess of truthfulness…I am not bitten by the honesty bug. I have earned all this in the war, on the strength of my wrist…my sword…"

Ahilya tried to maintain her calm and took care to not destroy the progress she had made with Khanderao in one careless moment. "The wrists of the Subhedars and their swords are for protecting their people. Yet, you can still declare this loot, deposit the rightful percentage into the State treasury and then indisputably enjoy the rest, with pride and with dignity!"

"I do not need your advice about duty. If you can, why don't you fulfill your duty of being a wife and help me hide this treasure away safely?"

"You are my husband. I will most certainly help you, if you agree to declare this loot. Else, you will have to forgive me. I cannot put personal duty above my duty to the State"

Khanderao nodded and said, "It is best then that you leave immediately."

A numb Ahilya turned around…completely disillusioned by the present …having no more illusions for the future. She retraced her steps back to her own chambers…She placed her hand on her stomach and shut her eyes…She was expecting their second child…

5

The Jaipur throne conflict, drove a wedge, in the sturdy, long-standing friendship between the Holkars and the Shindes. The Holkars were morally bound to support Madhosingh and the Shindes believed that Ishwarsingh, the elder sibling, was wronged in this and offered him their backing.

Malharrao feared that the Holkar-Shinde friction could generate many a dangerous sparks and ignite many more flashpoints…and engulf the region in the flames of enmity. The Holkar-Shinde friendship was vital for the stability of the region. This matter could no longer remain unresolved.

Malharrao took the matter to the court of the Peshwa. Nanasaheb Peshwa himself camped in Rajasthan. In the battle of Bagru, which ensued for 6-7 days, Ishwarsingh was defeated. The Holkars were victorious. Indore was filled with victory beats and immeasurable wealth!

Around the same time in 1748, Ahilya was delivered of her second child, a baby girl. She named her Mukta…meaning, freedom. Hoping, that the Holkars would never have to see a day where two brothers would fight for the throne...or destabilize the region with their disputes...The Holkars, she thought, were free of these skirmishes...

Mukta's arrival seemed to herald a new chapter in the history of the Holkars. Shahu Maharaj delegated the entire mission of expansion in Karnataka, to Nanasaheb Peshwa, who in turn relied heavily on Malharrao Holkar. This meant that Malharrao spent almost all his time away from Indore. During this period Shahu Maharaj's health began to deteriorate. Consequently, Nanasaheb began to frequent Satara, further entrenching Malharrao into the Karnataka missions. In the year 1749, Shahu Maharaj passed away and Ramraje ascended the throne.

The political scene kept Malharrao away from Indore and therefore, Ahilya was immersed in administrative responsibilities. As a result, the elders in the house were busy bringing up her two children. Time was breezing past. Some days were gentle and cool but most days were stormy.The next year witnessed the suicide of Ishwarsingh. 1750-52 was marked by the conflict of the Jodhpur throne. Malharrao spent the better part of those two years resolving the family feud there.

Ahilya and Baiji spent many a moments together... discussing...deliberating...planning...pondering, but above all supporting each other. Khanderao was absorbed again in wine, women and his intoxicants. Malerao was almost eight years old ...Mukta four ...and their mother, about 27...

Mukta was a delight...a lovely child! She was interested in art, music; reciting poems, learning numbers...But Malerao seemed to be different...

He found happiness in being notoriously naughty... destructive...breaking things... Ahilya could not discount his behavior as boisterous...or boyish games...she was worried, truly and deeply worried. She was determined to exert herself on improving him.Every day, early in the morning, she started assigning two hours to Malerao. Telling him stories from the epics, Ramayana and Mahabharata... telling him stories of courage, honor, grit, valor, truthfulness, dedication...She would proceed to her work only after this coaching session!

One such day, she reached her workplace. A place she had been coming to, for the past twelve years now. Politics, accounts, communication was her life. She had a dispatch from Malharrao waiting for her. She opened it...

Malharrao gave her the details of the political equations in the North and the South. The region of Rohila was acquired along with fifty lakhs. But the disagreements between the Marathas and the Jats were on the rise in the North. To the South, the Nizam was playing games! He would plead for truce as soon as defeat was in sight and simply delay paying indefinitely when the time to disburse neared. This was frustrating the armies as the entire action in battle was then rendered futile.

Malharrao urged Ahilya once again to be generous with the army...to never forget that all victories, taxes, wealth, gold, gems were collected on the strength of these very soldiers. They deserved priority, reciprocation and gratefulness.

Ahilya could visualize Malharrao struggling hard, rushing from North to South with the Holkar flag flying high. She put the letter away and looked up towards Khanderao's quarters. Ironically, she saw the colorful dupattas of Khanderao's women...unfurling stories, that history would never be proud of. Every evening, Ahilya would return home and lying in her bed, would wait, late into the night, for the sounds of the dancers' ghungroos from Khanderao's quarters to go silent. The silence would then haunt her...with visions of Khanderao in bed with those very dancers...

****

The month of Shravan arrived with monsoons, rains...swings and songs, festivals and Pujas. On one such festive occasion, some Brahmin priests were invited to the palace. The rituals of the ceremony were over. The priests were courteously ushered into the sprawling dining hall. Flat wooden rectangular seats with pretty brass rivets were placed on the floor neatly in a row, for the priests. Sparkling silverware of plates and bowls lined the seats. Multihued rangoli motifs on the floor, defined every individual plate, with its floral patterns…giving each priest an exclusive and distinctive embellished place. The priests were requested to occupy their seats. Two rows of eleven priests settled down facing each other for lunch, on those wooden seats. The women of the house displayed their reverence towards the priests by serving them personally. Copper finger bowls with rose water and petals were offered to the Brahmins. They washed their hands, collected their 'Dakshina', a voluntary monetary offering for their services, and prepared to leave. Baiji and Ahilya escorted them to the main door and thanked them. They turned back…happy and contented. Other than the absence of Malharrao, the function lacked nothing. The two women started walking towards the Diwankhana when suddenly a commotion broke out!

A couple of priests were shrieking in pain …Baiji and Ahilya rushed back. The priests were hopping, holding their feet…attempting to sit down…No one was ready to answer, as to what had happened. The servants stood there, looking down, speechless. From the corner of her eye Ahilya spotted Malerao, behind a pillar…laughing…

"Scorpion!" shrieked a priest… "a poisonous scorpion in our footwear…" Ahilya's head was thumping. She fell at their feet, apologizing profusely. The royal Vaidya was sent for. Medicinal pastes were made…applied on the stings. Herbs were being crushed…roots were being scrubbed on stone surfaces with liquids and honey to make potions and lotions.

As Ahilya looked on helplessly, she felt her anger now rising. She paced swiftly towards Malerao, pulled him out from behind the pillar and slapped him hard for this prank! The boy groaned in pain and let out a loud scream. She was trying to get a grip on her anger but her hands were mindlessly thrashing Malerao…

At that very moment, the door to Khanderao's room upstairs… flung open. Khanderao was drunk. He could barely walk. He somehow stumbled downstairs…and grasped Ahilya's wrist. "How dare anyone raise their hand on my son…the heir of the Holkars? No one dare …."Before he could finish his sentence, Baiji arrived there. Her stare was enough to control Khanderao. She stared at him and then Ahilya's wrist. "let go of her wrist" , Baiji's voice was loud and clear. Khanderao jerked open his grip to release the wrist of a tremulous Ahilya…He then took Malerao with him and left…

Ahilya sank lifelessly into a chair nearby. Everyone …the servants…the Vaidyas…the priests…the other women… everyone, was staring at her. She knew this incident would be whispered throughout Indore now…

Now in his father's refuge, Malerao resumed his pranks with a vengeance. Every two to three days, Ahilya had to deal with a new episode…more bizarre than the previous one. Malerao would at times, fill cow's urine in perfume bottles, chilli powder in red kumkum boxes, put salt in drinking water, pour gum on seats…and some games were even more hideous and cruel. His laughter would then cascade through the palace… Everyone was fraught with strain and anxiety. Only Malerao would be amused!

Ahilya was losing her appetite…and her peace. Malerao's growing pranks were tearing open the seams of Ahilya's tolerance and patience. Malerao did not stop shocking her, with his disparaging…destructive behavior.

The festivities at the palace were being clocked in an atmosphere of apprehensive terror. Priests were refusing invitations. If they did accept invites, they treaded carefully…unsure as to when a ball may be flung at them from some corner or a catapult may be used to spurt something on them. Despite these threats, people would dare to come and not complain…only and only for Ahilya.

Every week Ahilya would receive a letter from Malharrao. The arrival of a letter spelt a spurt in activity… errands… deadlines…couriers…correspondence…spy codes…firearms, food, money and all other arrangements to be calibrated.

Today too, a letter had arrived, bringing with it good news, that Malharrao would return soon…maybe at the end of the Hindu Calendar month of Bhadrapad , which fell ,around September. Ahilya forwarded the letter to Baiji as was the usual practice. She finished reading and replying to the other letters…sent a few reminders on payments…summoned Gangoba Tatya ,Govind pant, Ganesh Vitthal to give out further instructions…the list was endless…

Ahilya returned home, freshened up and went to the temple. Baiji was waiting for her there. Ahilya expected Baiji to be beaming today…Malharrao was to return after so long. She looked at Baiji…and…

"Is anything wrong?" asked Ahilya, "Has Malerao…"

"No no!" Baiji interrupted, "Khanderao has sent for you. He wishes to see you tonight."

Ahilya was calm. "Alright.I will go."

Ahilya changed the topic and the mood. "Did you read the letter?!! This year's Diwali and Dussehra festivals promise to be brighter and happier!" Baiji still hesitated but then gave Ahilya a slightly vacant but a broad smile.

Late in the evening Ahilya had a bath. She wore a white sari with a gold border. Applied her red kumkum spot in the centre of the forehead, a dot of turmeric yellow haldi below the kumkum…wore a double string of pearls and her 'Mangalsutra'[10] of tiny black beads and gold pendant, in her neck.

She went to inform Baiji that she was on her way to Khanderao's room. Baiji was mesmerized by the lustrous look. Wheatish complexion, expressive large eyes, wavy hair… Baiji nodded. Ahilya left. Baiji continued looking at her…a bright personality eclipsed by the dark deeds of her husband and now unfortunately, her son too…

Khanderao stood up as Ahilya approached. She greeted him politely.

"Am I looking at the full moon or is it indeed Saraswati…the Goddess of learning, dazzling in a white sari?"

"I am not beautiful", said Ahilya. "I am an ordinary woman. You have many beautiful women surrounding you…"

"They are … 'Kama' or lust personified. You are 'Karma' personified…Karma Yogini…and seduction by intelligent, brilliant women is always more charming!"

Ahilya obliged him with a forced smile. Khanderao recognized that and came straight to the point, "I blundered the other day, didn't I? I realize, I should not have behaved the way I did. But you were spanking Malerao and I could not bear that…"

The Karma Yogini was a mother too. A mother, concerned about the well being of her son…a son who was to carry forward the Holkar reign…inherit all the wealth…and he necessarily had to be worthy of deserving that wealth and title…

"I did not enjoy thrashing him. I rapped him but his wounds still hurt in my heart. Yet, he needs to be disciplined… trained …groomed…he cannot be spending his entire day watching bull fights and bird fights…those poor animals…"

"Ohhh! Those are signs of masculinity!" said Khanderao defensively.

Ahilya despaired. "I wish I could agree with you. He needs to spend time educating himself …writing, reading, reciting shlokas, and attending scripture sermons…"

"I am a man of ill repute. The Holkars evidently owe their good repute to you…similarly…" Ahilya did not allow Khanderao to finish what he intended to say. She also did not appreciate his self denigration…

"Accepting mistakes requires far greater strength than

rectifying them. You recognize your faults. It will therefore not at all be difficult for you to improve on them, if you show just a little determination." She continued, "Destiny has offered you everything. A Subhedar father, an erudite mother, wealth, a son who will benefit immensely if you lead him by example…a wonderful daughter… In this game of life, Destiny may deal you a generous hand or a poor hand but ultimately how you play your cards, determines your success or failure."

Khanderao was quiet. "Alright. Give me one more chance. And this time, you accompany me on my mission. I promise to bring accolades to the Holkars this time."

Ahilya was straight forward in her response. "Bajirao Peshwa has set a precedent by allowing Mastani to accompany him on missions. But in retrospect…now that I reflect on it, I maintain, that I am not in favor of wives or women accompanying men on battlefields. The army needs to focus only on combat. Women not only become enchanting distractions but bring on additional responsibilities. Their tents need to be guarded. Additional facilities need to be provided. More food and water supplies….Well, but if women were to help in first aid, nursing, handling arms, food… it would be reasonable. But merely accompanying men, living in tents, eating and being merry…A strict no .The forces must be lean."

Khanderao looked upset. "Why not speak plain, that you are not keen on going with me?"

Ahilya pondered for a few moments. "I will come but I will handle the cannon carts."

"Settled then!" agreed Khanderao, "I will establish my worth…"

"Nobody doubts it…"reassured Ahilya

"Neither will you." Khanderao concluded. At the break of dawn Ahilya returned to her room.

****

The Navratra festival was two days away. The sweetmeats to be made on each of those nine days had to be planned. Food menus had to be deliberated. Invitations to the Brahmins and priests were dispatched. The musical instruments were to be bedecked…the jewelers had to polish gold ornaments…the silver mounts and saddles, of horses and elephants, were to be buffed up… the ghungroos adorning the cows had to sparkle… the brass umbrellas, spears, flagpoles , had to shine…Temples were being whitewashed. The deities had new brocades adorning them… Ahilya completed approving these details and proceeded to her workplace.

She was studying the detailed, wall mounted, political and topographical map of the region. The rivers… mountains… roads…Rajputana…Vidarbh…She had received intimation that Nanasaheb Peshwa's younger brother, Raghunathrao, was planning to visit Indore. Ahilya looked at Gangoba Tatya. "What is the information? Which route is Raghunathrao expected to take?"

"Apparently, the entourage is set to arrive on the thirteenth day of the month of Bhadrapad …"

Before he could finish his sentence, Indore was filled with the sound of bugles! A signal, that Subhedar Malharrao had arrived.

Ahilya was overjoyed! She rushed back to the palace…Malharrao was being welcomed by Baiji with a tray full of numerous oil lamps…

For just a moment, as she looked on, she fantasized… Khanderao returning like this….victorious…and she, welcoming him… A dream….

She touched her father-in-law's feet…hard times had left a trace on his worn out face…he blessed Ahilya and told her that all his war stories would have to wait until the next day. He was tired and wanted to rest. Ahilya smiled and nodded in agreement. She was, in fact, amused to see Baiji, Harkuaai…in fact, all his four wives decked up in new saris, flowers in their hairdo…for Malharrao! Even Khanderao was present to welcome his father.

Next day Malharrao opened the gates on all the stored anecdotes…War stories, cascaded into the family room and flooded everyone with myriad emotions…at times like soft bouncy waters, sometimes roaring…sometimes swirling… everyone drenched in the sprays of emotions…pride at victories, anger at betrayals, surprised by alliances and shifting loyalties…friendship with Bhonsales, Nimbalkar's treachery with the Peshwa, truce between the Nizam and the Peshwa, expansion up to Khandesh…

Warm saffron milk was served by late afternoon. The intermittent trickle of visitors was now a steady stream and the family convention had to be dissolved…

****

The next day, early in the morning, Ahilya was nervous. Malharrao was to review all the papers…reports…accounts… tax recoveries…complaint redressals and justice delivery systems…. She reached the workplace before Malharrao. She stood up as soon as she saw him approaching. Malharrao greeted her. She was about to start taking him through the papers when he told her to carry on with her work and that, he would send for her if required.

Ahilya knew …Malharrao would now validate and corroborate everything thoroughly. He would enquire in his own subtle way about the respect received by old and trusted hands, veracity of accounts, goodwill with subjects, and appropriateness of the language used by Ahilya…everything! Ahilya spent the day on the edge, restless…hoping she was not summoned…

The evening was closing in. She looked outside her window. Malharrao was returning. She missed a heartbeat. He was walking swiftly...Calling out to everybody on his way …ordering them to gather in the Diwankhana... Baiji... Harkuaai...Renu , Anjana, Khanderao...

Ahilya's blood started rushing to her head with apprehension...Malharrao clapped twice...she now felt faint...Before Ahilya could blink, a man walked in with a tray. On the tray, in a velvet box, was a four string pearl necklace with a pendant in the centre, bearing the symbol of the Holkars on it. Malharrao picked it up and put it in Ahilya's neck!

Malharrao's smile of appreciation said it all! Just as all the women were about to crowd round her, to pore over the necklace...Malharrao said, "I have only one question. When already enough and more concessions have been provided to the villagers...why have you sanctioned such huge additional amounts to the sub units of those villages?"

Ahilya felt a surge of confidence swelling inside her... "I believe, unless the interior regions are developed, prosperity cannot be remitted and unrelenting expansion is impossible. Good water supply gives an abundant crop. Good crops ensure prosperity. Prosperity kills dissatisfaction and destructive behavior...leading to peace."

Malharrao was pleased. "I will never regret my decision of awarding you with this Holkar crest!" He said this and left.

Ahilya smiled in contentment! She had not let her father-in-law down.

The women now crowded around her...admiring the crest...Khanderao walked up to her and said, "Well done! You have achieved what I should have. You truly deserve to be called the heir of the family. The Holkars need you more than me. May you live long! In fact, longer than me..."

What he said disturbed Ahilya tremendously...and before she realized, tears were streaming down...Baiji's blunt glance at Khanderao was a silent whip of disapproval. Khanderao left. Everyone was attempting to calm Ahilya down. But Ahilya was shocked at her own reaction...the tears were real...she felt pain deep inside her…why? She wondered…She had not experienced the love her mother had told her about…yet…this ache? Was it fright, that on Khanderao's death, she will have to follow the tradition of Sati? Was she scared of death…or widowhood and the prospect of losing her right to live well? Did she want her children to have their father around or she just did not want a life without a husband? Ahilya sat in front of the deity at the temple…She could not comprehend her own emotions…She was just feeling weighed down by that sentence…

****

The festival of 'Navratra' [11] was in progress. Preparations for Dussehra were in full swing. Parade practices with horses and elephants, drill formations with swords and spears, throbbing circles of dancers looked like colorful flowers blooming …songs…bugles…drums…

It was late afternoon on the day of Dussehra. All preparations were on the mark for the grand Dussehra procession. Traditionally, Malharrao and Baiji would grace the golden mount on the first elephant…followed by the other members of the family, on the succeeding elephant mounts. Ahilya started walking towards the second elephant. Baiji invited Ahilya to join them on the opening golden mount along with Khanderao.

Khanderao acknowledged, but politely declined. He said he will lead the cavalry with the flag of the Holkars flying high atop the spear. "That would be more than fortunate for us!" replied Malharrao. Khanderao looked handsome in the yellow and red headgear…the representative colors of the Holkars. Ahilya smiled and joined her parents-in-law. The bold four string pearl necklace with the Holkar crest could not be missed by anybody.

The procession rolled out. The infantry…cavalry…the elephants…musicians…dancers…

The flag of the Holkars fluttering in the air…so was Ahilya's heart. The Sun's setting rays, falling on her face, were playing hide n seek from behind the fluttering flag…creating a light and shadow play of memories in Ahilya's mind…

Not long ago…she could see herself as a little girl, holding her father-in-law's finger… accepting the papers of the Subhedari. Time had forged its way ahead bringing glory to their dynasty through the numerous victories that Malharrao had to his credit. Just the mere sight of Malharrao, in his full battle gear, it was said, was enough to disrupt the enemy forces! Such was his command! Back home, Ahilya's mere presence was enough to energize their forces… such was her influence!

Indore was resonating with chants and chimes …erupting spontaneously…in praise of their chief, Malharrao and Ahilyadevi…Ahilya would get distracted by the Holkar flag… her attention diverting to the flag every now and then …

The elephant was swaying majestically…the mount responding to its rhythm…Ahilya rocking mildly in it…and the necklace sliding from side to side…reminding Ahilya of the heavy responsibility on her. The future of this very flag…crest…troubled Ahilya. Who would she hand it over to? Khanderao ? Malerao?

She looked around. A sea of people, looking up to her… She had to build their present…secure their future. Ahilya was lost in thought…

Baiji nudged her gently…drew her attention to the women lining the windows of their homes, greeting her with folded hands. Ahilya was mildly embarrassed that she had missed returning their greetings…Ahilya folded her hands and waved out to them all! She could see cheer breaking out in groups of women…

Ahilya had made up her mind…

****

The next two days blurred past, with so much pending work

to dispense. Just as work was closing for the day, they received a message from Raghunathrao.

Malharrao began to read it out aloud:

'To the Honorable Subhedar: posting my respects at your feet.

Kindly grant my urgent request to dispatch immediate army assistance. The pressing need arises to ensure timely contributions by the Rajputanas in the Ajmer region. There is dependable information that cannons will be provided to the Jats to fight this battle. Allow me the liberty here to offer you a word of caution on the Jats and the Emperor of Delhi. It would be my good fortune if you could make it convenient to join us at Bharatpur around 'Makar Sankrant' and bless us on the occasion. Urge you to dispatch army assistance immediately under the lead of Khanderao for now. Trust your generosity and plead you to forgive me if I have erred before. Bless me always…Raghunathrao'

The letter triggered furious activity. Malharrao instructed Ahilya to return to the palace and inform Khanderao immediately. Ahilya nodded and left immediately. Preparations began to gather momentum…sweets and savories with long shelf lives were being prepared. Grains, provisions and silver coins were being filled in large jute bags. Clothes, medicines, ointments, herbal pastes and other first aid was arranged for. The horses were washed and brushed. Lemon and chillies were hung on arms cache to ward off evil eyes… threads blessed by the deity were tied by the royal priests on the arms of the people ready to depart. Baiji was going around motivating everyone with some concluding words of caution and counsel …The traditional farewell of oil lamps was completed by Ahilya.

As Khanderao bowed down to his father to seek his blessings, he expressed his desire that Ahilya join him on this mission. Malharrao pondered for a bit and replied, "During the time of Shivaji Maharaj, soldiers or their sardars were punishable by whipping, if a lady was as much as even spotted in the camp. After the Peshwas took over, things are now different. Baiji too, did accompany me to Palkhed. But protecting women in times of war is an additional pressure. There would be extended meetings and discussions, critical situations...the journey too is long and difficult...But around Makar Sankrant , it is my promise that I will bring both, Baiji and Ahilya with me when I join you."

Khanderao looked pleased. Khanderao walked up to her to bid goodbye... Ahilya unwittingly hoped that Khanderao would tell her, that he would look forward to her to joining him...Ahilya smiled in anticipation. "When you visit me...do not forget to bring my other wives too..."Ahilya nodded vacantly...Khanderao left.

Malharrao looked worried. Ahilya waited for everyone to disperse...she had to find out why Malharrao was so tense...When Ahilya enquired Malharrao merely nodded and put his hand on her head...as if to bless her...Ahilya persisted with her queries...and gradually prodded him to answer. 'He was never comfortable allowing Khanderao to go for battles...'said Malharrao in a very heavy voice...

Ahilya did not want to be unkind to her husband...she assured Malharrao, "With encouragement from you, he will surely excel...Please do not be unforgiving to your own child" An apprehensive Malharrao answered with unease, "There is not an ounce of doubt that Khanderao can be very capable, if he pledges to. But there is a very subtle distinction between courage and madness. Courage without caution is madness and battles are not won on courage alone. Impulse and impatience invite defeat and I fear that...because in that fear is veiled a deeper fear..."

6

For the next two months Ahilya trained to operate the cannons…manoeuvre them, loading ammunition, sealing and firing. Malharrao would watch over the training imparted to her by Ganesh Vithal and Ramaji Raghav. Malharrao seemed rather pleased with the progress. Ahilya bowed down to touch her father-in-law's feet to seek his blessings on completing her training. She expressed her gratitude and said, "You are not just my father, you are my mentor… my teacher, my guru! I owe you a 'gurudakshina' [12] as is our custom …But... I am too small to offer you anything…" Malharrao let out a hearty laugh and seemed to humor Ahilya, "Modesty is a good ploy to wriggle out of presenting to me, my rightful gurudakshina, is it?!" And then on a serious note he added, "You have already more than repaid me, my child…by dedicating your life to the state…and not letting me down…But don't you worry! I will not let go of my gurudakshina…let me think… of something worth demanding!"

"It will be my good fortune. I promise to keep my word…"Ahilya smiled too…

Just then Khanderao sent a message saying Surajmal Jat had refused to comply with the payment of one crore…and instead replied 'take 40 lakhs or prepare to fight'. They had seiged the fort but needed urgent assistance…

Malharrao put the letter down. "I will leave immediately. You women leave after Makar Sankrant. Sufficient security guards will ensure your safe passage" Malharrao left that evening.

****

Makar Sankrant was celebrated…sesame and jaggery sweets were prepared…haldi kumkum ceremonies …coupled with a gesture of distributing curious, inexpensive gifts to the womenfolk was accomplished! Charity to the temples and 'dharamshalas'[13] was done....the significance of every festival was cherished in good spirit at the palace!

After the festival, without any delay, the palanquins left the palace. Banaai and Harkuaai stayed back with the children. Baiji, Dwarkaai, Oodabai and Ahilya were together. The two mistresses of Khanderao were in another palanquin...passing their time playing a game of dice. Ahilya was inspecting the region...fields...crops...rivers...water canals... spies... information collection systems....

If she detected anything amiss anywhere, she would immediately stop and send a notice to the administrator-in-charge of the region.

The landscape outside the palanquin transom began to change face slowly...they were now approaching a strife-ridden area...barren scorched land...maimed bodies strewn about emitting a foul smell of decomposed flesh. Traces of a fierce battle were etched all around...the mood turned somber...the tales of pain wrenched everyone's heart, streaking in, a throbbing twinge of repulsion for war...

The entourage made cautious enquiries...changed routes frequently to mislead lurking dangers...before finally reaching the camps. Everyone was more relieved than joyful at finally seeing each other safe ...

Now a daily routine was established at the camps. All through the day Ahilya would be engaged in inspection, training and other wartime activities. At the end of the day, Ahilya would bathe...pray to Lord Shiva and seek his blessings for the well being of everyone...and after the Puja send 'Prasad'[14] to the tents of Malharrao, Raghunathrao, Khanderao...and also to the Shinde's tent. The women's camps were segregated...Khanderao lived with his mistresses in a separate tent.

The siege would not end. There was no sign of truce anywhere. No one would enter or exit the fort. Both parties had dug their heels in the ground.

On that one particular day, in 1754, Ahilya had her bath as always…prayed to Lord Shiva and decided to distribute the Prasad to all the tents personally. Baiji was glad at her decision… and suggested to her that she should do this more often. Visit Khanderao's tent. She confessed to Baiji, "I do not go to Khanderao's tent because I am not as large hearted as you are. You have accepted your husband's wives, as your sisters. I am unable to do so." Baiji smiled knowingly… "This is the story of every woman. Don't I know that he has nine other wives? But remember, no one has the status that you have. And then you have your rights too, as a wife…"

Ahilya nodded and left for Khanderao's tent with the 'Prasad'. She entered the tent and was shocked at what she saw. Khanderao was intoxicated …so were his mistresses. There were clothes strewn all over the place…Ahilya turned right back and returned to her tent.

The scene at the tent, kept flashing back and distressing Ahilya for more than one reason…It troubled her more, that, at night when the seniors huddled together to strategize, discuss and plan victory … when the soldiers strived hard, away from their families…Khanderao chose to skip those conferences and indulge his own desires…

Ahilya spent a restless night. She also feared for his safety. When at war, he needed to be in control of his senses…being intoxicated on opium…wine…women…Ahilya shuddered. She had to do something. She had to protect her husband…

She bid her time until the next day. Ahilya decided to have a conversation with him. She entered his tent. Khanderao's eyes were bloodshot; from last night, she thought. He could barely balance himself. Ahilya steadied and said, "You invited me to see your courage and valor…and what do I see here? It hurts me deeply, to see you in this inebriated condition…"

That very instant an angry Khanderao stumbled across the tent. "Who says I am inebriated…look…look at me ….I can go and fight right now!Demonstrate my courage…" Khanderao was swaying.

"Stop!" Ahilya pleaded… "this is not the time to go out on the battlefield. No guards…no weapons…no security cover…wait!!!" Ahilya tried to prevent Khanderao from going towards the battlefield.

Khanderao pushed Ahilya aside…turned around and mumbled… "Heroes venture where ordinary men fear to tread…" Ahilya ran after him…calling out to Baiji… Malharrao…

But Khanderao charged out beyond the boundary lines…and before Ahilya could even breathe, a shot rang in the air , originating from the fort…not missing its target…and piercing straight... into Khanderao's body…Ahilya screamed loudly…people came rushing out of their tents. Malharrao froze. Baiji buckled to the ground …Ahilya moved slowly towards Khanderao. He was dead, on the spot. Ahilya sank next to him…her body was losing its sensation…vision seemed to blur…she was stunned into silence…ears felt like stones…engulfed in a vacuum. Beyond…she could see blurred images of people crying… muffled sounds of women thumping their chests… everything around her began to spin….

The news of Khanderao's death spread like wild fire. People despaired at the thought of Ahilya now having to follow the tradition of 'Sati' and bid them farewell too. Crowds began to assemble…there was complete shock and utter gloom…

Khanderao's body had now been carried back to the tent. Ahilya was now calm. She was preparing herself to fulfill her duty as a wife…follow her husband in death…give up her life on the pyre of her dead husband. She believed this was her one final chance now, to redeem herself, for all those times when she had not supported Khanderao…

Baiji was desperate, trying to beseech Ahilya with her pleas to reconsider the decision…Baiji tried to reiterate to Ahilya in more ways than one, about the fate of her children after her...Mukta...Malerao...Ahilya calmly told Baiji that she had been a wonderful mother and a mentor to her...she trusted Baiji with her children...and had nothing to fret about...

The crowds outside were swelling...sounds of people wailing ...filling the air ...Malharrao entered. He looked frail and crushed...He seemed to have aged a decade in one day...He was in fact shaking...with tremor in his voice...and tears in his eyes, he was trying to focus. He folded his hands, sank onto his knees, put his head down on the floor in front of Ahilya's feet...

Ahilya snapped out of her numb daze. She stood up instantly. The man she revered the most was falling at her feet. A man of the stature of Malharrao, was indeed imploring ... begging her to change her mind...dedicate her life to the service of the people.

"I have done whatever I could, as long as I could...but now destiny has sealed my fate...Please let me go..." appealed Ahilya...

"Ahilya...by following this cruel tradition...you will merely be remembered as a dutiful wife who followed her religion...but have you considered what would happen to the thousands of people who will suffer...their homes will be plundered...looted without an able administrator...you cannot be selfish and sacrifice the well being of so many people, simply for a personal fulfillment..." Malharrao tried all pitches...but Ahilya seemed to be intractable on this...

Finally, Malharrao made a feeble attempt to sound strong. "This is my time, my child..."he cleared his throat, gathered himself, shut his eyes and without looking at her said... "This is my time, to ask for my 'gurudakshina'. I ask you for just one thing in return for all that I taught you...as your guru...I ask you for your life...Do not attempt to live forever by embracing death but embrace life, even if it may seem like dying a thousand deaths...You are giving up your life, in both events...one by dying and one by living...I beg you to choose the one by living…"Malharrao's knees were buckling under the pressure of this uncertainty… "Now you understand why I dreaded Khanderao going to war…I dreaded this moment… Ahilya…please…have mercy on this old man…" and …Malharrao collapsed.

Baiji rushed…the Vaidya rushed…Ahilya's head was spinning…thoughts were whirling in her head…She remembered how Baiji and Malharrao had tutored her. Today they were shaken, not by the loss of their son but by what the loss of their son meant to them. To them, it meant the loss of their daughter-in-law…they were crying for her, not their son. She was filled with grief for them…their tears…their appeals…In the corner of her mind, she was also reminded of Khanderao's behavior….his drinking, womanizing…too many emotions crowding her mind. She shut her eyes, trying to sift through her emotions. Was she trying to run away from life or run away from death?

Ahilya sat there for a long time…no one spoke anything…Ahilya then stood up, inched towards Khanderao's body .The weight on her heart visible in her walk as she dragged herself…She looked at Baiji and Malharrao. They could barely breathe due to anxiety…fear of an unexpected decision looming large in their eyes…

Ahilya steeled herself. She looked at Khanderao's lifeless face and announced her decision. "I was never your favorite. Yet, your Ahilya, the Ahilya you knew, dies this very moment and goes with you today. I will wear only white clothes and give up all pleasures of life. The rest of my life will be dedicated to my people…the people of this country." Ahilya slumped near the body and just let her emotions out…she did not know how long she cried…She removed all her jewelry…pearls, bangles, nose ring, earrings…she tied all of it in Khanderao's shawl…

A huge pyre was prepared. Khanderao's body was placed on it. The pyre was lit… …Ahilya covered her ears and was banging her head on the wall trying to block out the screams of the women burning alive …as Satis. She kept thinking of the two Muslim wives of Khanderao…Did they not want to live? They wore the white saris...smeared their foreheads with kumkum…adorned garlands in the neck…they did not hesitate even once. They had a smile on their face as they accompanied their husband on the journey beyond this earth and forward…Did they experience true love? The union that her mother had spoken of…? How was true love after all, thought Ahilya to herself…Share everything good or bad with your husband and go with the flow, or stand up at times, even against him…try to reform him and do the right things…Why did she not get that love…

The cacophony of the drums and pipes could drown neither the screams of the women burning alive nor the turmoil in Ahilya's head…What kind of an inhuman, cruel tradition was this…how could people bear that...could they not hear anything? The thunderous chants of people, 'long live sati!' long live sati!' were deafening her eardrums and blowing her brain apart…

****

The Jat realized what a grave mistake he had committed, in firing the shot that killed Khanderao. He was shaking like a leaf. He was certain that Malharrao would now avenge his son's death. He tried to pre-empt disaster by sending his headgear to the Shindes symbolizing surrender. In a bid to prevent escalation of conflict, Shindes accepted it, meaning end of enmity. When Malharrao heard about the pardon and truce, he was furious and also disillusioned with his dear friend, Shinde. ..But he thought it prudent, to make allowances for differences, in the Holkar-Shinde alliance. Only a seasoned statesman knows that the enemy always looks for chinks in the armor and as soon as they spot one, they attack. He knew better than to allow personal tragedies to eclipse strong political alliances. He thought to himself... 'The Jat is going nowhere ...and I am here too...but will wait for the right time...'

Malharrao returned to the camp. He could not bear to see Ahilya dressed in white...no jewelry...no kumkum...He mustered the courage of his lifetime ...to merely cast a glance at Ahilya ...who sat on the floor...her head resting on her knees...teary and numb. Malharrao's voice softened. He took a few steps in her direction and stopped...folded his hands and said, "Ahilyabai, I will remain indebted to you forever. I know I have stood in the way of your religious duty as a wife...but I will be answerable to God in his Court of Justice. The sins, if any at all, will be on me...only me...not you my child." Saying so, without as much as waiting for a response, Malharrao turned around and stepped out of the tent...starting his journey to Mathura for further rituals...leaving behind a grieving Ahilyabai in Baiji's care...

****

The war was stalled...tents dismantled. The women left for Indore. The palanquin of the two mistresses returned empty. Ahilyabai's eyes were misty...their thoughts haunted her.

Indore was shrouded in gloom. Some people were chanting the names of the women who went Sati with Khanderao...singing their praises. Nobody said anything to Ahilyabai...yet she felt, as if the glances of some staunch religious people following the palanquins, were piercing her back...their quiet glances questioning her...

She got off the palanquin and quickly entered the palace. The incriminating silences of some people were lashing her core...She rushed to find Mukta and Malerao...she hugged her children and simply broke down. Everything that had built up inside her was easing out...Baiji , Harkuaai...no one could console her. They just huddled around her, patted her and watched helplessly...living her moments of pain with her as she quietened gradually…

People started trickling in, to offer their condolences. The sardar women…the Jahagirdars…Baiji had lost her son too. But Ahilya sensed that people seemed more keen to see her…stripped of all her jewelry, color, kumkum. Some women even seemed to suddenly find their own miseries less aggravating in comparison to widowhood… 'At least, they were not reduced to living a black and white life…'was their secret thought.

Human emotions can surprise us. Good occasions make others feel bad sometimes, and bad occasions at times, can make them somehow feel good, about their own lives. Ahilya thought, most often, it is neither men nor religion, nor the system…but a woman, who is another woman's worst enemy. Many women made their displeasure known to Baiji about Ahilya not following the tradition of Sati…

Baiji stood strong. She did not wish to validate their displeasure by trying to offer explanations. But Ahilya felt she was being condemned…though she had lived for the larger good. Surprisingly, the two Muslim mistresses were elevated to a high pedestal, for following the 'dharma' of dutiful wives…despite living a life of intoxication, alcoholism, lust, and squandering of royal wealth…

Baiji recognized Ahilya's unspoken dilemma and glanced at her reassuringly at regular intervals. Ahilya drew strength from Baiji's unfaltering support…

The visitors' flow waned. Baiji reached out to Ahilya and said just one thing. "Ahilyabai, public memory is short. One day, Indore will resonate with praises for you…and your benevolent reign. The secure tomorrow of these very people rests on your sacrifices of today…and they will be indebted to you forever."

At night Ahilya entered her room. Ahilya lay in bed…exhausted by the sheer swiftness of events as they had occurred. Khanderao's quarters were in darkness. No sounds coming from there. Did she miss those very sounds she so detested? Ahilya spent hours sorting out her feelings…It was in the wee hours of the morning that Ahilya wanted to shake off all discarded thoughts…She had to look ahead. She had to focus on Malerao. Now, there were no conflicting influences on him in the palace. She had to prepare him to take over the rule and the benevolence of his grandfather. She was full of determination. But only destiny knew what lay in store for her…

****

Ahilya received many letters of condolences …also from the Peshwa….the Badshah…an apology letter from the Jat…Ahilya was going over the letter she had received from Malharrao that morning, informing her that Khanderao's ashes had been immersed in the Yamuna river. She sat down on the chair…shut her eyes and rested her head on the backrest…thinking about what Malharrao had written to her further…he had said… 'You looked like Goddess Lakshmi…bejeweled… on your wedding day and after…Now, it pains me to see you bereft of color… but I now look upon you as Goddess Saraswati, white, pure, knowledgeable… Everything now rests with you…the well-being of the people, the wise employment of wealth…the growth of the region…

She noticed that Malharrao and Baiji too, had started referring to her as Ahilyabai…now, at the helm of the Holkar family. Ahilya felt weighed down by some indescribable burden…

****

The political climate in the Marwar region was getting inhospitable and frosty. Ramsingh was a weakling. He was usurped by Bakhatsingh and later, after his death, by his son Vijay Singh. Ramsingh had the support of the Shindes…and Vijay singh was Madhosingh's son-in-law. Madhosingh, had come to power with Malharrao Holkar' support…

One more time, the Shindes and the Holkars seemed to be pitched against each other. Malharrao was disturbed by this feud. After all, both, Shindes and the Holkars were the Sardars at the same court and owed their allegiance to the Peshwas.

Towards the North, Sujaa-ud-daulah ascended the throne at Ayodhya, spreading unrest between the Hindus and the Muslims. Mosques were being built by demolishing temples. Hindus were reinforcing their rights by demolishing mosques and re-establishing temples. Ahilyabai was anguished by this deadly game of one upmanship. 'All religions preach equality, peace and tolerance…so what was all this about…' she thought…

****

Six months had gone by. The silence at the palace pronounced Khanderao's absence at every step. Malharrao had returned for the six monthly rituals, to conclude the death rites of Khanderao. The Puja commenced. Ahilya sat in a white sari. Ahilya listened intently as the priests mentioned with due respect the names of the deceased ancestors …then of Khanderao and then of his wives who left for their heavenly abode along with him on the pyre. Every name was mentioned except Shabnam and Shakina…the two Muslim wives.

Ahilya apologized as she interrupted Antoshashtri to enquire if they had forgotten the names of the two Muslim wives. There was silence. No one spoke. They simply looked at each other. Ahilya questioned again…Antoshastri cleared his throat and said firmly that those two women…their religion was different and hence their names had been omitted!

Ahilya was dismayed. "Those two ladies were the wives of my late husband…wives, who most willingly and happily embraced death along with their beloved. The two women reduced themselves to a pinch of ashes with my late husband...and, we are not willing to as much as even acknowledge their existence and pour two spoonfuls of water in their memory on this mound of rice in this ritual? If it was acceptable to have them as wives in his life, they must be accepted in death too. I will consider this ritual incomplete and unfinished if we miss out on mentioning their names."

Malharrao and Baiji were taken aback. One of the priests said resolutely, "Kindly excuse us, but this breaches the tenets of our religion."

"Tenets of our religion?" Ahilya repeated. "Who created this? We, human beings have. So then find a way out. Shabnam and Shakina were two living beings. They too had a soul...and they did not evade this tradition of sati on the basis of religion...they could have. But they did not. They dropped all religious differences and perished with my late husband. Despite this if you are unable to perform rituals in their memory for the peace of their souls ...then I regret to announce that I will have to go to the Maulavi to pray for the departed souls...and unless I complete this ritual, I will not eat a morsel of food."

Tension was palpable in the room. The priests listened with abated breath...other visitors were barely breathing... Ahilya got up from her seat, went to Malharrao and requested him to resolve this.

Malharrao was pensive. Everything had come to a standstill. He looked at the priests and said, "Antoshastri, I request you to kindly pour water in memory of the two Muslim women..."

The priests all murmured under their breath and expressed their displeasure. Some also feared being ostracized.

"Then...in that case," roared Malharrao, "you are all welcome to move into the palace along with your families and live in our protection! Ahilyabai is speaking the truth and from her heart. The true essence of following 'Dharma' or religion is to follow your conscience. God created human beings ...and human beings created religion. Religion was created to bring people closer not to divide them. The importance of religion cannot override the importance of human relationships."

He looked at Ahilyabai with great pride and permitted her to proceed to offer the names of the two women...Ahilya said... "Shabnam Khanderao Holkar and Shakina Khanderao Holkar..."...and the rituals were complete.

****

One day Mukta entered Ahilyabai's room...jumping with joy...displaying two exquisite yardages of silk...One was peach colored with delicate gold paisleys and the other was a fresh sapling green with pretty red roses embroidered on it. The fabric was soft, seemed to be rare and expensive. Mukta wanted her mother to make her a dress out of it. Ahilyabai was rather surprised and wanted to know where she got the fabric from. Mukta replied that her brother had presented it to her. Ahilyabai found this rather unusual and proceeded to find Malerao. She looked for him everywhere. As she approached a small secluded room, she could hear Malerao and his friends whispering inside. She pushed the door open and stood there aghast...Some friends ran away throwing the game of dice halfway...

Ahilyabai knew she had to be patient. She had to talk to the child and not instill fear. She had to explain to him that playing dice at this young age was not a good thing...She walked up to him and sat him down...hugged him and tried to talk to him...find out about the silk pieces...the game of dice...

Malerao relaxed. He felt assured that his mother will not punish him and spoke up...the truth poured out...his father would take him to his quarters ...teach him the game of dice...he had even tasted alcohol...he took Ahilyabai and showed her the hiding places...Ahilya saw a small box...with trembling hands she opened it...and there they were! The small tablets that Khanderao was addicted to! Ahilyabai's eyes were full of fear! She asked him, "Do you know what this is?"...Malerao smiled and said, "Oh! You have to eat very small portions at a time…" Ahilyabai sank in her chair…That explained the slightly longer sleeping hours of Malerao…it was not due to exhaustion from his training sessions!!!

"…and those silk pieces?" Ahilyabai dreaded the answer… "Oh! The women in father's quarters used to give us those…"

The boy was barely ten …Ahilyabai was numbed…she was reminded of the day, the Holkars had received the papers of the Subhedari…she was barely 9-10 years old and Khanderao was 12-13 …and Khanderao had slept all day long…

Ahilyabai was alarmed…shaking inside with fear…She knew she could not trust herself to deal with this…This needed a lot of patient investment of time…and that was the one thing she did not have …time…her time was taken up by her work…She knew she would have to depend on Baiji for this...a patient handling…for success…

****

The first death anniversary of Khanderao was two weeks away. Malharrao placed a letter in front of Ahilyabai…She looked at Malharrao and opened the letter not knowing what to expect…It was a letter from her brother, Shahaji Chaundikar. It was a scathing comment on what had transpired at the six monthly death rituals of Khanderao. The letter strongly condemned the unusual inclusion of Muslim women in Hindu rites and therefore requested his exclusion from the invitation list if the same drama were to unfold at the first death anniversary too. The letter concluded with a sarcastic suggestion, urging Ahilya to embrace the other religion rather than desecrate this religion!

Malharrao looked at Ahilyabai. She sent for her assistant to write out the reply as she dictated with stern conviction, "Kindly inform him that there will be no change in the way the ceremony was conducted. The women who charred themselves to death with my husband will be duly and respectfully remembered. I fail to understand how praying for the departed souls is either unusual or can desecrate any religion, albeit, everyone is free to choose what they wish to do"

Malharrao smiled with admiration for Ahilya's conviction.

Friends and family gathered for the solemn occasion. Ahilyabai's mother arrived from Chaundi. Her father and brother were conspicuous by their absence. The head priest was present. Many other pundits declined...some were purportedly travelling...some unwell...some had personal contingencies... Ahilyabai was aware of the real reason.

Some relatives even posed questions on her being religious at all...Ahilyabai set their doubts to rest by proclaiming that, "She is guided by religion, not blinded by it". Someone had the audacity to comment on Ahilyabai herself being impious as she had not followed her religion on the tradition of sati...Malharrao chanced to hear that. Malharrao stopped in his path. Turned around, faced the person and stared at the one who had said that... he announced in a loud voice...as he continued to stare...saying, that if anyone ever uttered a word about Ahilyabai not following Sati...he would personally set them afire...there and then! Malharrao had never made statements like these! Everyone froze. No one even dared to breathe. The silence was more deafening than his declaration...

People tiptoed around and spoke in whispers throughout the rest of the ceremony...the guests too left at the earliest convenient opportunity.

Before long, the palace wore a lonely look...and then ...out of the blue...a story , that, 'Khanderao's quarters were haunted,' started doing the rounds! Trusted people...like Anjana, Renu, Raghoji, Bhagoji claimed that they had heard the sounds of ghungroos at midnight, on dark no moon nights...Everyone whispered about unfulfilled wishes...ghosts...spirits...This news fanned out throughout Indore. People were frightened to pass by that side of the palace...Ahilyabai too was a bit shaken by the accounts of her close aides...

Before Ahilyabai could steady herself, the news of two more events pulled the rug from under her feet. Vijaysingh orchestrated the murder of a brave sardar...Jayappa Shinde. After a dip in the water, Jayappa Shinde would shut his eyes to pray. The killer, disguised as a beggar, exploited that moment and attacked.

Second, Madhosingh, poisoned Govind Tamaji, the lawyer of the Peshwas...

Both these events crippled Malharrao's strength. Malharrao mourned the casualty of the Shinde- Holkar friendship in this deceitful death of a courageous sardar. Malharrao felt terribly let down by Madhosingh and his son-in-law, Vijaysingh.

Even after Khanderao's death, despite being let down by the Shindes themselves, Malharrao never fought against them. Many feelers were sent by opportunistic foes of the Shindes... attempting to deepen the Shinde-Holkar chasm. But Malharrao's answer to them all, was the same...That, they both owed their allegiance to the same throne ...the Peshwas...and so will never fight against each other. 'The Shinde-Holkar divide was the most unfortunate page in history. A true friendship soured in the game of political alliances and loyalties...' Malharrao truly regretted this...A dear friend lost...the cost of lost friendship, dearer...

****

7

A quiet, hurt, Malharrao in mourning, departed for southern missions...leaving everything behind in Ahilyabai's charge...A widowed Ahilyabai, barely 30, in white, stripped of her jewelry and instead straddled with responsibilities requiring an iron hand...dedicated herself to the service of the people...replying to heaps of letters, dispensing justice...demolishing trouble and building a strong social order…

It was a tiring day…and Ahilyabai returned home in the evening…Today, Ambadas, the son of their priest Raghodas, was to hold the first reading session of the great epic Mahabharata at the palace. Harkubai cautioned Ahilyabai against the reading of Mahabharata, but instead advised her to arrange the reading of Ramayana. "Mahabharat is all about politics, deceit, lust, betrayal…Ramayana is about love, duty, commitment… triumph of good over evil…" said Harkubai…

Ahilyabai smiled. She said… knowledge is never good or bad. How you use it makes it good or bad…Mahabharata is also brimming with valuable lessons…

"…and how is that?" asked an amused Harkubai

"It teaches you that prevention is better than cure…it teaches you, never to disregard even the slightest of problems because if you do…then they come back to bite you with greater force and precipitate complete destruction…This epic cautions you on, how greed for power can become a rising sandstorm…how silence can lead unsuspecting people into quicksand…how arrogance and ego can drag you to abysmal lows…" Just as Ahilyabai was talking about Mahabharata, Ambadas arrived, accompanied by a Tantric.

Ahilyabai looked at him with surprise. Ambadas introduced the Tantric as an expert in exorcising ghosts. "I have heard about the sounds at midnight and …" said Ambadas. Ahilyabai hacked the conversation, saying, "I do not remember having extended invitations to exorcists. If I ever feel the need to employ such services, I will certainly send for him. But for now, he is welcome to join us as your guest". Ambadas proceeded to read the first page of the Mahabharata…

****

The dark no moon night was four days away. Ahilyabai informed Harkuaai about her plan to go to Khanderao's quarters at night, to examine the veracity of the stories ...Ahilyabai thought to herself, 'if at all spirits exist and I happen to meet the ghost of Khanderao or the Muslim women...I will ask them if they have any unfulfilled wishes..' She also wanted to know if there was indeed any significance to the crows staying away from the rice mounds, at the death ceremony rituals of Khanderao...

Harkuaai offered to accompany Ahilyabai. They both decided to keep this visit a secret and tell no one other than Baiji...

It was a no moon night. Dark...Ahilyabai and Harkuaai made an excuse of visiting Depaleshwar and instead went to Khanderao's room...and hid behind the curtains...On Baiji's insistence, as ample precaution, they carried with them the religious symbol of 'aum', a small idol of their God and holy water for protection...as well as some candles and lights.

The time was almost still...moments were passing heavily as darkness started creeping around them. They could hear the crickets buzzing in the stillness...an owl would suddenly startle them by scratching the silence with its screech...their hearts were in their mouths...midnight was closing in on them...and ...unexpectedly, they could smell the burning of incense sticks...see some smoke... the two women held each other's hands and tried to look at each other in that darkness. Their hands were frosty ...feet were cold too...and yet, they were breaking out into sweat as they gradually began to hear soft sounds of ghungroos. Slowly, the tempo quickened...they heard a male voice... "Shabnam....Shakina...begin the dance..." Ahilyabai and Harkuaai were motionless...their skin goose pimpled...heart almost stopped beating and blood rushed to their head...tilting and rolling the room around them...

Ahilyabai had to draw strength out of her every pore to collect herself...She was well aware that Harkuaai was barely holding on to her consciousness...She was certain that Renu, Anjana, Raghoji and others must have gathered in the courtyard below as they always would, on a no moon night to hear the sounds of the ghungroos from a safe distance...She had fulfilled all her duties as a wife except following sati... 'If that is haunting the spirits', she thought, 'then I need to confront this once and for all...'

She was herself feeble at the joints...the sounds of the ghungroos had peaked...she took a deep breath...and determined to settle this ...she lit a candle and bolted out from behind the curtains...and...what she witnessed stunned her...She let out a piercing shriek...as she lost consciousness... her scream knocked Harkuaai out and brought Baiji rushing into the room....

Both the unconscious women were carried to the main palace. The royal Vaidya was immediately sent for...someone was sprinkling water on them...another thrusting onion halves under their noses...in the hope that they would somehow regain their consciousness. The royal Vaidya got busy with the mortar and pestle and his herbs, while the palace was busy churning out ghost stories...with grainy details... beliefs... opinions... experiences...questions...reprimands...perspectives...

Ahilyabai opened her eyes and assured everyone that she was not obsessed by spirits. But she kept staring at the ceiling...quiet...the sounds still ringing in her ears. She shut her eyes. The ghosts were from within the house... They were her own son, Malerao and his friend Sudama...frightening everybody. The moment they saw her, they jumped out of the windows at the back, and escaped through a route designed by them.

She only told Baiji and Harkuaai about it. Baiji later assured Malerao of complete secrecy on this incident if he indeed did mend his ways...

A year and a half had passed by. The sounds of the ghungroos had stopped. Indore was now brimming with stories of how Ahilyabai's good karma had driven the ghosts away. These were the very people who had unkind words to say to her when she did not follow sati. Ahilyabai smiled to herself. She had a lot to learn…about the fickle mindset of the people…their shifting opinions…and at times resolute approaches…She knew just one thing…Be honest and true to what you think is right…and she got back to work in all earnestness.

A letter from Malharrao arrived…narrating the story of the Nizam's defeat, despite betrayal by two of Malharrao's allies, Murarrao Ghorpade and Muzzafarkhan. The letter also described the combat power of the foreign cannons. They had captured regions that would bring in ten lakhs into the Holkar treasury. Ahilyabai was pleased. But the stories that followed wiped that smile away. Malharrao had intended to mend distances by offering his condolences to Dattaji Shinde. Instead of granting an audience, Dattaji sent a reply, 'Will meet you in heaven now' … devastating Malharrao, and distancing the two families further. Just before ending the letter, Malharrao left Ahilyabai completely uneasy…He wanted to discuss the marriages of his grandchildren…Malerao, now 12 and Mukta, merely 9…

Ahilyabai shuddered with the thought of Malerao's marriage…Just then, Gangoba Tatya arrived with stories of the escalated menace of the Bhil tribal community…looting travelers and passers-by.

Ahilyabai sighed, "Gangoba Tatya, how do the Bhils dare to persecute, loot, the travelers…? The answer is simple, she reckoned. "Not without protection from the local law and order authorities!" She was informed by her spies that morning, that, the local officers were getting a proportion of the loot in exchange for protecting the Bhils! She directed Gangoba Tatya to dispatch strict warning letters immediately to the authorities maintaining law and order in the area as follows: 'If anybody is found to have any connection with the Bhils, they will face cancellation of their rights and withdrawal of the authority vested in them. No explanation will be entertained. The travelers have to be guaranteed safe passage. A patrolling unit must be established on every road. In the event any loot occurs, the chiefs, in charge of the region, have to not only repay the travelers back but also bear a fine…'

Ahilyabai stood up. "What kind of people are these Gangoba Tatya who enjoy harassing others…." And Ahilyabai was reminded of her own son…

****

Ahilyabai was concerned... The nuisance of the Bhils had not subsided. She consulted Baiji... who had no suggestions to offer either…Ahilyabai was pacing up and down… all of a sudden her face brightened up. She turned to Baiji and said, "You have read Mamanji's letter too…the very thought of the children getting married shook me up! But herein lies an opportunity…just like the days gone by…why don't we set a condition for Mukta's marriage: 'anyone who can contain the menace of the Bhils will marry Mukta!' It will at least assure us an intelligent, capable, fearless son-in-law…" Baiji pondered…adding that she had some well reckoned families in mind…

"The family may be well reckoned…" reinforced Ahilyabai, "but the boy has to be worthy …Mukta has to marry the person, not the status or wealth. After, all Baiji, when you married Mamanji what did he have with him other than his valor? Nothing! He built it all up…I would value qualities not wealth…"

Baiji nodded in agreement and advised her to discuss the plan with her father-in-law.

The next day …was business as usual. Ahilyabai was steeped in work when suddenly she heard a commotion. Looking out of the window, she noticed a crowd in the square near the main palace structure. Ahilyabai quickly tidied her papers and left for the palace. The distance of a barely forty yards, seemed like a mile to her as she quickened her pace. Ahilyabai was more than shocked to see Malerao lashing a boy with a whip…She rushed there like a lightening and intervened. She plucked the little boy away and threw one arm around him in protection and held Malerao's whip with the other. Before Ahilya could react any further, Malerao darted off like an arrow…slicing through the crowds…

Ahilyabai's blood rushed to her head! She looked around at the crowd and questioned them with derision, "Not one of you had the courage to stop this heinous act?" Her pitch was now shrill…and she demanded to know what this was all about. When she understood that the lashes were showered because the friend had broken a wooden toy …Ahilyabai could not prevent herself…She picked up the whip and proceeded towards Malerao's hideout. Baiji stopped her… "He is your son…" she said. Ahilya replied, "The boy who he thrashed is also someone's son…so, do not stop me…Malerao has to be punished for this reprehensible behavior…"

****

Malharrao arrived in a celebratory mood! As soon as he stepped into the palace, he told Ahilyabai to bring him some sweets…and he announced the good news…that… he had found a match for Malerao!

Malharrao said, "We will have two weddings after the monsoons…Malerao's and Mukta's.! You will get a son-in-law and a daughter-in-law…and I will be relieved of my responsibilities!"

"…adding to mine!" quipped Ahilyabai. 'who is the girl….what is her age…her family…' queried Ahilyabai to keep the conversation going. But deep inside, there was emptiness…nothingness…She knew that the little girl's destiny was to be like hers…

Malharrao informed Ahilyabai that she was the daughter of

his friend, Bahaad. "Her name is Maina…a little girl…with innocent large…clear…lotus eyes…with brilliance just like yours!"

Baiji arrived with trays full of more sweets. She was excited at the thought of getting a granddaughter-in-law! Malerao's wedding …and then to look for a match for Mukta…

Maina and her family were to visit them the next day. Baiji started giving out instructions …preparing for a grand welcome. Ahilyabai barely smiled and left the place using a ploy, of some work. She kept thinking of those unseen…large…innocent clear eyes of some little girl somewhere…

Baiji sensitively conveyed Ahilyabai's thoughts to Malharrao …on how to find a match for Mukta…the person who could contain the menace of the tribal Bhils. She wished to marry Mukta to courage, not to family prestige…

Malharrao was pensive…he agreed …A well known family cannot assure a courageous match. But a courageous boy can bring glory to any family. "Look at our own family…" said Malharrao. Baiji hesitated but expressed her doubts… "What if the boy turns out to be a Muslim…a Pathan…or from lower caste?" Malharrao looked a bit worried…but he merely said, "Why don't you ask Ahilyabai this question…" knowing fully well that Ahilyabai must have already contemplated that…

"I did…" said an embarrassed Baiji.

"…and?" Malharrao was curious to know Ahilyabai's response.

She said, "Virtues do not have a caste…courage has no creed…" and then she asked me, "Baiji, our bodies are made of five elements of nature (Panchmahabhootam)…Do fire… sunlight…water… wind…earth…have a caste? If not, then we cannot have castes either!"

Malharrao smiled with deep satisfaction. Their own caste, 'Dhangar', was reckoned as illiterate…low caste in the social order…he knew, under Ahilyabai's reign all this was set to change for the better!

****

It was late afternoon that day…After siesta time, Ahilyabai ordered for some warm saffron milk with powdered nuts and cardamom to be served to all in the family room. The inadvertent rap of Malerao's whip, as she had intervened, was stinging on her arm. The thoughts of Maina …and those innocent eyes that wrapped her heart, made it feel sorer.

Ahilyabai offered Malharrao the glass of milk and said… "Tell me more about the Nizam' defeat…" Malharrao looked surprised! He said, "I presumed you would rather want to ask me more about tomorrow's visitors and Maina…" Not waiting for Ahilyabai to react…Malharrao continued and spoke about the treachery…and then suddenly he remembered something!

"Yes! I must recount two stories. First…Anubai Ghorpade! An extraordinary woman who commands her own regiment! The other…the power of cannons! I have already left behind one of our best men to study and learn the techniques. After he returns, I am certain you will utilize his expertise to create many more trained, skilled people …"

Ahilyabai was galvanized to hear about Bajirao's sister, Anubai Ghorpade! "I am going to start training and recruiting women…and create a women's regiment in Indore too!" Ahilyabai's imagination was fired by the visions …and details of executing this idea!

Meanwhile Ganesh Vithal, Bharmal dada, and others had arrived to report to and update Malharrao on various political and monetary issues. Ahilyabai took their leave and stepped out of the Diwankhana. All around, hectic preparations were in progress for the visitors next day. The chandeliers were shining…cushion and bolster covers were being refreshed, carpets rolled out…perfumes poured in oil lamps…fresh flowers speckled…rosewater sprinklers placed…Ahilyabai seemed distant...disconnected...Malerao had been sleeping all day... Malerao showed no desire for education. Despite all efforts by Ahilyabai and Baiji, they could not channelize his energies ...or groom him to be the next Subhedar. Mukta was barely nine...the hunt for her groom would have to wait for a couple of years...

Ahilyabai was restless all night. Quite early the next day, Appasaheb Bahaad arrived with his family. The little girl tugged at Ahilyabai's heart...wavy dark ringlets of hair, framing a round, fair face, large clear lotus eyes and a charming smile on her rose petal-like lips. Ahilyabai found it hard to believe that an incredibly adorable doll, at such a young age, could narrate stories from our scriptures for two hours at a stretch, at temples... this girl...for an undeserving son like mine....?

A warm welcome...followed by lunch and matching of horoscopes...Ahilyabai felt a huge weight inside her chest...she was silently sighing heavily...and found it almost difficult to breathe...

Nobody made much of the fact, that Ahilyabai left the room with Renu. She went upstairs. Sent Renu back to Maina's parents... requesting them, to meet her upstairs, in confidence.

The parents came up...tentative...not knowing what to expect...dowry demand probably...they discussed between themselves...As they entered, Ahilyabai put all doubts to rest.. "Please do sit down..." She offered them some juice. "Why do you appear so worried...I want nothing from you...no dowry!" She smiled lightly ...just to diffuse the tension. "Your daughter's beauty reminds me of moonlight shimmering over rippling waters...calm...bright...pretty...But it is my misfortune to caution you that this marriage to my son, may eclipse this child's destiny...your daughter is like a little Goddess incarnate...but Malerao..."

"Why! He too is blessed with good looks and we are certain with many virtues too..."

"If he was virtuous, I would not have summoned you for

this meeting. Let me speak plain. My son is extremely mischievous…at times viciously unruly…"

Maina's parents interrupted her, "At this age all children misbehave…he will grow up and certainly prove himself…"

Ahilyabai found it hard to choose her words… "He drinks alcohol…uses opium tablets…cruel games like an animal fight…has a bad temper…"Ahilyabai spurted all out in one breath!

To her surprise, the parents were calm… "The descendants of the Subhedar have to be strong… even cruel at times…they hear stories of torture, valor…blood curling battles…what else would you expect them to become?"

Ahilyabai was exasperated…It was not easy for her either to describe her son in this manner… Finally she said, "Look, your daughter will never be left wanting for love from me …or Baiji…But I have no assurances on Malerao…You are therefore free to refuse the match"

Maina's mother spoke, "Marriage and responsibility are known to reform even the worst. Given the free will, men have enjoyed since times immemorial, can anyone, anywhere give assurances of a man's character? They are free to do what they please and when they please…At least here, in your house, we are assured of even handedness and fair dealing…She is assured of love from you…I would rather that she is safe in your house than insecure elsewhere…Be kind enough to accept Maina as your daughter-in-law…"

Ahilyabai was speechless… "Alright then, as you please…"

****

Just after the monsoons in 1756, Malerao married Maina in a simple ceremony. Maina was looking divinely delicate…exquisite jewelry…exclusive clothes… expensive gifts from the Peshwas…fitting return gifts…

Ahilyabai had no role to play in the religious rituals due to her widowhood. She was lost in her memories. The lemon yellow dress...Subhedari papers...the wedding...the wedding night...the glass of saffron milk...emerald armlets...that last night together in a white sari...

At about 31, Ahilyabai was a mother-in-law..Malerao and Maina came as a wedded couple to seek her blessings. She poured her heart in it...and wished them a long, happy wedded life and good luck always...

****

Abaji Sadashiv retuned with the expertise and detailed awareness of employing cannons in warfare. Ahilyabai got busy with arranging training and imparting skills to people. Baiji was reveling in celebrating all of Maina's first festivals in the household...Makar Sankrant...Holi...New Year...

Maina had found a friend in Mukta. The two were growing to be best of friends...sharing stories... games... secrets... Fourteen months just glided past...

Antaji Mankeshwar had been repeatedly sending messages from Delhi requesting for additional forces for the North. The rumors of an impending attack by Abdally on Delhi were growing thicker. Northern regions needed to be protected. Discussions were gaining pace. Plans were being sketched. Raghunathrao too arrived in Indore for consultations. Abdally was demanding two crores and the Punjab region. It was suspected that Abdally would find an ally in Najeeb Khan.

Ahilyabai was of the opinion that the joint forces of the Holkars and Raghunathrao should, without further delay, march towards Delhi...provide support to Antaji Mankeshwar. Punjab had to be fortified. If that crumbled, the rest of the country would be under threat. Ahilyabai urged the two warriors to set off immediately and they did so with huge forces...

The expenses of such a huge force were herculean. Malhararo therefore decided to take a detour to Rajputana to collect taxes which he thought would help sustain the expenses of the army.

Raghunathrao was against this. At the end of three months, an exasperated Raghunathrao said, "You are 44 years older than I am…You should know better than to go around collecting taxes, when we should be moving towards Delhi!" At the end of May, as tax arrears were collected and Malharrao neared Agra, explanations were demanded for his delay…, "You have come now? Abdally has already looted jewels worth 25 crores…massacred people…kidnapped Hindu women…So many women consumed poison, some jumped into flames, others bit into diamonds to escape molestation…" Raghunathrao felt anger rising inside him…

"Madhosingh and others sided with Abdally…Peshwas were at Shrirangpattam…and you arrive so late? Messages after messages…pleas after pleas were sent…and you come now? To lock the stable door after the horses have bolted??!!!" the Jats continued venting… "Antaji Mankeshwar struggled to hold fort with weak forces…every house was looted….temples marauded…people beheaded. Heaps of corpses and chopped heads were piled on the roads…It was a 'holi' played with the bloodied waters of the Yamuna river…Raghunathrao could hear no more. He covered his ears, not sure if he was livid with Abdally more or Malharrao more.

Later, in the month of June, Vithal Shivdev, managed to capture Najeebkhan. Most rulers were in favor of killing Najeebkhan, but ultimately Malharrao's suggestion of releasing him, albeit, in exchange of a huge sum was accepted by all.

The huge sum was instrumental in wiping the debts out and additional, immeasurable riches were gained. But this success came in as too little, too late. Not enough to wipe away the ignominy of the Abdally episode. The disgrace heaped by Abdally, engraved in History, as a 66 year old Malharrao's erroneous judgment, had now brought disrepute to the Holkars…

****

Ahilyabai's spies were bringing in stories. She could not believe that Malharrao had erred…that he spent three months collecting taxes on the way when people had no shelter…nowhere to hide…when Vrindavan, Gokul, Mathura were burning and being looted…Ahilya was upset…shattered…also angered by this discredit to Malharrao.

Ahilyabai had no time to breathe. North was burning, South had become treacherous, and the nuisance of the Bhils went unbridled. There was chaos everywhere. Ahilyabai had reached a decision. Well guarded shelter homes, wells, roads, temples had to be built…where people could hide safely in times of war. Arrangements had to be made for the protection of the common man. Ahilyabai drew plans and ordered immediate implementation.

Ahilyabai, in all this, neither had the time nor the energy to protect and guard Maina from fourteen year old Malerao's spiteful pranks and sadistic games. The day she discovered that Malerao had loosened the knots of the swings on which these girls played…just to see the fun…she thought it best to send Maina to her parents' home till she reached adolescence.

****

A couple of months later, Malharrao returned to Indore. She saw a frail man…Ahilyabai touched his feet to seek his blessings. She looked up and noticed that he had aged abruptly. Ahilyabai was filled with compassion for the aging, courageous Subhedar. She advised him to rest and left for work. This time she did not want to hear the war stories….

Ahilyabai looked at the accounts. Collections ran into crores. Jewels…silver…gold…so much wealth. But it did not make Ahilyabai happy. It had come at a massive cost…

She went to Malharrao the next day. One third of the loot had to be deposited with the Peshwas. It was unsual, she thought, that the Peshwas should be under crushing debt when the treasuries of their sardars are overflowing. The rivers of wealth were not flowing into Pune…they were flowing into private treasuries. This seepage had to be sealed. She had to initiate that beginning. She urged Malharrao to go to Pune at the earliest to submit the accounts and deposit their rightful share…

Malharrao's ill health delayed his departure to Pune by a month and a half. When Baiji and Malharrao left for Pune, Ahilyabai spent restless days and nights…She wanted no one to ever doubt the integrity of her father-in-law…She wanted him to be remembered as a heroic, courageous, upright, fearless man down the generations…

****

Two months had passed by. Ahilyabai was keenly awaiting Malharrao's return from Pune…and just then she heard the bugles blow…a signal that Malharrao had entered Indore. Mukta rushed to greet her grandparents. She was happy to hear that they had visited Maina on their way back and that she was well…She missed her sister-in-law in all their play games…

Malharrao and Baiji freshened up. Everyone got together for some snacks and refreshment. As Ahilyabai moved towards Malharrao to serve the juice, he stopped and looked up at her, smiling affectionately. "Ahilyabai…" he said, "you were right. The news about the wealth I had accumulated had reached Pune before me…spreading discontent….based on the misgiving that I would not deposit the fair proportion in the Pune treasury. Nanasaheb and Bhausaheb were surprised to see me! I stood there with folded hands and apologized for being late but then committed one third portion of the collection to the throne of Pune."Ahilyabai's face lit up with a wide grin. Malharrao continued, "I am not just proud of you my child, but will remain indebted to you for pushing me, to go to Pune… disallowing temptation…" Ahilyabai had tears in her eyes… 'a great man becomes heroic, not because he makes no mistakes, but because he accepts and rectifies them', she thought. "I am proud Mamanji that your repute flies high with our flag"

There was a letter she had to share with Malharrao…from Dattaji Shinde …thanking Malharrao for putting behind their differences and for protecting and supporting him in the North, in the battle …in tackling Najeebkhan. Also suggesting that if the Jats, Rajputs and other sardars were to unite, defeating Abdally and Najeebkhan would not be difficult at all…and thereby urging Malharrao to take charge and guide everybody in this mission…

Malharrao had always insisted and strived for that unity between the Shindes and the Holkars. He knew very well, that it was not just of utmost importance, but, in fact more than enough to contain, not just Abdally…Najeebkhan…but any other enemy…He was glad the Shindes were now speaking his language of internal unity...

Ahilyabai finished reading the letter and suggested that after the monsoons that year, Malharrao should proceed to the North. Malharrao disagreed saying, the kingdom was expanding and he would have to visit Jaipur-Udaipur before going northwards.

Ahilyabai was firm. She asserted strongly that the North cannot be left unattended at any cost. It offered easy entry to externals powers into the country…that had to be priority. Malharrao looked at Ahilyabai with great respect…as he admitted with pride that she had now surpassed him in understanding political priorities…and that he was now aging … "I have no hesitation in leaving all this behind, in your able hands…" a grayed Malharrao looked satisfied…

Malharrao looked tired as he sat down. Ahilyabai sat next to him. Malharrao looked at Ahilyabai and said… "Today the kingdom owes its existence to you. I owe my expansion and aspirations to you Ahilyabai, and I know, all this has come at the cost of your personal happiness…and I seek forgiveness for that. I am guilty on one count…that I plucked you out, a brilliant little girl, at a tender age, from your village, to marry my good-for-nothing son…all for the love of this kingdom. I enslaved you, to work for the welfare of the people…I did not allow you to know any better…in life" Ahilyabai was taken by surprise by this poignant talk by Malharrao. She did not know what to say…all this had turned too intense but Malharrao seemed to feel lighter…Before Ahilyabai could respond … Ramaji Yadav, arrived to take Malharrao and Baiji on a scheduled tour of the ammunition factory. Malharrao took a deep breath and stood up to leave. Ahilyabai was surprised at herself as she showed them around… 'when had she learned all this…' she thought, '…fortunate that her life had a purpose! But what would happen after her…?' She did not dare ask destiny that question…

****

8

Malharrao had left on his mission. There had been no news from him for a while now. For the last 7-8 months Baiji had been suffering strong bouts of Asthmatic cough. The mortar pestles were busy churning out medicines… mixtures…potions. Massages, dietary routines, thousands of well wishers and visitors, were all stifling her normal routine. Malerao was delighted with so much distraction and the crowds! He would hide on the first floor and pelt pebbles, marbles, on their head…spray powdered black coal or pink gulal on people dressed immaculately…and then laugh out loud…

Ahilyabai was busy handling her duties on all counts when a horse rider shot inside the palace like an arrow. The entire security of the palace was alerted. The rider held the saffron flag of the Marathas. Soldiers threw a ring of security around

Ahilyabai. She steadied herself and swiftly snatched a weapon from a nearby location. She shot back a threatening look at the horse rider and took a hostile stance as the rider got off the horse…

"Who are you? Identify yourself immediately and declare your intention else you will not leave this place alive!" blurted out a watchful Ahilyabai…

The man got off and kneeled down. He was out of breath. "I have a lot of news for you and very little time… but need to speak with you in private…"

"I am Maloji Shinde. Abdally is flooding the North with his army. The movement of his troops indicates a fierce impending battle …we need Malharrao's help right now…" Ahilya was stunned. But Malharrao has left for the North…Ahilya's heart was beating fast…Where was Malharrao?

Maloji Shinde clarified… "Malharrao is occupied at Udaipur and Jaipur! This was Najeeb khan's ploy…to provoke Madhosingh and keep Malharrao engaged at Udaipur-Jaipur…so that he gets time to pile up his forces and gather more might…

Ahilya lost her cool… "But where is Antaji Mankeshwar? Hingane? Could nobody see through this ruse?

Maloji pleaded… "I have tried unsuccessfully…therefore I have left the battlefield and come straight to you. Please give me a letter in the name of Malharrao urging him to proceed North towards Delhi without any delay. There is utter chaos up North…tens of thousands of Muslim forces are entering our country…men are being massacred…there is loot and plunder…"

Ahilya looked furious. She knew right away that sparing Najeebkhan was to be her father-in-law's gravest political blunder… Ahilyabai was now determined. Ahilyabai ascertained a couple of vital facts from her spies. She knew this was not the time for exchanging letters. She decided to go herself. Instructions were issued. The Army was readied. Ahilyabai, Maloji Shinde and one thousand horses started galloping towards Jaipur…An unwell Baiji, was to follow in a palanquin with adequate security. Though, on the last leg of the journey, Ahilyabai brought Baiji on horseback.

The entourage had just about reached Malharrao's camps in January of 1760, when the sad news of his dearest friend Dattaji Shinde's demise broke out. Malharrao broke down…tears rolling down…finding it difficult to hem in his grief…Malharrao crumbled on the ground…

Ahilyabai merely looked at Malharrao. She did not feel like saying a word to him or consoling him… 'What good are these tears now…'she thought to herself… 'When wisdom… protocol…political judgment all indicated that Malharrao should have first marched to Dattaji's support rather than go to Udaipur-Jaipur to solve the tussles there…'

Dattaji Shinde challenged the Muslims even as he fell…saying… "I will fight you till the end…revive me now...and I promise, you won't survive…" ["bachenge toh aur bhi ladenge!"]

Baiji noticed Ahilyabai's reluctance and moved forward to console Malharrao. Baiji calmed the grieving Malharrao … and said, "Be proud that a young Dattaji gave such a stiff fight. To what avail are these tears now … you should have been with him…reinforcing his army. Despite repeated pleas, you thought it prudent to solve the Jaipur- Udaipur intrigue first? Do not dwell on what has happened …You must now avenge the death of Dattaji and protect the injured Janakoji."

With Baiji echoing her sentiments, Ahilyabai found courage to speak directly. "Had you reached here two months ago …the picture would have been different, Mamanji…You should have…" Malharrao snapped her sentence short. "Anybody and everybody takes the liberty to pelt stones at an aging lion…so are you…"

But before he could say anything further, Dattaji's wife, Bhagirathi arrived there…barely able to walk, in this final, ninth, month of her pregnancy…supporting her unborn child in her belly as she walked…She was unable to maintain, neither her posture nor her composure…

She looked at Malharrao and said, "My husband had relied heavily on your help. Every time he saw clouds of dust rising…he would expectantly say… 'Am sure that is my uncle, Malharrao approaching with his army! Now let me see who dares to clash with us…'.He would be instantly energized with hope…But it is too late now…" She broke down. Malharrao now truly understood the damage his delay had done…Malharrao was shaken…Bhagirathi was distraught… not sure what she should regret more…her late husband's disappointed trust or the disappointment of her late husband's trusted uncle…

Janakoji's wounds were being treated…Janakoji's wife Kashibai too arrived with heroic stories of her efforts to save a wounded Janakoji…

Reports indicated that Durani's army was approaching in their direction. Malharrao suggested that they all cross the Chameli river to safety. He had to now ensure the safety of Bhagirathi, Dattaji's unborn child… the other women and Janakoji. But Janakoji refused to retreat to safety…Insisted on defending his land…braving the approaching army.

Baiji looked at Malharrao… "You are revered for your courage and fearlessness. Do not choose disgrace at this stage in your life. Without your support and presence Janakoji will not succeed. I have full faith in your victory…and…it is better to give yourself up defending honor than preserve yourself for a life of disgrace and regret…"

"What do you suggest, Ahilyabai?" asked Malharrao.

"I am strong enough to safeguard the women and children. But the security of the kingdom rests on the edge of your sword…"

"Alright then!" roared Malharrao! "We go right away"

Oil lamps were readied… 'tilaks' made on the forehead…betel leaves presented…good-byes were said. Kashibai was distraught…Bhagirathi numbed…Ahilyabai and Baiji kept gazing in the direction of the departed armies…till the dust finally settled.

A few trusted horseriding warriors were left behind. All the women started their return journey. Midway, on the banks of the Kunwari river, the tenth day and the twelfth day death rituals of Dattaji were completed. Many priests and pundits from the nearby places crowded around…the mounds of rice were placed on the river bank. But, not a single crow ventured near them, let alone peck at the mounds of rice…suggesting an unfulfilled wish of the departed soul…

A 35 year old Ahilyabai stepped forward. With folded hands, she looked up at the sky…closed her eyes, concentrated and said out aloud… "Dattaji, you fought bravely. Do not worry about Bhagirathi. I promise you, I will ensure she delivers your child in as much comfort as possible. I will protect the mother and child and personally guarantee their safe passage home, to Ujjain…"

As soon as Ahilyabai made this announcement, the hovering crows swooped down to partake of the symbolic mounds of rice…Bhagirathi broke down…her journey with the young Dattaji spanned barely a year and a half. But she had countless stories to tell…of their love …togetherness… Ahilyabai listened…searching for some comparisons…but found herself grappling with darkness.

Ahilya felt lonely and depressed…She now wanted to reach Indore to Mukta…and maybe even Malerao…That evening passed by, dull and disinclined…Baiji's Asthma was nagging her… Just then Kashibai came rushing…Bhagirathi had gone into labor. Arrangements for midwives and other preparations for the delivery were in place.

Bhagirathi was getting hysterical, thinking of her dead husband...and with every teary outburst she was pulling the child in, rather than pushing it down...Baiji was getting impatient and worried. Ahilyabai sat down beside her, held her hand and pulled her through the delivery procedure...A bonny boy was born.

Ahilyabai bathed the mother and child with warm water, wrapped the baby in soft warm clothes...tied a scarf around Bhagirathi's head to avoid lightheadedness post childbirth... created a small fireplace near the bed. Baiji put together all the traditional medicinal herbs and prepared measured dosages to be administered to the new mother for proper lactation... disinfection and spinal strength. Syrups were boiled... powdered medicines given in jaggery pellets...

The dull tents in the camps had to celebrate this happiness that had streaked in! Ahilyabai stood up...smiled...blew the conch, announcing childbirth! Bugles were blown...sweets were distributed...On the fifth day, the palanquins left for Ujjain. True to her word, Ahilyabai personally escorted the mother and the newborn to the safety of their home.

All the women hugged each other, said their good-byes. Ahilyabai told the Shinde family that she was always just a message away...and like a sister to Bhagirathi, now and always.

The Shinde-Holkar ties were cemented by providence in this unique twist of fate!

****

The entourage reached Indore. In Ahilyabai's absence, Oodabai had overseen the palace...and looked after Mukta and Malerao. Ahilyabai held Oodabai's hands...and thanked her generously for the support in looking after her children. She acknowledged that this support allowed her the liberty to work for the people... "I am indebted to you, for the love that you shower on my children…" said Ahilyabai

Oodabai smiled but looked a little worried. Later in the day, when all the chores were accomplished…Oodabai wanted to speak with Ahilyabai…She expressed her reservation on Malerao, who had discovered a new pesky way of harassing people. Ever since he had learnt horse riding, he would get astride a horse and gallop threateningly towards groups of women…girls...or even old men…and when they would scatter away in fear …he would spit out red betel leaf solutions and laugh out loud…people feared to protest…

Ahilyabai was shocked into silence. She looked at Baiji. But before she could say anything, Mukta came in rushing to her mother! "Where are you, mother? Why do you go away? Why can't you stay at home like aunt Oodabai? I love that she is around the house all day with me…."

Oodabai patted Mukta and said, "Your mother has greater things to do. She has to rule the kingdom, make roads, temples, gardens for you to play in…your grandfather needs your mother's help!"

Mukta immediately replied, "Then take me along too! I too will learn to rule like you!

Ahilyabai hugged Mukta … saying, "God bless you!" She kissed her on her forehead…and looked up. Malerao had entered the room. He had changed in these four months…he looked so much like his father. The same gait…same style…

Ahilyabai struggled hard to keep her calm. "You are forbidden to ride a horse henceforth…"

"Oh!" he snapped. "So my dear aunt has squealed to you, is it about that old man?"

Ahilyabai first warned Malerao that he could not be rude to his aunt and then questioned Oodabai about 'the old man'?

Oodabai fumbled for words. She confessed that she could not gather courage to tell Ahilyabai about it.

Malerao looked threateningly at his aunt, as she blurted out the truth that an old man named Phadke was trampled to death under Malerao's horse…

This had crossed all limits…a death…in fun?! She charged towards Malerao…held him by his arm…Malerao tried to get hostile but as soon as he noticed movement among Ahilyabai's guards, better sense prevailed and he did not defy her any further.

"Come with me…right now" ordered Ahilyabai sternly.

"But where…"demanded Malerao trying to resist her.

"To ask for forgiveness, from the Phadke family. You seem to be able to show your strength only against the weak. Try me!"

Malerao continued to look at his aunt…now verbally threatening her…

Ahilyabai stopped. Turned around and slapped him tight across his face. Stood there staring back at him. Malerao was thrown off balance. Before he could regain his stability, Ahilyabai dragged him with her…saying if he did not obtain the forgiveness of the family, she would have to treat him as she would any ordinary citizen…and that meant…

Baiji got up and handed a pouch of 5000/- to Ahilyabai, to be given to the widow of the old man. As soon as Ahilyabai reached the Phadke house, she sincerely apologized after her son and asked for forgiveness.

The widow, quiet, merely blessed her…saying …Malerao was 'her' son and that was reason enough, to forgive Malerao.

Ahilyabai was thoroughly ashamed as she handed over the compensation money to the old widow…The palanquin returned to the palace.

****

Ahilyabai had entered the treasury after months. Work had piled up. Tax arrears had to be collected. Some sardars had not made their specified contribution to the army…complaints had to be looked into…letters, messages, correspondence…

The rulers were so engulfed by battles and wartime activities that the security and conveniences of the common man were being compromised. People were living in constant fear and uncertainty. The Bhils were exploiting the strife ridden times and harassing the travelers more than ever…Ahilyabai was revolting inside against these wars.

Forts had to be repaired, funds had to be raised. People had to be protected. Arrangements had to be made for Dwarkaai and Banaai to go on a pilgrimage. They deserved a break too…Ahilyabai was exhausted…

She pulled the complaint box and emptied it on the table. The first complaint was from the widow of the Phadke family. 'How do you propose to punish your son for killing someone? Order death by trampling under the elephant's foot or hanging until death?'

Ahilyabai kept staring at the paper blankly…hoping that their visit and the widow's forgiveness had put that question to rest.

****

The accumulated work kept Ahilyabai occupied for two months…and one day, she received a letter from Maina's parents saying she had come of age…matured…and that arrangements could now be made for Maina to go to her husband's home…and begin their marital life…

Ahilyabai felt as if all her energy had drained out of her body…her heart dropped into the pit of her stomach. She sent for Oodabai…discussed it with Baiji…Ahilyabai said things had deteriorated even further since their marriage…and she could not dare to bring Maina and hand her over to Malerao as his wife. She feared for the girl's safety…She was not going to ruin that little girl's life…

"But people will talk…and Maina's family will have to

answer a lot of awkward questions..."warned Baiji

"I have a suggestion," said Oodabai. "Why don't we be honest and explain to them...and request them to delay sending Maina by two more years? Let us bide some time...and find a solution in the meanwhile"

Ahilyabai was sorely relieved... "Yes!" and she slumped in her chair out of mere fatigue ... "this can be done"...

The very next day Oodabai packed Paithani saris...nose rings...earrings...sweets and left personally to visit the Bahaad family with the proposal...

****

Ahilyabai's spies could not bring her any information about Malharrao. There were misleading rumors floating around, about his locations...she was beginning to get worried when she received a letter written by Malharrao himself dated March 14. A letter detailing the furious battles up North...the massacres...cautioning her about the dangerous times ahead...the imperative call for supplementary funds... the letter also named the people who had gone down fighting...Malharrao expected that personal condolences be offered to the families of the martyrs...

Ahilyabai urgently sent out messages about the death of the martyrs...She herself accompanied by Baiji , visited their homes to offer condolences...

The homes were seized by pain...tears...sorrow...the widows were distraught...insisting on sati...Ahilyabai patiently convinced them against sati...

One more time Ahilyabai felt repulsed by war...She was exhausted...and she spent the next day, just lying down in her room...

****

The summer heat of April-May was roasting the palace

walls...and within these walls was hectic activity. Grains and pulses were being sun dried...salt, turmeric...chilly powder, were being pounded...chips and other long lasting savories made from fermented wheat, potatoes were being stored...jars of pickles...bottles of jellies...kept everyone bustling around.

Ahilyabai had lost her sleep on the news of Abdally , Najeebkhan and Shuja-ud-daullah uniting to form an alliance...She was busy on that front...

The Monsoon rains came streaming in, sprinkling freshness and greenery around. It was breezy...cool...a respite from the dry heat...the smell of wet earth travelling from afar...The rains were pleasant, swinging in festivities and sparkle...

The entire palace would wake up in the wee hours of the morning...bathe before sunrise and arrive at the place of worship, as the veil of darkness lifted with the orange flourish of the early sun rays... lovely oil lamps twinkling at the crack of dawn. The temple and the palace would be reverberating with the chanting and mantras. The scent of fresh flowers was carried on the whiffs of sandalwood incense sticks and burning camphor...A fresh beginning to the day would keep Ahilyabai going through the long and dreary day...dealing with letters, complaints and dismal news from her spies.

At the palace, Malerao was annoyed with his grandmother, for allowing his mother to keep his wife, Maina, away from him for a year or two more. He walked in to his grandmother's room forewarning her, to bring Maina by the end of Monsoons...

Baiji gestured to him... inviting him inside to sit next to her. She tried to chat with Malerao, to enthuse him to improve his ways...encourage him to help his mother in her work...

Baiji wanted to say more but Malerao stunted her attempt by his outburst, "Do not teach me about good deeds and religion. What happened to my mother's religion? She should have gone with my father... on his funeral pyre...but instead, she pushed the other women into the fire and is blissfully enjoying the power of controlling this region…!" Before he could finish, an angered Baiji stood up, saying, "Don't you…"and lunged forward to slap him across his face…

Malerao, a strong, young boy of 15, merely blocked her hand and she reeled back on her own force, lost her balance and sprained her ankle. "Don't 'you' forget …" warned Malerao, "I will become the Subhedar one day…dread that day…" Baiji sat down …numbed…shocked…trembling…

Ahilyabai walked in…home, after a tiring day. The air was tense. Dwarkaai and Banaai told her what had happened. Ahilyabai turned back… went straight to Malerao's room. Malerao had put his feet up…he looked at her and continued to play with a top (a toy)…Ahilyabai began to speak…and Malerao interrupted her… "It would be in your best interest if you traced your steps back…" Ahilyabai could feel the anger rising inside her. She continued to move towards him. Each step, definite and resolute. "What makes you believe that you will be the next Subhedar? No education…no swordsmanship…no credence…yet this conviction! Drop this arrogance and apologize to your grandmother right now. And if this is how you plan to behave, I am not bringing Maina here ever… is that clear? Go and apologize NOW."

Malerao did not move. "Now! I say!.."shrieked Ahilyabai. Malerao moved very slowly…stood up…made a face… "You also tell the old woman to stay out of my matters…just raising my voice will be enough for her to collapse…"

Ahilyabai could not put up with this anymore. She snatched a whip lying in his room and lashed him. One strong blow before he could even blink. The second blow was on its way when he trapped the whip in his hands and tugged at it. Ahilyabai lost her balance momentarily…but she did not let go of the whip. She firmly balanced herself back. The whip remained strained hard between the two of them…their gaze fixed on each other. There was shocked silence.

In one lightening move, Ahilyabai tugged the whip and then let go of it! Malerao lost his stance and reeled back. Ahilyabai turned around swiftly, stepped out of the door…swirled around and shut the room door from outside…locking it. Guards were posted outside his room. He was served food and water but could not step out.

A few days went by…Malerao showed signs of softening…he promised his mother and the grandmother that he would improve. Malerao was still under surveillance…but was being allowed a few concessions. He was quieter now…

****

Less than a month had gone by after the Ganapati festival and one day a palanquin arrived at the gates of the palace. Everybody's hearts stopped beating…was it an injured Malharrao? Everybody dropped their work and rushed towards the palanquin…and just then Maina stepped out of the palanquin. Everybody resumed breathing…with a collective sigh of deep respite…and moved in to welcome her, and her parents.

Ahilyabai invited them inside with respect and honor… offered refreshments and fruit juices. Later , lunch was served on Ahilyabai's insistence, breaking social custom, where the bride's parents do not eat, or even drink water in their daughter's marital home unless and until she bears an heir …a son…to the family. Ahilyabai insisted that she did not believe in customs that distanced people rather than bring them closer…

After lunch Ahilyabai said, "If you had informed us of your visit, we would have welcomed you with magnificent splendor… melodious music playing right from the city limits.

The parents looked perplexed and exchanged surprised glances… "Did you not send us the letter through Sudama, our son-in-law's best friend...to bring our daughter? In fact, we did find it a little unusual that you would bring Maina into the palace this way…but the times are uncertain… war…battles…we thought…" Maina's mother interrupted her husband…realizing that saying anything further would be unfavorable and wrapped up the subject by saying, "after all, it is time now that the girl starts living in her husband's home…adapting to the ways of this household…we now leave Maina in your care."

Ahilyabai, instantly knew what had happened… Malerao had surreptitiously sent the letter through his friend. Ahilyabai said nothing. She made arrangements for their return journey …gifts were exchanged…goodbyes were said… Ahilyabai's heart went out to the poor girl and her eyes started welling up. Maina's mother did not miss the moistness in Ahilyabai's eyes. She said, "The tears in your eyes reflect the concern in your heart. I am certain my daughter will be safe with you."

Ahilyabai felt a huge load on her shoulders…seemed heavier than that of the treasury…As they left, Ahilyabai went cold with fright … 'How do I protect this girl from Malerao….' Baiji noticed Ahilyabai's apprehension and advised her not to dismiss the possibility that marriage may change Malerao…make him, responsible…Baiji substantiated numerous examples where marriage had brought about a positive change in people and urged Ahilyabai to have faith in the Lord…

****

At daybreak a messenger arrived with a confidential letter from Malharrao, written on September 20, 1760. Ahilyabai took the letter to Baiji and both women read it together. The letter chronicled the ongoing political developments… Malharrao was disheartened with the treatment now meted out to him, by the other forces which were gaining ground at the court of the Peshwas. Malharrao's hair had grayed in the rough summers spent in protecting and serving the Peshwas…but no one respected gray anymore, he protested. His advice was going unheeded...The younger blood was arrogant, disregarding experience and loyalty...diplomacy was at its bankrupt best. The last sentence in the letter wrenched their hearts. Malharrao said, he was now told to visit the Peshwa's Darbar only when invited... "After spending years on barren land and rough terrain, living in tents, this is what I get...Do not have the mental energy now...A dull feeling seems to weigh me down and harsh words seem to tear my heart apart... desire family support in this hour...."Malharrao was disenchanted and disillusioned...

Ahilyabai and Baiji exchanged frozen looks in silence...eyes moist...a lump at the throat was choking Baiji. Ahilyabai broke the silence. "Do not waste time thinking. You must leave, to be with your husband. He needs your support to shore him up now...I will make arrangements for your departure"

Ahilyabai ordered a palanquin seat to be strapped atop a camel...summoned her soldiers from the safety and protection division. By mid-morning preparations for Baiji's journey were in full swing. Bags of provisions were sewn, silver seat anchored, other loose ends tied. Around noon Baiji was set to leave. But Ahilyabai was restless. She had never stayed without both Malharrao and Baiji. She bowed down to touch Baiji's feet to seek her blessings and she just broke down...curling up at her feet, unable to get up, covering her face...trying to stifle the sounds...tears flowing incessantly. Baiji hugged a troubled Ahilya, calming her down. Everybody had gathered to say their goodbyes. Baiji left late that afternoon, leaving Ahilyabai in long, dark, shadows behind her...feeling anchorless, lost.

****

9

The festival of Dussehra went by, heralding Diwali. It was Maina and Malerao's first Diwali. Malerao had been behaving himself lately. But deep inside Ahilyabai was distrustful of her son. She used to keep a watchful eye on their movements. She would observe Maina's expressions... peer into her eyes at every opportunity trying to mark reflections of any anguish...determined to act quickly if she spotted any...Ahilyabai did not know what she should feel...There was profound responsibility...unfamiliar hope... strange guilt ...unknown fear...

Preparations for Diwali got underway. Saris for Renu and Anjana... blouse pieces for others, uniform and clothes for the men folk, headgears for some. In line with the protocol of seniority, gold rings, brooches, pearls were distributed as gifts. The priests were presented with shawls as a mark of respect. Paithani Saris and jewellery for all the other wives of Malharrao. Ahilyabai did not have Baiji to share and discuss... She truly and deeply missed Baiji.

Just as she was thinking of Baiji and Malharrao, a letter dated 3 November, arrived. Ahilyabai opened it impatiently. Other than the news that Dattaji Shinde's killer, Kutubshah was captured alive, no other news was heartening. The same deadlock in the North and recurring disregard of her father-in-law by the younger order in command...Ahilyabai was upset. A straight forward man who had contributed monetarily as well as strategically to building this expansive empire...today was being disregarded...his judgment questioned...opinions dismissed!!?? She conceded, surely, sparing Najeebkhan was a grave mistake made by her father-in-law. But who does not make mistakes in politics? And can that one mistake wipe out the goodwill of a lifetime? A life spent, striving only for one thing, the expansion of the Peshwa rule. No one in a thousand years could cast a doubt on his intentions...and that made all the difference...It is always the intention behind the act rather than the act itself that always must matter.

Ahilyabai was simmering inside yet helpless....She wanted

to support her father-in-law in this hour but did not know how to achieve that. She was restless …could not concentrate on her work. She decided to retire early. Before retiring, as was her ritual, at least once in a day, she would spend some time with Maina…observe her…talk to her…assure herself of the girl's uncertain wellbeing.

Maina walked in. Her walk was a little slow…smile faded…eyes dull…Ahilyabai touched her forehead. She seemed to have fever.

"Are you not well, my child?" asked Ahilyabai. Maina said nothing. Ahilyabai held her and helped her sit. The girl winced in pain. "What is the matter?" asked Ahilyabai again…Maina nodded, "nothing…"

Her eyes….Ahilyabai's heart began to sink. Maina had covered both her shoulders with her sari pallu…like a shawl. Ahilyabai's heart was now thumping. She brushed the pallu aside from her shoulders…and…slumped into the chair. There were bruise marks on the girl's shoulders…neck…and some partially hidden under the neckline of her blouse. Ahilyabai looked closer…noticed her swollen lips…It was as if a lightening had struck her. Ahilyabai struggled up on her feet…her mouth was dry…her breathing interrupted…The silence of 20 moments seemed like a score gone by…Ahilyabai took a deep breath… "when did this…why didn't you…how…" Maina came rushing into Ahilyabai's arms sobbing sorely…hugging her so tight that Ahilyabai could not free herself to even speak. Ahilyabai was hesitant to touch her, even to console. Maina's body was hurting. The girl was in pain…mentally and emotionally.

Ahilyabai was furious with her son. She wanted to slap him hard. This boy was never going to reform himself. She hated herself for trusting the hope, that Baiji sowed in her. Now Malerao was never going to set his eyes on this girl again. Her first instinct was to condemn him to the dungeons.

Ahilyabai sent for Oodabai to come to the palace

immediately...as she assured a fearful Maina...calmed her. Ahilyabai sent for the vaidya. In the meanwhile, she applied soothing anti septic lotions on her Maina's body...fed her some food...juices...

Ahilyabai rued the fact that mothers taught their daughters to comply with everything that their husbands demanded...to never say no, simply for marital success. Mothers told their daughters... 'be tolerant, patient...and then all turns out well in the end...' This was our culture...our advice to women! Ahilyabai made up her mind. She was going to initiate this change. Encourage women to speak up...

Oodabai rushed in after getting an urgent message from Ahilyabai. Maina was lying on the bed. Ahilyabai was quiet...sitting by her bedside. Oodabai looked at Ahilyabai's dark, cloudy eyes...guilt written all over her face...

In that instant, Oodabai knew...her worst fear... She tip toed close to the bed. Ahilyabai looked at Oodabai with the saddest eyes...helplessness...anguish...

Not a word was said. Ahilyabai pursed her lips, her body limp...breathing with great difficulty and effort...Every breath sounded like a sigh. Oodabai knew. She hugged Ahilyabai ...who sobbed and sobbed ...blaming herself ...responsible for Maina's condition.

Maina's eyes were now dry. Oodabai was speechless. She kept looking at Maina over Ahilyabai's shoulders. It was a while before anyone spoke. It was Ahlyabai. She told Oodabai to take Maina away to Depaleshwar with her...safe...away from her son's brutal instincts...till she could make up her mind on what to do with Malerao. Arrest him...exile ...or a death sentence. He already had a murder charge...and now this...

Oodabai made arrangements in the cover of the night...to take Maina away to safety without much discussion. Ahilyabai stood there...looking at Maina's silhouette, as it disappeared into the darkness. The little girl who told love stories of Radha-

Krishna…Nal-Damayanti…young soft dreams crushed in broad daylight…dissipating in that darkness…

Malerao asked about Maina. Ahilyabai did not think his questions merited any answer. She just replied, "Safe…somewhere…"She had to control her anger and take the right decision about Malerao.

In all this, a beggarly looking man…torn clothes… unshaven…arrived at the palace gates. Ahilyabai wondered…a beggar…riding a thorough bred horse?! Unusual. A traveler? A spy? A soldier…?

****

The beggarly man showed her a symbol…a ring worn by the Subhedar…Ahilyabai froze, not knowing what to expect or what she was going to hear…

There was a message from Malharrao. He needed assistance…Reinforcements…The situation near Panipat was grave. The soldiers had no food supplies. Help from the South…the Peshwas was yet to arrive…

Ahilyabai impatiently took the sealed message and rushed inside to read it. 'Please arrange to immediately dispatch 50,000 soldiers and one Crore to me. We are under siege from Abdally. Reinforcements from the south are unreliable. Without a moment's delay, take all available ammunition and cannonballs from the Indore factory and personally come to Gwalior immediately to oversee operations. You have brought prosperity…now is the time to protect it. Baiji's asthma is worsening in this siege...If I survive …we meet. Else martyrdom…Blessings to all'

Ahilyabai did not have the time to be alarmed. She gave instructions to verify the authenticity of the beggarly man and to take care of him …food …water…bath…

As soon as Ramji Yadav arrived, she left for the ammunition factory. She returned and tried to persuade Malerao to accompany her to Gwalior...but to no avail. He refused. Ahilyabai put together as much as she could... forces... money... ammunition...food ...and left for Gwalior, leaving behind Banaai, Dwarkaai, Harkuaai and Mukta...all to their destinies... The future of the country was at stake.

****

Gwalior was more discouraging than Ahilyabai had anticipated. She met Bhagirathi, Dattaji Shinde's widow. Jayajirao too had lost his life fighting this battle. The numbers of widows in the territory were growing every day...In all this it looked rather out of place that Nanasaheb Peshwa was busy getting married to Radha, a daughter of a moneylender called Bakhare. 'What does one make of this'... thought Ahilyabai to herself...Does this mean all is well with the army or that Nanasaheb has no knowledge of the fierce battle ensuing at Panipat...?

Finally, one day, in the January of 1761, Ahilyabai was relieved to see Malharrao with his army approaching her. Janakoji Shinde had been captured by the enemy and held hostage...One lakh people had lost their lives in the battle of Panipat...Malharrao was proud of Ahilyabai for the reinforcements she had brought in but he ordered her to return to the safety of Indore immediately.

Ahilyabai returned to the palace. Mayhem had swallowed the palace. Hundreds of soldiers who had lost everything in the Panipat war...maimed...hungry...sick...wounded...no food , no water, collapsing outside the palace , begging for care and help...

A shocked Ahilyabai swung into action. The kitchen fires were ordered to keep burning all day and all night. Women were employed to cook for these soldiers. Blankets and clothes were distributed. The royal Vaidya was called in with his disciples. Medical care was given to the wounded. Lotions, ointments, tablets, were being administered...

Ahilyabai would take rounds every few hours to enquire after their well being. The anguish among the soldiers settled down…They had gory, heart wrenching stories to tell of the carnage at Panipat. Ahilyabai was assuring people but her own words were sounding hollow to her. Nothing could justify the pain and anguish of the soldiers… Every step convinced her of the futility of war…This had to end, she grimaced…

The very next day, a very disturbing news reached her. Nanasaheb had done the unthinkable. He had confiscated the palaces and other properties of the Shindes and the Pawars, as a penalty for the defeat at Panipat! Ahilyabai was not inexperienced…She recognized that a similar fate awaited the Holkars…

Quick on the heels of this news, Malharrao returned with Baiji to Indore on horseback! He was fuming. As he was getting off the horse he condemned the confiscation…and regretted how the young leaders like Bhausaheb disregarded rules and caused mayhem .It was not poor leadership but the disorder that caused the mayhem and carnage…

Ahilyabai had never seen Malharrao so disillusioned. She tried to sustain the moment by saying, "Mamanji, your courage and valor has an edge sharper than the sword. It will not be long before you will have erased this blemish…and…" just then the news of the arrival of Nanasaheb at the gates of Indore broke their conversation! Malharrao immediately rode towards the city limits to welcome them!

Greetings were exchanged with an undercurrent of bitterness…on either side. The entourage arrived at the palace. Lunch was served. Everybody was in mourning for the loss at Panipat. Simple meals…no music...no pomp…

After an uncomfortable lunch, punctuated by forced smiles, everyone moved to the Diwankhana. The air was apprehensive. The odds of impending fiery exchanges, were frighteningly high. Everyone seemed distracted…silently rehearsing their lines of accusations...explanations....counter questions...options...

Nanasaheb occupied his high seat while Ahilyabai sat on a white durrie on the floor. Ahilyabai looked in control and determined to defend her father-in-law. The glow of her confidence outshone the other bejeweled ladies in the room who had accompanied the Peshwa.

Nanasaheb spoke. "Panipat was a disgrace. Many trusted people lost their lives on the battle field. But you seem to have survived." Nanasaheb took a pause. "What does this mean? A secret pact with Najeebkhan?...to save you, in exchange of old favors?"

Malhararo tried hard to keep his calm and succeeded. "I pushed my limits. Bhausaheb defied the established protocol and all hell broke loose. And today after years of service, my loyalty and integrity is being questioned? Ahilyabai herself had arrived with reinforcements and controlled the cannons for a brief period...."

The Peshwa, interrupted Malharrao and looked at Ahilyabai. "I have heard great praises about Ahilyabai..."

Ahilyabai was not interested in tracing her praises...her focus was restoring her father-in-law's dignity.

Ahilyabai smiled mildly, thanking the Peshwa for his kind words and then replied very humbly, "If I am what I am, the well deserved credit goes solely and only to my father-in-law who has been in your service all his life...dedicated to heralding victory after victory for nearly 40 years now. It will not be long before this lone defeat at Panipat will be made good. His sword commands that power!"

Malharrao was both proud, that his daughter-in-law stood strong by him....as well as hurt, that the Peshwa did not. With mixed feelings in his voice and resignation in his tone, he said, "Ahilyabai...why recommend my integrity when one defeat has eclipsed decades of victories...Its time now that I leave everything in your able hands and proceed on a pilgrimage..."

For a brief while, the conversation steered away to acknowledging Malharrao's might...yet, in the end, the Peshwa made demands of huge amounts as penalty from Malharrao for the defeat. Malharrao pleaded...saying... he had himself suffered tremendous losses... "Where do I..." the Peshwa interrupted Malharrao very curtly, and in a menacing tone, said, "I confiscated the palaces of the Shindes...with you...I am being kind enough to ask..."

That was the last straw for Malharrao who had been struggling to tender the respect that an employer should deserve. His annoyance was apparent as he raised his voice a trifle... "Not withstanding the poor treatment you have meted out to the Shindes, I am obliged that you are 'asking' me. I have seen twenty five summers more than you have...and if you call me family, how appropriate is it for you to penalize me like this? I considered myself family when I offered 30 lakhs in lumpsum towards your debt...all that forgotten with just one defeat? I beg your pardon but I will be unable to give you anything..."

Before the Peshwa could ingest the remark and respond, Gopikabai, his wife, hustled to take the steam off the situation... "Malharrao, my husband is in mourning and a little unsteady with his emotions. You are the pillar of this kingdom. I apologize on his behalf...do not be offended by what he said...and now, it is time we take your leave..."

The palanquins left. Unenthusiastically yet, not breaking tradition, Malharrao walked 50 steps with the palanquins and turned back. Everyone was quiet. No one spoke.

Four days later, a scroll arrived. The non-residential palaces and properties of the Holkars were confiscated. Malharrao was bitter. Baiji was crest fallen...her ill health deteriorated further. She was bedridden. Malharrao had to regain his lost status...avenge this disgrace.

****

For almost 5-6 months, till June 1761, Malharrao reestablished rule over Bundelkhand, Rajputana, Malwa. He gave tough fights in Gwalior, Jhansi, Datiya, Bhadawar…He was like a man possessed.

In the meanwhile, on June 23rd, 1761, Nanasaheb Peshwa passed away…and on 17th July 1761, his son, Madhavrao ascended the throne.

Malharrao never for a moment lost sight of the fact that his loyalty lay with the Peshwa…whoever it was…and whatever happened…

He wrote a condolence letter without any delay and promptly received a reply too from Madhavrao.

Ahilyabai was delighted to receive that reply. She wanted to read it out to Baiji whose health was on the downslide…energies depleting gradually…sometimes bouts of Asthma, another time high fever…Malharrao was informed about her aggravating health.

That day …Ahilyabai wanted to read out the letter aloud to Baiji.

"Respected Malharrao…"

"Are you listening, Baiji?" Baiji lay in her bed. Ahilyabai confirmed Baiji's attention and continued to read. "…My greetings and respect offered at your feet. You have been relentlessly striving for the prosperity of our region. Restoring order in the north, in a mere 7-8 months, using strength and diplomacy effectively, is no mean achievement. Your experience and contribution is priceless…your advice even more valuable. In fact, had your advice at Panipat been heeded, disgrace would not have come our way in the first place, let alone the inglorious words uttered by my predecessor. You are a father figure not just to me but to the people too. I humbly request you to put the past behind and shower your blessings on me…"

"Did you hear that Baiji…Baiji…?"Ahilyabai woke her up … read the scroll again and again…making sure that Baiji heard all that she read out, even as Baiji was in and out of consciousness…

Baiji had heard every word…her husband's respect had been restored… "Baiji…our palaces have been returned to us…the Holkar flag flies high on them now…Baiji…do you understand what I am saying…?"

Baiji nodded…she wanted to see Malharrao…he had arrived. He sat next to Baiji. Baiji smiled…a smile of satisfaction…her eyes spoke everything…

Malharrao lifted Baiji's head…put it on his lap and looked at her. Baiji could barely whisper… One last time she wanted her husband to put kumkum on her forehead…a symbol of true lasting love…building hope that if there was a life after , it was a promise to meet again…another time…another life…bid goodbye to her in this life…

Everybody had started pouring in…Oodabai, Harkuaai, Banaai.. Ahilyabai had locked herself in her room. She wanted to cry…just cry…loudly… She buried her face in the pillow stifling spurts of tears…just crying till she was breathless and exhausted. Baiji was more than a mother to her…a mentor…her strength…her companion…her guide… gone…forever…never to come back…

Malharrao and Oodabai knocked at her door. Ahilyabai came out…forlorn…distraught…crying uncontrollably… breathing deeply and then letting out streams of tears till she could no longer breathe …almost as if her breath was locked inside her chest…

Malharrao braved her tears and spoke. "Ahilyabai…steady yourself…come…"

"Come..? Where? Take me to one place where her memories will not haunt me…Mamanji, you will soon go on your mission…leaving me behind…here…in this palace…where every step …every corner…every turn…will remind me of Baiji. Take me to a place where I can escape this. You have your companion…your sword…I have lost my mother…"

Oodabai consoled her…after all Baiji had spent more time with Ahilyabai. Even Bajii's own daughter, Oodabai, did not feel what Ahilyabai felt for Baiji…

Malharrao had no time to mourn. He had to get back to his mission. Ahilyabai was unhinged inside. Baiji was gone. Malharrao was ageing. Malerao was not growing up…

Ahilyabai pleaded with Malharrao to take Malerao along with him. If he was to be the future Subhedar…he had to learn to be a soldier first…

Malharrao was reluctant to take the only heir…But Ahilyabai convinced him, saying, "What good is a life, if not lived well? Please prepare him for his duties"…she begged.

An even more reluctant Malerao was initiated into the regiment. Malharrao and Malerao trotted out on horsebacks together. The entire palace, placed their hopes on that moment…hoping to see a turnaround in Malerao on his return…

The political scene had metamorphosed in the last 2-3 years. Everyday new developments…fresh allies…new enemies. The British had used business and economy to burrow their way into politics. The Marathas were clashing with the Moghuls in the North…defeating the Nizam in the South. Differences between Madhavrao Peshwa and his uncle Raghunathrao were creating chasms…opening up opportunities which the British never failed to exploit. Shuja-ud-daulah and Gajiuddin were sitting on the fence…at times siding with the Holkars and at times with the British.

Ahilyabai spent more and more time working…after Baiji passed away who would she come back to…? No one to share…discuss…laugh with. Ahilyabai brought Maina back to the palace. Mukta and Maina were once again spending happy times together…

…and one day, Malerao, now a young handsome boy of

twenty, entered the palace on horseback.

****

1765

The rigors of war, the grind, had channelized Malerao's energies. There was a huge change in him. Mukta was now 17, engrossed in her education. For once, personal life seemed promising for Ahilyabai…

Malharrao needed an uninterrupted stream of funds… money…supplies…Ahilyabai was exhausted…wanted to get away…She decided to go personally with the requisition and also to meet Malharrao who had barely visited Indore in the past 2-3 years. She touched his feet, seeking his blessings and expressed indebtedness for the promising change in Malerao.

Malharrao was a trifle surprised to see Ahilyabai. He asked her why she had left Indore. Ahilyabai looked tired and older than the forty summers she had weathered. The incessant work had taken a toll on her. Baiji's loss was showing in her eyes…

"I wanted to get away…see you…and take a short pilgrimage of four days on my way back…I feel fatigued"

Malharrao raised his voice… "What!? Is this any time for pilgrimage? The camps here need funds…soldiers….supplies. How could you even think of going on a pilgrimage! New spears….swords need to be made. Today our treasury has 84 lakhs …all on the strength of this sword! And Ahilyabai, I have crossed seventy! Who should be tired? You? Or me? Go right back to Indore…employ 1000 more people…send me more arms….and…."

Ahilyabai had tears in her eyes. Malharrao softened… apologized…explained the precarious political position and how much he depended on her support behind the scenes. He could not have achieved any of what he did, had Ahilyabai not sent timely supplies…arms…water…food and other needs of the army. He was now old. His left hand was seriously wounded in the battle of Mangaloor, suffered injuries on his head damaging his ear drums, sending intermittent shooting pain…knees were giving way… "Its time for me to feel tired my child…not you."

Ahilyabai …knew…understood. She looked at her father-in-law, "Come back to Indore as soon as you complete this mission. Give me the good fortune of looking after you. You need to rest now…"

Malharrao had tears in his eyes. "Do not tempt me with these worldly affections Every time I think of you …the children…I feel weak. I want to shed even the last drop of my blood in the service of the Peshwas. After me, take care of the kingdom…the people…work for them…"

Ahilyabai found it very hard to leave that day. There was a strange sense of impending end in the way Malharrao spoke. She was uneasy…dragging her feet as she prepared to leave. Malharrao kept looking at their fading silhouettes till the tears in his eyes made everything look like a blur…shaky images …of a lifetime gone by…of life as it had bypassed Ahilyabai…

****

Ahilyabai on her return journey was lost in her childhood… in the things that Malharrao taught her…how Baiji would save her from Malharrao's punishments for not learning the tables of ¼ , ½ and ¾ … and for incorrect accounting!! The gifts she received when she excelled in her studies…her talks with Baiji…the good days and bad…all beaded together in one thread…Ahilyabai's heart was heavy with memories…like dark clouds wafting on breezy times… one moment, cool and fresh …teary droplets another…

****

Ahilyabai reached Gwalior. The news of a joint attack by Shinde –Holkar at Gohad reached her. She immediately sent a message through her spy to Ramaji Yadav in Indore to give an impetus to the ammunition production. She immediately employed one thousand people, expediting the fabrication of spears....swords, shields. People were working day and night assembling hand grenades, cannonballs...She prepared an additional army of 3000 soldiers...

Ahilyabai was contented with her own work and thinking to herself how pleased Malharrao would be with her prompt actions...and say, "All this is good...but tell me how much is 17 times 1/4th ?!!" She was still weak at her tables...and Malharrao would always tease her about it! She smiled to herself...and turned around...

A messenger was standing there with a scroll. She opened it. It read:

'Respected Ahilyabai, with deep regret, I inform you that respected Subhedar, Malharrao passed away on Tuesday, the 20th of May (1766), at Alampur. We await your arrival for the last rites. Your trustworthy, Mahadji Shinde'

Time just stopped for Ahilyabai. She stood there like a statue. Frozen in that moment...reading it...blanking out...again reading... fading in and out of shock.... disbelief...numbing reality... staring at the message...one moment, the message did not seem to sink in...and the next moment, she felt everything around her sinking... She simply felt light headed...with blurred images of people around her...distanced, muffled sounds...

Messages were sent to Indore...Dwarkaai, Banaai, Harkuaai, Oodabai...all arrived. The palanquins left. Ahilyabai herself got astride a horse and left for Alampur, with the security of the Shinde forces, to pay her last respects to her mentor...teacher...guide...

The horse stopped outside the tent...where Malharrao's body was placed. Suddenly, Ahilyabai's energies drained out...her legs had no strength....the horse was restless, tapping its hooves

...in anticipation for the rider to get off... Finally, after a long time, Ahilyabai drew courage from her deepest breath...walked inside the tent...

Malharrao's body lay there... frail... wounded... scarred...having weathered over 70 summers...leaving behind a trail of glorious victories, unswerving service and towering integrity...with an expression of relief... with his subsequent success, after the ignominy of Panipat ...

An 8-9 year old Ahilyabai...walking down ...holding her father-in-law's finger...the praises...the fun...the punishments...the marriage...training...snapshots of her life passed by her in that one moment as she crumbled at his feet...Uncontrollable tears just streaming down a blank face...she put her head on his feet...washing them with her tears...

Mahadji said...in the moments before he faded away...he said... 'please convey to Ahilyabai, my deepest respects and blessings...as I shut my eyes, I see the dazzle of her brilliance...my hope resting on her...am now at peace...'

Ahilyabai was now completely shattered...unable to stifle the sound of her tears...the tent spinning around her...But the storm had yet to hit her with full force...more was yet to strike her...

A pyre of sandalwood was prepared and Malharrao's body was placed on it. Oodabai, Sitabai were weeping in a corner. And...Ahilyabai was unmanageable when she saw Dwarkaai and Banaai come out dressed in white saris ...vermillion smeared on their foreheads...prepared for Sati... Ahilyabai pleaded desperately...she was shaken. The palace was going to be empty. In one stroke she was going to lose three people around whom she had woven her life after Baiji had passed away...

But the two women were adamant. Ahilyabai was on her knees...trying to dissuade them. Harkuaai was away in Khandesh and also, not a legally wedded wife and so could not go sati...The two women calmly sat near Malharrao's body...as Malerao lit the pyre...The drums started beating loudly...deafening music...Ahilyabai covered her ears and shut her eyes tight...

****

10

Ahilyabai returned to Indore. The palace looked different...felt different...dull, no activity...bare rooms.

There was no Baiji to share her feelings with...Dwarkaai was gone. Banaai not around, to oversee palace activities...kitchen chimney was inactive with Harkuaai away...no stories to hear from Malharrao...The air in Indore was gloomy...no discourses or hymns at the temples...

Harkuaai arrived dressed in a dull, plain, earthy colored outfit, befitting a widow in her religion. Harkunwar...no one knows where she had met Malharrao ...but had fallen in love with him...married a sword and had symbolically become his wife. She sat in the centre of the room, beating her chest...crying out loud , as was the custom for mourning ...Renu, Anjana, Raghoji, Bhagoji had tears in their eyes as they went around their chores in the vacant palace...quietly.

Monsoons had set in...with heavy dark clouds. Ahilyabai did not feel like even getting out of her room... not even to meet visitors, to accept their condolences. Entire Indore was in mourning...except one person...Malerao.

Malerao was excited...energetic...brimming with enthusiasm...he was after all to be the next Subhedar. There were only two more days for his coronation. The papers for his Subhedari were to arrive on 3rd June. He had no time to mourn. He had to order carpets...chandeliers...A new decorative splendid throne was being carved out of pure silver. Ten oil lamps, each five feet high, with thick flames were to be set up.

The entrances and aisles were to be lined with flowers and potted plants, entwined with delicate creepers in brass filigree, with two dozen oil lamps intricately placed amidst them…

Gangoba Tatya tried to caution Malerao… "Your mother, Matoshri Ahilyabai is in mourning…so is entire Indore…the Peshwas too desire a simple ceremony…I suggest a subdued ceremony would be rather appropriate…" Malerao snapped at Gangoba Tatya who responded by being silent but proceeded to Ahilyabai and narrated the incident.

Ahilyabai was angry…disheartened…worried …all at the same time. She sighed in helpless exhaustion… "When authority and arrogance come together, it spells the beginning of the end…"

On the 3rd of June, Ahilyabai woke up with a start…to the sound of bugles, drum beats and celebratory music! She immediately ordered the music to be stopped! Malerao came rushing down only to see that the reluctant musicians had disappeared from there. He was about to go after them but Ahilyabai's one look was enough for Malerao to retrace his steps then …but he ensured that he brought his own friends to play the music during the ceremony later…

Abaji Yadav represented the Peshwas. Malerao was given the Subhedari clothes, head gear…brooch…the seal…the flag…Malerao ascended the throne…

Ahilyabai was transported into the past...reminiscing the function held years ago…

Every guest was served a simple glass of saffron milk as the function concluded. Ahilyabai was accepting condolences from some and congratulatory messages from the others…

Later, as Ahilyabai walked back to her room she sensed a scuffle in the adjoining room. She started towards the room and reached the door. Ahilyabai went cold…

Malerao wielded a whip in his hand as he spoke threateningly with Gangoba Tatya, questioning him why the expenses of the function were put under personal expenses…

Gangoba Tatya had his back towards the door as he explained that the Peshwas desired a simple ceremony and hence the expenses on the lavish decorations were to be considered as unapproved. The rest of the expenses would be deemed as State expenses. Malerao cracked a whip in the air and turned …and was taken aback for a moment when he saw Ahilyabai at the door.

Ahilyabai was furious…livid, at the indirect hint in Malerao's action and humiliation of Gangoba Tatya. She walked up to Malerao …unexpectedly snatched the whip from his hand and cracked it louder in the air. There was silence. "I ordered him to do so", she thundered, "…and without a moment's delay you will apologize to Gangoba Tatya …a father figure here…for even daring to speak to him in this manner"

Gangoba Tatya took off his head gear and placed it at Ahilyabai's feet…requesting to be relieved from his duties…

"Not at all! Absolutely No! In fact, Malerao will now apologize this very moment and place the head gear back respectfully…"

She looked at Malerao …he had never seen such a menacing look before…but he was on a high, tendered by the authority of being the Subhedar…and he laughed…laughed out loud…saying, "Matoshri, remember you are now talking to the Subhedar…" But before he could say anything further… Ahilyabai's voice resonated loud and clear, "Of course yes! But let me caution you…never ever forget that you may have the authority but I have the power! The power to recommend to the Peshwas to revoke your Subhedari this very moment! It will take just one message from me! Do not ever make the mistake of believing, that my love for you can be greater than my love for the people and their well-being!"

Ahilyabai's words struck Malerao like a lightening…Mukta, Maina and some others had gathered there…Malerao was spluttering with rage…But he had no choice…he did as he was told…trailed by Ahilyabai's steady glance…

Maina, now sounding grown up with her experiences and her position as the Lady Subhedar, tried to diffuse the situation and stepped forward… "Even our grandfather used to work on Matoshri's advice…and Gangoba Tatya's advice. If we too draw from their vast experience, you will be the most adored and successful Subhedar…" Before anyone could blink their eyes Maina's innocent efforts were sabotaged by a resounding slap across her face…from Malerao.

"Malerao!" Ahilyabai lost her restraint and in reply, lashed Malerao with the whip in her hand… "You will apologize to Maina right away…"

Malerao laughed loudly…a psychotic laugh… "Apologize to her???.."

"Malerao…"warned Ahilyabai, "…she is your wife and the lady Subhedar now. You dare not treat her like this!" Malerao flatly refused.

"Alright then…", she held Maina by her hand…and said, "Unless and until you apologize, Maina is not entering your quarters…"

Malerao continued to laugh… "I have far more beautiful women I can bring into my quarters…" Ahilyabai left with Maina …returned into her room. Maina's parents had heard what happened. They came to Ahilyabai's room and requested to take Maina away for a month. Ahilyabai nodded and arranged for security at the Bahaad residence.

Ahilyabai knew…she had to act now…and act quickly…

****

In a rather unassuming rectangular hall at Maheshwar…a darbar was held. Ahilyabai made an announcement. "The setback of Panipat is now behind us. We have been engaged with war and consequently, disengaged, from the internal law and order system. The Bhils have exploited the situation. We now have to focus our energies on containing the Bhils in the region. Today, people have lost faith in our ability to protect them from the Bhils. Fear has become greater than faith…and we have to make every effort to restore peoples' faith in us…Today, in this darbar…I make an announcement. Anyone who is courageous, strong, and can fight the Bhils, bring them to book, will be eligible to claim my daughter Mukta in marriage."

There was pin drop silence in the darbar. The reward was such, that it could make your life …but the task such that could take your life. People merely glanced at one another…gauging response…chances…

In all this, a young bright boy stood up. He offered his respects to Ahilyabai and said, "I will do this. I will do this. I am well trained in the use of sword, spears, dandpatta [15]…but I cannot do this alone. I need support… soldiers… funds…" Ahilyabai nodded. The young boy declared, "I take up your challenge here and now. I will show you my face again only after I have fulfilled this task…else consider these my last greetings at your feet…"saying so, he bowed again and swayed his right hand thrice…in a traditional greeting, the mujra. Tukoji Holkar whispered to Ahilyabai… "Matoshri, what about his caste…creed…family?"

"He seems to belong to the family of the courageous. His credentials are his bravery…and intention to serve the people. I know no other caste… What is your name, young man?"

"I am Yashwant. Yashwant Phanse"

"May God bless you! May you be successful!"

****

Muktabai and Yashwant Phanse were married in a splendid ceremony. The Bahaads brought Mainabai along with them for the wedding. Ahilyabai's maternal uncles arrived from Choundi. The absence of Malharrao and Baiji dampened Ahilyabai's enthusiasm yet she welcomed the braveheart Yashwantrao in all glory …commending his courage and goodness. Yashwantrao

Phanse had shown extraordinary courage and strategy. He was rewarded with a few villages and a designation on behalf of the state. The other gifts were showered on him from Ahilyabai's private treasury.

Breaking tradition yet again, Ahilyabai performed the kanyadaan. The guests were aghast…a woman…and a widow at that…performing kanyadaan! But no one dared say anything…as Ahilyabai asserted very strongly… 'those traditions and customs which bring people closer should be followed in good faith. Those that take you towards darkness become blind faith…Let us break those and move towards the light of knowledge…'

****

Ahilyabai handled the Bhils in the most unusual manner. When Yashwantrao Phanse booked all the Bhil leaders and presented them in court…Ahilyabai did not sentence them to death nor condemn them to jail. Instead she offered them jobs in her government…gave them the designation of 'Nayak' and the entire responsibility of the protection of travelers was now theirs. They were to get regular salaries from the state and be in the service of the State.

The Bhil leaders too, were invited for the wedding with respect and pomp. The Bhils were now getting not just money but also prestige. They were never going to let go of this prestige for the greed of money. In one brilliant, strategic stroke Ahilyabai had created a band of loyalists, willing to protect the internal law and order.

As the function concluded…Sardar Wagh approached Ahilyabai…offering his granddaughter, ten year old Peertabai in marriage to Malerao! Ahilyabai was shocked and dumbfounded. Sardar Wagh was aware of Malerao's ill mannered ways…yet, thought Ahilyabai, how can anyone offer their little girls to Malerao…

But Sardar Wagh explained. The girl had lost her parents. He was ageing and did not have a wife. The girl would be orphaned after him. He would rather, that she remained in Ahilyabai's care…

Ahilyabai remained reluctant…But a veteran sardar from Malharrao's time…one of his daughters had gone Sati with her husband, Khanderao. Sardar Wagh had been a great loyalist, desiring to merge his riches with that of the State…He did not allow Ahilyabai to refuse. But Ahilyabai insisted that Peertabai would continue to live in her own house at least for a few more years…Sardar Wagh accepted the condition. After all, he thought, she would be the Subhedar's wife. No one would dare to harass her. Her safety was guaranteed.

Before Mukta's wedding celebrations wound up, Malerao too was married to Peertabai.

****

In the past 5-6 months, Ahilyabai had spent most of her time at Maheshwar. Indore felt different now. She did keep a keen eye on Indore…but it was not like it used to be when Malharrao's courage shone bright and Baiji's breezy presence helped make Ahilya's days pleasing. Now, with Malerao's antics, living at Indore was stifling, suffocating, uneasy…

Malerao would wake up at any time he pleased…eat as and when he felt like…aimlessly ride on horsebacks…go hunting. At night, alcohol…massages by women, a different 'daasi'[16] at his service every night…but Heera was his favorite. Most of his nights were spent with her.

Whenever Malerao was not under the influence of alcohol or his potions, Ahilyabai would try to instill Malharrao's values in him saying, 'Malerao…when in power, never discard compassion…always respect grey hair and experience…work for the people…manage money…Take advice from Tukoji…God has chosen you to take this forward…be loyal to your destiny…'

All her words would fall on deaf ears, yet she hoped ...some day he would improve or at least get tired of this frivolous lifestyle and seek some fulfillment in life.

Ahilyabai had arrived in Indore that day with Mainabai. She was in discussion with Tukoji Holkar. Malerao had spent five lakhs in six months from the private treasury. Before that, other than Mukta's wedding expenses, the private spending was a mere two lakhs in two years...and now ? Five lakhs in six months!!!?? Ahilyabai was not going to allow that. She ordered Tukoji to lock the personal vaults and hand over the keys to her. Tukoji nodded...

All through the meeting Ahilyabai sensed discomfort in the room. Tukoji was not looking into her eyes as he spoke. What was he trying to hide or avoid...

Ahilyabai looked steadily at Tukoji. His gaze was unsteady...shifting around the room. Ahilyabai kept looking... straight ...following Tukoji . Finally Tukoji sat down...head lowered...gazing at the floor...lips pursed. He took a deep breath and looked up into Ahilyabai's eyes. There was silence.

That look....Ahilyabai broke into cold sweat. She knew she was going to hear something terrible...something unprecedented.

****

She kept looking at Tukoji. She had stopped breathing. Tukoji could not meet her eyes as he spoke.

"Matoshri...steady yourself...this may shock you... but..." Ahilyabai cut short his preface sharply, "Come to the point! Speak up!"

"Well...the palace has witnessed a killing yesterday..."

"What??!" a shocked Ahilyabai sprung out of her chair and stood up. "Who... how...?" she fumbled for words...Tukoji continued... "In the room near the stables...Malerao killed his favorite consort Heera's lover...a craftsman. He pleaded for mercy…Heera begged for forgiveness…but in the cruelest manner he chopped off the man's arms and legs in front of Heera…to teach him a lesson for falling in love with her"

Raghoji and Bhagoji were witness to the heinous crime. Ahilyabai darted towards the room. The walls had blood sprayed on them…the floor had crusted blood telling the gruesome tale…She confronted Raghoji and Bhagoji, "Why did you not stop him?"

"We tried. But he was under the influence of opium. Bhagoji tried to stop Malerao …but could not and lost three fingers in the bargain" Ahilyabai looked at the chopped fingers of the man who served the family for decades…She was ashamed.

The dying craftsman cursed Malerao as he fell…said he would haunt Malerao …return to avenge this death… The next day Heera consumed poison and died. She too cursed Malerao…with a menacing warning that she would haunt him.

Ahilyabai's heart felt like stone. She turned around and went to the temple. She sat there for a long time…

Ever since, Malerao had been disturbed. He would run around the palace as if escaping spirits. He would wail at night and hide under the bed sheet while sleeping…throw away glasses of milk insisting there was blood in them. Malerao would not sleep for days on end. Ahilyabai sent for the Royal Vaidya who tried all possible medicines and treatment to calm Malerao down. Finally he said, "Matoshri, I have tried everything that our science advises. I can do nothing more to help him. If you wish we can call some other well known vaidyas from…"

"No…I am sending for no one. You give him whatever you wish…but just do one thing…end his pain…do something whereby he can sleep…peacefully…"The Royal Vaidya administered a potion…and Malerao fell asleep…the first time in three months…

Everyone sat down for dinner. No one had eaten well in weeks. Dinner was over. Harkubai took a plate of food for

Malerao…she returned saying Malerao would not wake up…

Ahilyabai said, "Let him sleep…he hardly eats…he sees Heera's face or blood in the plate…let the medicine take its effect…" Ahilyabai got up. Just then Raghoji came rushing…. "The Subhedar is not moving…nor… breathing…"

Everyone went to his room. Malerao lay peacefully. The pain had ended. Malerao was no more. Ahilyabai stood there…like a statue…face expressionless…eyes dry. She stood there gazing at his face for the longest time…one last time…

****

All the relatives gathered at Indore. The families of the Bahaads and Waghs arrived…shockingly insisting that Mainabai and Peertabai follow the tradition of Sati…blaming their destiny. Ahilyabai was aghast. Those little girls…Peertabai was just 11…They had their entire lives ahead of them…this could not be their destiny…

Ahilyabai asserted herself. She hugged the girls saying she would not allow sati… "This is just a convenient ploy for society…what better way for men to get rid of women than to just push them into the funeral pyre?! No responsibility and also no one to stake a claim in the properties!!" Ahilyabai was agitated. "Those women may want to live…find partners…so what better way to deal with it than to deny them their right to live!! This is inhuman…barbaric…I will not allow this." The petrified girls hugged Ahilyabai for their life…literally.

The families of those girls were not willing to relent. They insisted it was ordained in the religion.

"What religion are you talking about? When a man loses his wife he remarries in less than a year! When women lose their husbands, they are killed in less than a day??" Ahilyabai was getting hysterical. But the religious grip on people was very strong. Many other relatives now found strength… to speak what they had always wanted to but had dared not. Now

Malharrao was not around …they had no one to fear…

They all told Ahilyabai that religion was not within her dictates. She had made her choice. She should allow others to make theirs. Ahilyabai was slapped shut. She knew the only way was to ban sati by law. But that would take time…specially by a court dominated by men…In the meanwhile…her little Maina and Peertabai…

The girls did not know the meaning of marriage…they did not know what sati was…they just knew something terrible was to happen…and only Ahilyabai was against it. A pregnant Muktabai was standing in a corner…against the wall…seeing her best friend Maina...disappear amidst a large crowd…glorifying them…praising them…

Ahilyabai and Muktabai shut their ears...There were drums beating and cacophony outside…but the turmoil inside was louder…Ahilyabai could still hear…and then the noise began to seem distant…faint…as Ahilyabai collapsed…unconscious…

When she regained consciousness she was in her room… It was all quiet outside. She lay in bed staring at the ceiling. When she would open her eyes, the screams engulfed her…when she shut her eyes tight, the visions crowded her mind…

Muktabai was 20 weeks pregnant looking after her mother in that empty palace. Ahilyabai could not live there anymore. She decided to move her base to Maheshwar.

****

PART II

11

A shattered Ahilyabai...looking much older than her 42 years... frail health ...worn out by personal losses, sat alone in her room reliving her life...going over the events... emotionally exhausted not knowing what else could lie ahead...

Oodabai and Harkuaai entered. Ahilyabai wanted to share a few moments of peace with them...but she sensed that was not to be...Both women looked worried...

Oodabai sat lightly next to Ahilyabai and said... "Vahinisaheb..." she hesitated...voice softer and tentative... "I have information...that Gangoba Tatya has sent a letter to Raghunathrao (Raghobadada)...that everyone in the Holkar family is in mourning...and that the property now has no heir. This is therefore a golden opportunity to come with your forces and take control...It was Shivaji Gopal and Ravji Mahadeo who cautioned us."

Ahilyabai was shaken to the core... She stood up. Gangoba Tatya? An old trusted hand...? She did not have the luxury of even mourning in peace...She had to act quickly! Ahilyabai looked determined...she had to protect the Subhedari...even in her frail health she knew, she could not lose another moment. She sent for her trusted people, or those, she believed she could still trust. But before anyone else could arrive she sent a letter to Tukoji Holkar…

'These are difficult times for the Holkar family. You are a part of this family and Malharrao had trusted you with my son. I have no hesitation therefore in placing my trust in you. Consider this of utmost importance and leave for Maheshwar at once on receiving this letter. I would like to designate you to be the next Subhedar.'

After this she dispatched 27 letters to the Gaikwads, Pawars, Shindes…

'Today I have the task of protecting the Holkar kingdom…that which was built by Malharrao brick by brick. But destiny has been rather unkind to the Holkar family and I need your support like never before. The Holkar family maybe heirless but most certainly should not be mistaken to be rudderless. An heirless kingdom becoming a soft target is not a good precedent. Nobody has seen the future! God forbid… but any of you could be in my situation in the future. I invoke your friendship with Malharrao and request you to send your armies to back me up and assist me in protecting his inheritance.'

The very next day Ahilyabai called for a meeting. Shivaji Gopal, Rajaram Ransod, and also Gangoba Tatya…all old, trusted hands…Ahilyabai looked everyone in the eye. No hint of mourning or weakness in her voice. She hit the nail on the head as she began to speak. "Let there be no misconception… that being a woman I am in any way weak or helpless. If I decide to don the armor and jump into the fray on the battlefield…be assured, even the armies of the Peshwas may find me more than a match. So let there be no doubt about the future of this Subhedari. Let no one be tempted to walk the path of treachery or rebellion…And, if you hear of anyone harboring such intentions it will be in your best interests to inform me about the same." She then looked at Gangoba Tatya and said, "Gangoba Tatya, you are the most trusted hand here. Do you have wind of any such plot being hatched?"

Gangoba Tatya's face lost all color. He said, "I have been keeping ill health. You sent a message for an urgent meeting …so I have come. But I am in no condition to participate in this discussion. With your permission, I would like to take your leave. I will return late this afternoon once I feel a little better and we will prepare our response strategy in case of any eventuality."

Ahilyabai nodded. After the meeting, she sent for her son-in-law, Yashwant Phanse. She explained everything to him and said, "The armies of our allies will arrive…but the responsibility of leading them lies on your courageous shoulders." Yashwant Phanse assured Ahilyabai and left.

****

Tukoji Holkar arrived on the 6th day after the letter was dispatched to him. All sardars sent messages, one after the other …confirming army dispatches. The Gaikwads sent 20,000 soldiers. There was not one sardar who could disregard Malharrao Holkar's goodwill or his favors! The Peshwas too trusted Ahilyabai's judgment and sent their approval seconding Tukoji Holkar as the Subhedar designate.

In a neat, appropriate and beautiful ceremony amidst bugles and flowers…elephants and camel processions Tukoji Holkar was given the seal, symbol and papers of the Subhedari.

Gangoba Tatya who had disappeared that day had not returned to work yet…

****

The very next day, Ahilyabai put together a women's regiment of 50 soldiers and wrote a letter to Raghoba and Gangoba Tatya, who were understood to be approaching Maheshwar.

'It is a matter of shame that anyone should attempt to exploit a person in mourning. I will shatter the dreams of every person seeking to seize my kingdom. I am on my way with a regiment of 50 women ...eagerly waiting to meet you. If I lose, I go down honorably in history. But if you lose, it will be to a regiment of a mere 50 women soldiers!"

As soon as Raghoba finished reading Ahilyabai's letter he knew he had made a grave tactical error... and the very next minute Tukoji Holkar's message reached him...warning him that if he dared to turn and cross the Kshipra River, he would be welcomed by a sea of soldiers

Raghoba knew he was checkmated. He used his good sense and sent a reply back assuring Ahilyabai that there was some grave misunderstanding! He insisted that he was approaching her merely to offer his condolences...and planned to leave his army behind and come alone...!

...and he did exactly that! Visited Ahilyabai...offered condolences and left. Gangoba Tatya sent a word that he had left on a pilgrimage towards Pune.

Oodabai hugged Ahilyabai...who profusely thanked her informers and loyalists. A magnificent dinner celebration was arranged. Each one was honored and rewarded generously. Ahilyabai appreciated their service and reiterated gratefully saying that kingdoms owed their existence not to the might of their armies...not to the strength of their funds...but to the loyalty of its sardars...

****

That very day Muktabai was delivered of a baby boy! Ahilyabai's brothers, Shahadji and Mahadji arrived with their wives...After a long time, the house was alive with people and the palace basked in happiness...warming Ahilyabai's heart, melting the coldness inside, into smiles...

Tukoji Holkar arrived to see the new born, with his wife Rukhma , who strutted around like a peacock , in her new found status as the Subhedar's wife...now travelling only in palanquins, speaking with a recently acquired edge in her voice…nodding stiffly at people greeting her, smiling suitably less and communicating more with gestures, steady stares and claps!

Tukoji Holkar, ever humble, never forgetting his modest origins, was the Subhedar. A clear understanding with Ahilyabai that he would be the commander of the forces but the power for all monetary and financial dealings with the Peshwas and the other sardars would remain vested with Ahilybai. He owed his allegiance to her. Tukoji never lost sight of the fact that she could have made Yashwant Phanse the Subhedar but she rightfully retained the rights with the Holkars and more importantly, acknowledged his existence. Muktabai too had a son now…an heir…

After blessing the baby, Tukoji narrated the episode of the arrest of Gangoba Tatya and the defeat of Raghobadada under the direction of the Peshwa himself.

Ahilyabai understood that The Peshwas had killed two birds with one stone. First, they managed to rein in Raghoba and Gangoba. Two, put to rest the fear that, Tukoji would drift towards Gangoba and Raghoba. Pitting them against each other, was in a way a test of Tukoji's loyalty and allegiance to Ahilyabai! Despite the compelling victory of Tukoji, the Peshwas still remained unconvinced. They appointed Naro Ganesh to look after the financial matters at Indore. Shivaji Gopal, Ahilyabai's trusted sardar was called to Pune to accommodate Naro Ganesh in Indore. This exchange was discomforting for Ahilyabai too.

****

Just a small family get-together and the baby was named Nathoba. A strong woman who had weathered vandalization by destiny was now protective of the small blessings in her life. Deep inside, Ahilyabai did not want a fancy ceremony, fearing evil eye…

Muktabai's son was a year old now. Ahilyabai had driven

the emptiness out of the palace. Muktabai would now stay with her most of the time as Yashwantrao was out on missions. Ahilyabai's brother, Mahadji too had moved to Maheshwar with his family. Shahdji's son , Ranoji Shinde Chaundikar was employed in Ahilyabai's service. Renu, Anjana, Ranoji, Bhagoji were now family. An army of 400 soldiers guarded the palace. The palace kitchen was churning out food, for over 200 people, every day. The palace was throbbing with activity again.

But Ahilyabai had to be alert. The differences between Raghoba dada and the Peshwas were peaking out…leading to flashpoints at many places…

****

Maheshwar was so close to Rajputana. The area was dotted with small Zamindars and Jahagirdars…all landlords… enjoying a luxurious, wealthy lifestyle…immersed in womanizing, intoxicated by lust…wine…wealth. Sibling rivalry was therefore the order of the day with legitimate and illegitimate heirs staking claim to inheritances and embroiling themselves in games of one upmanship…creating their own armies. Rajputana was scoring a new low every day …spreading unrest, distrust and infighting.

All this was not new. Earlier too Malharrao had sided with Madhosingh. Ever since, amongst others, Chandravat Rajput had nursed wounds of being wronged. Ahilyabai was now seen to be a lone lady. The Holkar army had marched to the North with Tukoji Holkar. What better opportunity for Chandravat than now! He planned his audacious moves and marched towards Maheshwar with an army of 25,000 soldiers.

Ahilyabai was disturbed by this news. The armies…Tukoji, Yashwantrao…all of them were away. She called for an emergency meeting.

"This is not the time for confrontation. We have barely 5000 soldiers at hand…" Bharmal dada interrupted her. "That's more than enough! I will march on them with 5000 and reduce them to dust."

"No doubt!" appreciated Ahilyabai! "I have no doubt that you have the power, courage and competence to reduce them to dust! Yet, it will come at a heavy cost to us. We will lose many men. This is a moment for truce…for peace. Let us concede 10-15 villages and save thousands of lives. Once our armies are back I will deal with his misadventure"

Ahilyabai always preferred to 'display' strength rather than 'use' strength to win battles .The threat of the impending use of potential power had greater influence than the actual use of power. She believed… Power was best used when not employed…

Rajputana was eaten up by infighting. Pune and Shaniwarwada infested by rotten politics. Ahilyabai knew she had to strive to protect the Holkar family from internal feuds. Little did she know what lay in store ahead…

****

Ahilyabai held Tukoji's letter applauding her wisdom of conceding 31 villages to Chandravat in a graceful truce. Ahilyabai was looking over the emerging skyline of Maheshwar. It had been four years now since they had moved to Maheshwar. Tukoji had spent most of those four years on missions. Ahilyabai reminisced her four years well spent as she appreciated the view from her simple but large living quarters atop the fort. Maheshwar looked pretty on the banks of the rustling waters of the Narmada River, defined by well constructed embankments with recesses of steps, leading down into the cool, clear, shallow waters. The banks were dotted with beautifully carved temples of Lord Shiva and Krishna…connected by frugally constructed pathways. The peaceful backdrop of these temples created a heavenly setting, for holding theological and religious discourses in the open spaces carved out around the temples, where people were treated to divine kirtans, sermons, chanting of mantras, shlokas, artis, music, mythological stories…

Nothing gave Ahilyabai more pleasure than to watch the silhouette of the well constructed city as the moonlit waters of the shimmering Narmada flowed gently. The peace and quiet at night was punctuated by the bustling activity of the growing trade and commerce during the daytime. The bazaars were brimming…masons, carpenters, traders were setting up homes around Maheshwar. The city was prospering …adding new business quarters which were being named after eminent people. Malhargunj …in memory of her father-in-law; Fansepura; Govindpura in respect of Govindpant…and so on…

****

As soon as Rukhmabai reached Maheshwar, after spending some time with Tukoji, she called on Ahilyabai. After a detailed narration of Tukoji's bravery, strategies, war stories…an impatient Rukhmabai remarked that none of the new business quarters were named after her courageous husband! Ahilyabai explained to her that there was nothing named after her either! "…that must be left to posterity!" continued Ahilyabai.

"How do you explain the one in your son-in-law's name then?"

"If you care to pause and notice you will realize that it is not in my son-in-law's name but in the name of his family…who own large chunks of land in the region!" Rukhmabai didn't seem convinced and declared that one day her son's achievements would compel Ahilyabai to name not one but many quarters in his name! Ahilyabai smiled. "With great pleasure! It will be my proudest moment to do so…and why small areas? I hope to name villages and towns after him!"

That brought a smile to Rukhmabai's face. She adjusted her sari, patted her hair, pursed her lips as if locking words inside, as she maintained that smile…dreaming of the power her sons would come to wield.

Ahilyabai gracefully enquired after her sons. Rukhmabai informed her that three of her sons were under the tutelage of the very learned, Pandurang Shankar. The youngest son, Malhar was with her…who she would very happily send away so that she could accompany her husband and spend uninterrupted time with him.

"Very well then…" offered Ahilyabai, "…send him to me. He will grow up here with Nathoba …after all we need to prepare the next generation to take over the reins…"

"Why would I let my son feel as though it was an act of kindness or favor that you allowed him shelter here?"

"Not at all!" said Ahilyabai. You can discuss it with your husband and let me know your decision. Nathoba is four. Malhar must be ten. They will train together and become stalwarts of the kingdom in the decades to come…"

****

Sakharam Dhongde had acquired expertise in silk. Ahilyabai invited him to Indore, provided him funds to start manufacturing and trading in silk. In four years, there were 100 people weaving Maheshwari saris. The hand weaving facilities were never idle now.

A business quarter for goldsmiths carving crowns, earrings and other ornaments for temple deities, was established. Silver vessels were being crafted in a unique way which would later on, come to be known as 'Maheshwari vessels'. "For any article to etch its place in the market..." Ahilyabai would say, "it had to have a distinctiveness" Saris and vessels from Maheshwar were to go down in history for their exclusive style.

Renovating old temples and preserving heritage sites was a project that was initiated by Ahilyabai. The first thing that Ahilyabai had done on her arrival at Maheshwar, was to start a Sanskrit school where 115 students were learning the ancient language and the Vedas.

Teachers, learned scholars would often visit Maheshwar and hold religious discourses to explain to the common man the metaphorical meaning in mythological stories. The sardars were assigned the job of collecting the best books and running a library in every region. She would also hold religious yagnas periodically as they were known, not just to calm the mind but also purify the environment. The incineration of sandalwood... dhoop...clarified butter...and the chanting of mantras were believed to clear the air of negative aura.

In four years, Maheshwar had become not only the cultural and educational hub but also a center of commercial progress! New construction, strong businesses, temples, libraries, dharamshalas, schools and other social developmental projects offered employment to people. Ahilyabai took personal interest in the welfare of her people...in ensuring that the basic needs of food, clothing, and shelter could be guaranteed.

Going to the banks of the Narmada was what she loved the most. Early morning, every day she would go there...survey the facilities...hold an informal darbar...meet people, listen to their grievances, offer quick redressals. This was something that gave Ahilyabai immense satisfaction...and she would rue the time spent in fighting wars...

Many a times Muktabai would travel with her mother to the banks of the Narmada to share not just her responsibility but also some very personal moments with her...the mother-daughter would talk about everything...even about the letters she would receive from her husband! For Muktabai, her mother was her friend, philosopher and guide...and for Ahilyabai, Mukta's relationship with her husband, was her only introduction to romance in a marriage. A marriage in which Ahilyabai had seen no caste or creed, no matching of horoscopes or identifying auspicious moments...a good marriage was all about the union of heart, mind, soul and body...

** { haach sansaar kharaa, naahitar nustaa pasaara} **

****

That day, Ahilyabai had called for a darbar. Santaji Laambhaate, Shivaji Shankar, Tukoji Mhaske, Bhagwat Kadam, and others were invited. These lines of commanders were the protégés of Malharrao Holkar. He had mentored them, nurtured them…helped them grow. All these courageous leaders were given the responsibility of certain regions which were under their control. Looking after the palaces… law and order… tax collection… spending an assigned amount out of it, on the upkeep of the army… Deducting their rightful share and crediting the rest to the Holkar's treasury, was their responsibility.

The darbar was no ornate place. No velvets, no silver thrones, no extravagance. It was a simple Diwankhana, lined with simple seating and in the center was a white durrie…on which sat Ahilyabai. A dusky lady, clad simply in white, yet charging the air by her mere presence. A strong personality with benevolence and conviction, rooted deep inside her.

" A warm welcome to all dignitaries gathered here. You have left no stone unturned in extending your support and allegiance to the Holkar flag. I express my deepest gratitude to you all…and welcome you once again here to your own home. When I say 'our' home, there is most certainly going to be warmth and undoubtedly, there will be dissent too. Each one of you gathered here, is an expression of courage, bravery and achievement. Yet, sometimes, this alone, is not enough to protect the motherland. We need to be cautious…we need to be united…not allow anyone to deter us, from our collective allegiance to the throne of the Peshwas. Any divisive element, who contemplates a move to destroy this unity, stands warned, here and now. Let us never forget the legacy that Malharrao bestowed upon us…"

Just as Ahilyabai was concluding her speech in these times of peace, a rider arrived with the news of the death of Shreemant

Madhavrao Peshwa at Theur on 18 November 1772…and that Ramabai, had chosen the course of Sati…accompanying her husband on his final journey.

The special darbar, concluded as a condolence meet. The sardars returned to their palaces. All commercial activities were stopped and Ahilyabai announced community readings of the Bhagwat Gita on the banks of the Narmada for the eternal peace of the departed souls.

****

The returning army of Tukoji Holkar sent up clouds of dust all over Indore. Ahilyabai got busy disbursing money to soldiers and rewards to the courageous. Naro Ganesh was fairly inexperienced at this job. He was besieged by people demanding more…larger shares…led by none other than Ahilyabai's own nephew, Ranoji Chaundikar! It was not until Ahilyabai herself addressed the soldiers and calmed them down that they accepted the payments…when, Ahilyabai impressed upon them how their families were taken care of, while they were away.

The matter was settled but what was unsettling was that her own nephew had incited the soldiers. As she retired to her room in the evening, Ranoji requested an audience, to pay his respects to her. Ahilyabai denied him audience saying he had already established his disrespect by instigating the soldiers …so where was the question of paying respect…

Ranoji obviously had a personal agenda and was brewing some divisive plots. As a response to this insult he immediately declared that he would resign from Ahilyabai's service. The issue escalated further with her brother and his wife supporting their son. She had no intention of stopping them as they threatened to desert her and walk out.

Ahilyabai called for the palanquin. She wanted to be alone…on the banks of the Narmada…soak her feet in the water…and allow her tears to flow into the Narmada...The rustling sound of clear waters helped silence the turmoil within…

Her own brother and nephew…rebelling and plotting against her…But on the banks of the Narmada, Mamanji, Baiji…Maina…all seemed to revisit her, crowding her mind with memories. The sun was about to set…reflecting its orange redness in Ahilyabai's swollen eyes….

****

Dark monsoon clouds showered the region with light rains…cool breeze bringing in fresh whiffs of wet mud in the distant green meadows. Events and festivals were sliding on the calendar smoothly. Ganapati festival was celebrated. Each day seemed to replicate the other. Ahilyabai would wake up with the early rays of the Sun...bathe…pray…meditate and follow 'Mauna Vrata', [the vow of silence] in the early hours of the morning, until her glass of warm saffron milk arrived. After that what would follow was an unending binge of discussions, checks, drills, reprimands, grievances….at times even past midnight.

On one such day, Ahilyabai received a letter from Tukoji which horrified her. On 30 August 1773, Narayanrao Peshwa, who had become the next Peshwa after Madhavrao's death, was murdered…following which, Raghunthrao had taken on the title of the Peshwa!

Ahilyabai immediately knew the conspiracy at Pune was certain to spread its web towards Indore…triggering treachery and betrayals amongst her sardars. She immediately issued a stern warning to all her sardars. 'Anybody assisting, sheltering Raghunathrao, would be declared a traitor and would be dealt with no mercy whatsoever.' She threatened each one with dire consequences if found or suspected to help Raghunathrao usurp the rightful unborn heir, due to be born to Gangabai, wife of the slain Narayanrao. Until then the administration was to be conducted under the seal of Gangabai, by the trusted lieutenants of the slain Peshwa.

****

For some time now, Ahilyabai had observed some unnecessary complications in the way money was weaving its way in the balance sheets. Some new patterns were emerging… unfathomable knits…twist and skip. It would take longer than usual to reconcile simple debits and credits. She could sense many knots under these new patterns. She decided to iron out all these creases when Tukoji was visiting her for two days. She came straight to the point.

"Subhedar, we are 300 people in this palace. Are your homes and families larger than this, that your private expenses cross 2-2.5 lakh annually?"

"You have made me the Subhedar and I have no choice but to answer such questions. The machinery of such a huge army does not run on water, Matoshri…" Before he could say a word further, Ahilyabai corrected him. "Need I tell you that we have separate supply channels for the expenses incurred on the army and one crore per year is not a small amount." Tukoji was not in a submissive mood either… "May I dare ask about the expenses on the temples, embankments, business quarters…" Ahilyabai stood up cutting him short that very moment! "Make no mistake! All this developmental construction that you are listing, has not drawn a single dime from the treasury. It has all come from the amounts set aside for charity and my private philanthropic funds. I am only ensuring that the money set aside for charity is indeed used for the welfare of the subjects."

Ahilyabai continued in a softer tone now, "Subhedar, you need to keep a keen eye on how and where the money flows…else the accountants will throw sand in your eyes very easily…"

"Are you insinuating that I have embezzled funds?" Ahilyabai took a deep breath and looked at Tukoji. Her jaw line was firm… "Look, I hate to ask you this…but I have come to understand, that you do have a mistress, Radhi. Can you explain the source of the money spent on building palaces for her…the elephants …the palanquins outside her home and all the other extravagance of flowers, scents, silks that are delivered to the palace…where do the payments go from?"

Tukoji was taken aback! He did not expect Ahilyabai to be so direct. Ahilyabai continued to caution Tukoji. "Look, we cannot sustain on what is saved. Fresh inflows cannot be constricted.35% of the loot won in battles must be credited into the treasury. I too am accountable to the Peshwas. Everyone knows that huge amounts are collected in the loot but proportionate amounts are not being reflected in the State treasury credits." Ahilyabai spoke of how Malharrao had bound her loyalty to the Peshwas in words and in deeds and that she would honor it till her last breath…

"I am only suggesting", continued Ahilyabai, "that as of now , about 50,000 to 75,000 seems to have been spent by you from the State Treasury for personal expenses. I am willing to write it off if you give me an assurance, that you will not use State money for private purposes, keep a strict eye on the monetary flows and reconcile the unaccounted expenses…" Ahilyabai patted Tukoji on his shoulder and said, "You are like my son…I did not enjoy saying this but as a trustee of this kingdom…I have to…" Tukoji nodded in appreciation but he did not have a smile on his face.The meeting ended with some refreshments and small talk …after all, a big amount of 3, 17,000 remained unaccounted for...

****

12

On 18th April 1774, the widow of the late Narayanrao

Peshwa, Gangabai, was delivered of a son! Ahilyabai rejoiced at this divine intervention…an heir was born! The title of the Peshwa would now be retained by its rightful heir...Sawai Madhavrao, the newborn son of Narayanrao.

Just as Ahilyabai shared her relief and happiness with her daughter, she heard some commotion at the main gate of the palace. She hurried to the window. Some unidentified messenger was demanding a meeting with Ahilyabai. The guards were denying him entry. Ahilyabai knew who it could be….

She sent a word with the sentry to keep the man outside and simply send the scroll or the message. As expected…a scroll from Raghunathrao…in fact a threat…to extend support to him against the newborn heir or that he would turn to the British for help…

Ahilyabai was enraged at Raghunathrao's audacity to even attempt this request. She picked up the pen and ink to send a fitting reply.

'Dadasaheb…ever since the times of my heroic and noble father-in-law, Malharrao Holkar, we have always owed our loyalty to the Peshwa throne and always will. It is indeed a disgrace that you could not support, leave alone protect Narayanrao Peshwa. And now, you even dare to harvest support against his heir? I would advise you to never ever dare to cross the Narmada and set foot on the banks of Maheshwar. As far as the British are concerned, be warned, that seeking their help would be your gravest mistake. Betrayal does not run in the Holkar blood."

Ahilyabai called the sentry and said, "Give the messenger some water and send this reply back with him" The sentry nodded. He made no mistake. 'Offer some water to the messenger' meant, escort the messenger out of the city limits under vigilance.

****

Unaccounted expenditure was touching new heights with every passing day. Gold coins, taxes were apparently flowing in but the books of accounts were dry. Where was all the fortune seeping through? Ahilyabai would plug one hole...discover another...She was exasperated. It was not the back breaking work that exhausted her but it was Tukoji being deceitful that broke her back.

Ahilyabai shut her books of accounts and closed her eyes. Her breathing was slow and stretched. Pulling in enough oxygen to stay alive seemed a daunting task...exhaling seemed easier...long sighs drained her stress out. Breathing almost seemed like a struggle. Breathing in was like mustering energy to continue...breathing out was easier...wanting to just let go...

For the last 5-6 days every discovery of Tukoji's transgression and misconduct drove a wedge in Ahilyabai's heart. She would let out a sigh...a sigh that drained her energies and her belief. That evening she went to the temple to sit in front of the deity, to renew her lost faith and energy...Little did she know, another blow awaited her round the corner.

****

Next day Oodabai and Harkuaai came to see her. Their visit was like an instant energy revitalizer! The three women connected over refreshing lemon drinks... news... chats... updates...Harkuaai cryptically conveyed to Ahilyabai that people were talking...saying...Naro Ganesh visits Tukoji's wife, Rukhmabai too often for comfort...

Ahilyabai froze for a moment...but then said, "Work, am sure, takes him there. After all, he is their accountant. And then, men can keep as many mistresses but if a woman, as much as even befriends a man, she is accused of the worst and these aspersions cast on her, haunt her a lifetime! People may talk...but we must be careful and refrain from such talk..."

"Vahinisaheb, this is a scorching topic of discussion among all the sardar women!"

Ahilyabai was quiet. Tukoji was away most of the time. Rukhmabai ...a stunningly pretty woman could attract anyone...

"Does Tukoji have any inkling of this? Is he aware of Naro Ganesh's visits to his home?" was all Ahilyabai asked. Harkuaai clarified that Tukoji trusted Naro Ganesh implicitly...the jewels and the ornaments from the loot find their way straight into Tukoji's home through Naro Ganesh...so also the money collected as taxes. Nothing gets accounted for, in the books... "Tighten your grip on the situation Vahinisaheb, before it is too late and the fortune of the Holkars, slips out like sand from your fingers" cautioned Oodabai.

The very next day Ahilyabai ordered an audit of the books. She pored over them for 15 days...also appointed Appaji Jagdev at Pune to send her information secretly about all that transpires there...Several stories about the numerous financial deals involving Tukoji and Naro Ganesh emerged...

What Ahilyabai could not reconcile was the story of Rukhmabai and Naro Ganesh, and Tukoji's love for Naro Ganesh...

****

Experienced and old loyalists were all praises for the nearly 50 year old Ahilyabai and her work. The ammunition factories, the cannons, the preparedness of the army, the security of the forts...the development of commerce, building of temples and embankments, dispensing of justice and above all her crystal clear articulation which stemmed from a strong conviction of loyalty to the Peshwas. There was never any ambiguity on her stand...no hiding behind words...sharp messages...strong actions, clever strategizing. A woman, who commanded respect, throughout the ranks of the army.

Ahilyabai now took charge of all expenses and authorizations. She had collected so much evidence that neither Tukoji nor Naro Ganesh could refute the allegation. Tukoji had not visited her in six months now. He found some excuse or the other to avoid confrontation. No confrontation…no interrogation…no compulsion to answer…Naro Ganesh on the other hand was sinking in the sea of evidence…no chance to keep his head above water. Yet, Ahilyabai could not make this knowledge public…not because she wanted to shelter the erring Subhedar, but to defend the throne from other opportunists. A strategic decision…a very good one.

****

Malhar and Nathoba were growing up faster in their new found companionship….playing, studying, learning Sanskrit shlokas… Ahilyabai too had her moments of happiness ringing in, with these two, prancing about noisily in the palace. Four months had gone by. There was no news form Appaji Jagdev. The last she had heard was about the thread ceremony of the little boy Peshwa.

Every day the markets and espionage circles were abuzz with new sketchy rumors. Ahilyabai had a hazy picture that there was a lot of activity at Borghat near Pune. The armies of the Shindes and other sardars had been commissioned to approach Borghat under Tukoji's orders. Spies kept her informed but Ahilyabai awaited news from authorized sources…and one day…Appaji Jagdev arrived himself! Ahilyabai's heart skipped a beat…

But the smile on his face put her anxiety to rest. "Matoshri, accept my greetings. Dadasaheb has been finally arrested at Borghat…after a fierce battle! Dadasaheb had taken help from the British on promises to share the spoils after capturing Pune. But our Subhedar, got wind of the plot and with the combined allied forces of about 80,000 soldiers, intercepted Dadasaheb at

Borghat. It was a vicious battle that dragged on for days. It was the courageous blow by the regiment of the elite 1800 soldiers led by Bapu Holkar which sealed our victory! Only 250 returned from the mission…but victorious… The honor of the Shinde-Holkar alliance was renewed. I wanted to give you this news personally!"

Ahilyabai folded her hands…shut her eyes…and remembered her father-in-law…Her decision to not punish Tukoji yielded results…the Holkar's loyalty to the Pune throne was demonstrated one more time and the legacy continued… uninterrupted

****

That day Harkuaai entered Ahilyabai's room with a very cheeky smile. Ahilyabai almost missed it but another quick glance and Ahilyabai asked her… "What is amusing you so much? Bapu Holkar's success?"

"Can you ever think beyond politics?"asked Harkuaai smiling widely. Ahilyabai put aside all the correspondence that she was skimming through…and gave her the attention she was seeking "tell me…what is it that you are struggling to keep inside you?!" Harkuaai in one swift move, closed in on Ahilyabai and whispered… "This is about Raghunathrao's beautiful wife, Anandibai!"

"Do not ever take his name…he is now under arrest" said Ahilyabai with a slight disdain and major relief in her voice.

Harkuaai raised her voice… "Again! …again politics?"

"Alright…", sighed Ahilyabai

"Your life is nothing but politics …so stop eating, drinking, sleeping politics…and listen to some entertaining stories!" Ahilyabai resigned herself to Harkuaai and said… "Amuse me!"

Harkuaai excitedly narrated how Ahilyabai's recognition makes Anandibai curious and insecure…and how she wonders if Ahilyabai's charisma was more attractive to people than her own classical beauty!

Ahilyabai heard Harkuaai out non chalantly…paused and said… "If your story is now over, I am thirsty …can you please send someone for a glass of politics to drink please?!!"

Harkuaai stared at Ahilyabai for a moment…and the two women burst out laughing at the uncanny slip of tongue! Muktabai, who was passing by her mother's room…stopped. She wanted to store this rare spectacle in her heart…her mother laughing out loud, heartily….

****

Ahilyabai was so excited and charged with the victory of Tukoji and Bapu Holkar that she started work the next day, with a new found drive and renewed vigor. Just like the stories of courage and bravery of the Holkars have stretched far and wide, she wanted the art and literature of Maheshwar to be talked about, across the country.

"Govindrao, I want you to contact eminent personalities and budding artists, poets, writers, sculptors and even Vaidyas. Send them an official invitation with my signature and seal, requesting them to settle in Maheshwar. Inform them that they will be assured of Royal Patronage and all facilities to establish institutes, deliver lectures and conduct research."

Govindrao nodded with great pleasure, "Most certainly Matoshri! I will accomplish this in the next 15 days! In fact…some learned pundits are here from Kashi and desire to meet you.

Ahilyabai stood up to receive them and offered them seats respectfully. They were four Brahmins from the seat of learning, of the North, Kashi. They folded their hands and said, "We are Ved Pundits but the Muslim invasions have made it impossible for us to pursue our study of the Vedas."

"How can I help you?" asked Ahilyabai with great reverence. "If you wish you can move to Maheshwar. All facilities will be provided to you by the fund set up for the promotion of Art and Literature."

The Brahmins appreciated her offer but politely refused saying it was not just about the four of them. It was a problem encountered by many others, their families and disciples.

Ahilyabai understood. She assured them that she would send her emissary Pundit Visaji Deshpande with a directive from her and have all facilities arranged for them in Kashi. The Pundits began to thank Ahilyabai …She was quick to suspend the vote of thanks as she said, "You may want to wait before you thank me. I would like you to know that my informers will indeed visit your facilities, ever so often. Sometimes as disciples…or teachers ...or even visitors. I will reassure myself that these concessions are indeed being used only and only for education and knowledge transfer…I am afraid but anything found askew will invite strict action…"

The Pundits smiled with satisfaction and said, "That gives us more reason to thank you then!"

That very evening, Visaji Deshpande left for Kashi along with the four Brahmins.

****

A sulking Tukoji and Rukhmabai, had recalled their son, Malhar, under some pretext. It was their way of registering their protest with Ahilyabai about the fund embezzlement allegations. The next Ahilyabai heard, was that Malhar was to be married! No invitation…Ahilyabai was deeply hurt. A white sari clad widow may not be welcome in wedding celebrations…but there were others too in the palace…She had always mentored Tukoji like her son and embraced Malhar as a grandmother would. No doubt that this entire episode of financial discrepancies had fermented the relationship…but then, the Vicory at Borghat had softened her feelings…but apparently not Tukoji's…

And after all, these disapprovals were in an official capacity…

personally, she did have affection for Tukoji…but he failed to recognize that…

Destiny had strung garlands of glory for Ahilyabai in her public life…but her personal life was a string of misfortunes. All her near and dear ones seemed, to somehow drift away from her…leaving her lonely...An otherwise strong Ahilyabai would these days, break down at the slightest nudge. Unill now, only the rustling waters of the Narmada witnessed and camouflaged Ahilyabai's tears…but now Harkuaai and Muktabai would spend days cheering up a dejected Ahilyabai…her walk was slower than a fifty five year old's, her voice subdued…the dullness in her eyes spread throughout the palace…A worried Harkuaai would watch over Ahilyabai hoping that these clouds of gloom would get blown away by some gentle, magical whiff….

****

…and a gentle whisper did indeed lift the dreariness. Harkuaai and Muktabai proposed the wedding of the 13 year old Nathoba to a pretty little girl from Mahadji Mama's side! This proposal injected some enthusiasm in the palace…but Ahilyabai was now wary of affections and attachments …she did not seem to have the strength to bear the pain that separation brought…

Soon the wedding date was set for, the especially auspicious moment of Aksha Tritaya. Ahilyabai ordered the best Paithanis, Maheshwari saris which had gorgeous peacock feathers embroidered on the borders…the jewelers crafted exquisite pieces for the grand daughter-in-law…

Yashwantrao Phanse's family as well as Ahilyabai's maternal side of the family …all arrived for the wedding. Shahaji came, albeit, without Ranoji. Ahilyabai took the opportunity to ease the strain between her and Tukoji. She sent an invitation to Tukoji, Rukhmabai, Malhar and the new bride with her personal signature and seal. All of them graced the occasion except Tukoji who was on a mission…

The wedding celebrations lasted for a week! Ahilyabai, Renu, Anjana, Bhagoji, Raghoji were exhausted looking after the guests. Ahilyabai distributed fabulous return gifts to them all, acknowledging their hard work and contribution in making the ceremony feel so warm, decorative and merry... so seemingly effortlessly.

Their bodies were tired but watching the 13 year old Nathoba and 11 year old Bala around the palace was a pleasure that energized their minds. The sound of the trinkets of little Bala would resonate in Ahilyabai's heart…reminding her, of her own childhood. She gave her all the love that Baiji had showered on her and Bala would come running to her whenever she was in the palace. Ahilyabai then would seem to forget all her worries.

Ahilyabai got busy celebrating all the festivals and ceremonies of the newly weds. At 55 now, Bala and Nathoba's love warmed her deepest motherly longings…The love of her grandchildren seemed to have rejuvenated Ahilyabai…

Muktabai and Harkuaai were more relieved than anything, to observe this change in Ahilyabai. There was now a guarded but sprightly bounce in her cautious walk at this age.

Visaji Deshpande had returned from Kashi after establishing a settlement called 'Brahmapuri' for the Brahmins there. He brought back with him impressive stories of their bright disciples.

Many of the artists and artisans who had received invitations from Ahilyabai to settle in Maheshwar started trickling in. She got busy establishing new institutes, libraries, ...She still had a lot to accomplish. Ever since she had heard that thousands of soldiers returning from Panipat had died of thirst, she had wanted to not only create shelter homes (dharamshalas) for the travelers and homeless, but also dig more wells. Plans were numerous. But the official treasury did not have the strength to shore up her plans. She had deployed a lot of her personal funds …

'This year the rains have been good', thought Ahilyabai… 'good rains mean a good crop…and a good crop meant a rich harvest for the royal treasury…' She was impatient to use those funds for the benefit of her people…for the development of commerce…and secure shelters for them…

****

That day, standing at the window Ahilyabai noticed a flamboyant palanquin with horses approach the palace. She was informed that the Shindes wanted a meeting with her. She observed Mhadji Shinde, with a slight limp…a souvenir of his bravery at Panipat, as he disembarked. Ahilyabai welcomed him with all due protocol. Refreshments…gifts for the newlyweds…return gifts of silk brocade and gold…small talk on political developments and discussions on the loss of Vasai to the British were over.

Mhadji Shinde made a reference to Tukoji. Ahilyabai was at her attentive best. She somehow knew what was coming…and sure enough, Shinde advocated that Ahilyabai recall Tukoji and restore his rights of access to the treasury and authorization of expenses. So this meeting was for a mediation…!

Ahilyabai replied firmly, "This wealth belongs to the Peshwas. I am in their service. Anyone who misappropriates it cannot be entrusted with safeguarding it." After all 2 crores were unaccounted for…

A few more pleas using different words…different tones…failed to convince Ahilyabai. She insisted, 'Tukoji is very close to my heart but he cannot go anywhere close to the treasury…'

Very casually then …in a rather cold voice…Mhadji said, "I request you to please keep in mind not just your affection for Tukoji but the fact that you are after all a lone woman pitted against men …and as men, we may want to attempt to solve problems using our ways…

Ahilyabai reacted without a moment's delay! "Of course yes…most certainly. You must try and attempt your ways…In fact, I would like to invite you to get a glimpse of our cannons, ammunition, arms and not just the preparedness of my army but their skills in warfare! You will indeed be assured that the late Subhedar, my father-in-law, left behind his legacy, albeit, in the hands of a woman but very safe hands…"

Mhadji Shinde got the thunderous message softly but clear. He hastily turned the conversation into a little speech of praise for the Holkar army, the ammunition factory, and so on…concluded the conversation …took her leave and returned to Indore.

At Indore he narrated the incident to Tukoji and Naro Ganesh. Naro Ganesh said, "Give me eight days and I will set things right!" But Tukoji refused. He could never commit such an act, he said. After all she had given him the love of a mother…

Tukoji dismissed the meeting, not realizing that the man serving refreshments in that room would overhear everything and relay the conversation to Ahilyabai…

Tukoji's response cemented Ahilyabai's faith in him but Naro Ganesh had to be watched. She was trained well by the late Subhedar. She knew this was not the time to act but watch…watch keenly.

She remembered her father-in-law as she performed the annual rites on his death anniversary. A woman… a widow at that, performing the rites was against the scriptures. But Ahilyabai followed her conscience. For her, Dharma[17] was the voice inside her. She was filled with old memories of Indore as she poured water over the mound of rice, symbolizing the spirit of the deceased person…

****

Harkuaai would always breeze in with a bagful of rumors

floating in the market! She strutted in looking rather pleased with some unpleasant news. "Reap as you sow!" she spouted out the words on a beat. "What happened?" asked Ahilyabai, rather anxiously. "Well, they say, the canopy at the wedding venue of Malhar was gutted in a fire...

Ahilyabai's heart sank...She knew that this meant a loss running into lakhs. Now she could expect long decorative expense sheets of the wedding costs. This fire was going to burn a huge hole in the Royal Reserves. She knew she would have to spend long days auditing those accounts...

Immediately on the heels of the wedding celebrations, Ahilyabai received news that Tukoji had left on Tipu Sultan's trail. No official word from Tukoji. Ahilyabai had fought many personal battles. She expected one more now. She had to prepare herself for it and this time, she decided, even the waters of the Narmada would not be privy to her tears.

She sent for Yashwantrao Phanse. "You are well aware of Tukoji's actions. My loyalties lie in safeguarding this inheritance and passing it on into safe hands...to a Holkar. May I therefore take the liberty of proposing, to adopt your son Nathoba? I do understand he is the only son of your family and hence if you have even an ounce of hesitation or doubt ...I will respect that and endeavor to find some other way out of this..."

Yashwantrao had no hesitation in giving his consent but he did have some other doubts. "In my books this would be a very hasty step, Matoshri. It would make for greater wisdom to draw Tukoji back into our fold rather than challenge him..."

Ahilyabai's voice betrayed her exasperation as she replied. "Seven years on various missions and four years as sardar...but no substantial addition to the Royal reserves! The Shindes and the Holkars own properties of equal valuations...but our collections are one half of theirs. How? No famines anywhere...yet the State is in debt. Even Tukoji's sardars complain that their fair share of loot never reaches them! He has not reported here in almost a year now! Reliable sources inform me that Tukoji has some plan up his sleeve…"

Yashwantrao knew, Ahilyabai had made up her mind. He gave his consent for the adoption and left. Ahilyabai sent for her private writing kit…the one with her personal seals.

6-2-1782

'In the service of Shreemant Peshwa…

Request consultation…

The infamous stories of Tukoji's personal life may have reached your esteemed self. At this stage in life, the daughter-in-law of the late Malharrao Holkar is today, compelled to write under oath, that I am bound beyond doubt, in words and deeds, to the throne of the Peshwa. The times are treacherous. The British have captured Vasai and were moving towards Pune, albeit, have ensured uninterrupted supply of resources to Tukoji to ward off that threat. But I have not seen any inflow worth mentioning in the last decade…the paperwork leaves a lot to be desired…the accounting practices do not come clean…

I write this, not to undermine Tukoji but rather to determine my loyalty. I urge you to verify my statements.

With this letter I also revive a request made earlier in the year 1779, to permit me to adopt Nathoba Phanse and prepare him, to take over as the future Subhedar. Tukoji will be retained as the commander-in-chief of the army.

The second request is regarding my late father-in-law's 'Khandaarani'[18], Harkubai . Harkubai has an accountant by the name Maniram. He is also related to Sumersingh, by virtue of the fact, that Maniram and Sumersingh's children are married to each other. Maniram has cheated Harkubai of ten lakhs and Sumersingh of his property. Maniram and Naro Ganesh are birds of the same feather…and of course, a friend to the manipulative Raghunathrao.

Tukoji gives me no reason to doubt his loyalty yet I do believe he is not in good company.

I submit these two requests at your feet…

In your service…as ordained by Lord Shankar… Ahilyabai.'

****

Rukhmabai, along with Malhar, and the new bride finally arrived to seek Ahilyabai's blessing. Ahilyabai too welcomed them warmly. Rukhmabai said, "It was Malhar who insisted that we should all visit you …so here we are!" Ahilyabai simply smiled. She did not want to examine the 'why s' and scrutinize the 'hows'…she was just happy that they had all come! She hugged Malhar and then the little bride. Rukhmabai made a face as she looked at the little girl… "Well, not a good beginning…the girl proved unlucky! The canopy at the wedding venue was gutted…" Ahilyabai looked sternly at Rukhmabai, and interrupted her monologue. "You have said it now…never say it again! Putting lamps on the canopy was foolish and dangerous. Why blame the poor child for it!"

Rukhmabai was quick to change the course of conversation to Muktabai. Nathoba and Malhar along with their brides were playing in the palace. Ahilyabai too played a few traditional games with the little girls…The palace was alive with their laughter like old times…

Gifts, saris, silks and gold necklaces were showered on Malhar's wife. Ahilyabai did all that a grandmother should, to pamper the new bride.

As the visitors were about to leave, Ahilyabai made a passing reference to Tukoji…saying… "Tukoji does not seem to miss his mother…but I am glad all of you visited us…"

Rukhmabai only smiled and said, "I am myself very upset with the Subhedar. He never spends time with me…always on missions…"

Ahilyabai did not think that was a complaint befitting a Subhedar's wife….

****

News from Appaji Jagdev was not encouraging…Ahilyabai was already being sidestepped by Tukoji. He was issuing instructions and collecting toll directly, emphasizing that the money be sent to him directly, skirting Maheshwar. Tukoji, as Ahilyabai had estimated, was now beginning to establish corridors of power in Pune through Nanasaheb who was acting on behalf of the nine year old Peshwa. The entire country was distraught with infighting. The British were gaining ground very fast. Gujarat was almost under their influence…Surat, Bhadoch, Jambusar, Dabhai were dotted with British platoons. The Gaikwad wada itself housed 100 British personnel… Baroda, Ahmadabad too, were in the grasp of the British.

The lawyer from Lucknow, sent word of the situation there. Seven representatives of the British arrived at the court of the son of Suja-ud-daullah offering him assistance to capture large areas in exchange for 2 crores. The son apparently put his own mother and grandmother under arrest, for one and a half crore cash... and jewellery, worth crores, was put at stake.

Around this time, the British sent four platoons to the fort of Gwalior. Ahilyabai received an imperative appeal for immediate assistance from Gwalior. She dispatched a 10,000 strong army under the leadership of Baluji Ingle and Rajaram Ransod to repeal the British attack. Despite being given so many chances, Raghunathdada, unfortunately, seemed to never mend his ways. He gave the army the slip and took refuge with the British at Surat. Not just this but he also dared to send two of his messengers, Maniyar Paarshi and Hanmantrao, straight to the King of England to request for independent military aid. His requests were repealed in strong words from England denying him any military assistance!

Nanasaheb was aware of these developments. With the help of the French and Hyder, he made all efforts to put the British under siege. The British knew that they could not fight the allied forces…and so on 17th May 1782, 20 kms from Gwalior, a truce was inked at Saalbai. According to this truce, the British had to withdraw their support to Raghunathrao and other than the island of Sashti (Salsette) all other regions had to be returned to the Peshwas. Ahilyabai was invited to this meeting where the truce was inked.

Ahilyabai struck a conversation there with Nanasaheb, assuring him of Tukoji's allegiance but cautioning him once again about his misappropriations. She also thanked him for ensuring the release of Harkubai's properties. Ahilyabai clarified that she did not fear being divested of power but she feared that the power would get invested in the wrong hands. "I am nearing 60 now...I would be more than happy to pass on the power and go on a pilgrimage. But destiny pronounces that concession, as an indulgence for me! I do not insist that the power remains with me but I will most certainly ensure that my father-in-law's legacy is not destroyed. Tukoji could add nothing to the treasury in 14 years. With your support if Tukoji gains further ground, we will both be equally guilty of being incapable of protecting what was created... and that I consider nothing short of a betrayal to the Peshwa throne and Malharrao Holkar's trust in us..."

The messages rang loud and clear in Nanasaheb's ears! He guaranteed Ahilyabai of his support ...

****

13

One day, Ahilyabai, was overseeing the palace arrangements. Nathoba was playing with another child. Ahilyabai went to the boys to strike a conversation. She realized the child was a little warm. And Nathoba had high fever. She sent for Muktabai and the Royal Vaidya...

Just as she settled the boys, Ahilyabai was told that a few Muslim messengers had arrived with some letter. Ahilyabai wondered …who they could be.…

Ahilyabai took her seat and sent for them. It was a group of four or five people. They entered and announced grandly, "Baadshah ka Inaayatnama laaya hai. Isko khadi taazeem dekar aapne izzat ke saath lena hai" ['This is a message from the Baadshah. You will have to get up from your seat and stand up in obeisance as you accept this message!]

Ahilyabai stared at the visitors…paused and looked at her minister. "Even the letter from the Peshwas, is received by my minister. If at all, I would stand in respect only for the Peshwas." She looked at her minister and said, "Mukundrao, kindly bring the letter to me if these people are willing to hand over the letter to you…else please see them off!"

Mukund Hari brought the letter. The messengers were left seething… Harkuaai who was observing this, looked at Ahilyabai with pride and thought, 'only she can do this…'

Nathoba was well now. No fever. Ahilyabai would spend hours at her workplace…replying to letters and messages… arbitrating complaints of her subjects, litigation… development work…religious discourses… community kitchens… constructing wells and ablution facilities… No one was allowed to bathe in the Narmada. Waters of the river were to be transported in copper or brass containers, balanced and hung on either ends of a rod. There were special porters appointed to transport and supply water in this manner. The water had to remain crystal clear…and not sullied.

The temples too were abuzz with Pujas…and chanting of mantras by 101 Pundits together… the Brahmins were given alms …the temple bells agog at dawn and dusk…kirtans and devotional songs were sung…programs by Bhil poets specially, the renowned poet, Moropant, were arranged…people would gather there to experience divine peace on the banks of the Narmada.

Almost a year went by. The festive months of Hartalika

and Ganesh Puja…then the 15 days of 'Pitru Paksha' when the ancestors were to be remembered and rituals for the peace of their souls were to be performed. Those 15 days, Ahilyabai would transcend into the past. The palace at Indore... Baiji… Malharrao… Khanderao's Mahal…Malerao's pranks…and would never forget the lover of Hira who was murdered by Malerao…She had built a 'samadhi' in memory of that artisan…

This year some Muslim fakirs also received alms and charity. "We believe Allah…God…are all one", she would say to them and urge them to discourage religious skirmishes…

****

Navratra followed…then Dussehra…Ahilyabai had a special chariot seat atop an elephant. Every Dussehra she would sit on it and step out onto the roads…showering greetings and gold flowers on the people…connecting in a very special way …waving out to them…

Nathoba , accompanied by his wife, held the Holkar flag as high as he could. Ahilyabai looked lovingly at Nathoba as the elephant swayed through the streets of Maheshwar.

That night Nathoba came down with fever again. Throughout Diwali, he had fever, every now and then. Amidst this anxiety came some excellent news…the news of the marriage of the young Peshwa. Ahilyabai received the invitation with warmth and respect from Nanasaheb… insisting that her presence was of highest significance.

Ahilyabai experienced a huge sense of relief and gratitude towards Nanasaheb who had, with support from Haripant Tatya, protected the young Peshwa from the political ferment in Pune. She shut her eyes and thanked the Lord for this day!

She was certain that she would not participate in the wedding celebrations. She did not wish, that anyone should feel uncomfortable due to the presence of a widow…

Harkuaai, Mukund Hari, and others advised Ahilyabai to

send wedding gifts separately, not with Tukoji. But Ahilyabai was firm. These gifts will be delivered to Tukoji and he will carry the gifts on behalf of the House of Holkars. After all, the gifts must be such that they uphold the honor of the late Malharrao Holkar…

In the January of 1783, for the wedding of Sawai Madhavrao Peshwa, two pairs of silk outfits including one with intricate gold zari work for the Peshwa, emerald and Navratna[19] embellishments for the headgear, two diamond bracelets, Clothes for the bride, One Jadau necklace and clothes for the senior family members were exquisitely customized and dispatched to Tukoji.

By the time Ahilyabai wound up her study that day, the news of the death of Hyder Nayak reached her. She sank into her chair. She recognized that the British would not let go of this opportunity to hoist their tactics again…

****

Amidst these lurking fears, the wedding of the Peshwa was celebrated with pomp and splendor. In some days, a letter from Pune was delivered to her. The letter affirmed that all heads of States were expected to make proportionate contributions towards the wedding expenses…and the Holkars were asked to deposit 2 lakhs. Tukoji had very conveniently forwarded the letter to Ahilyabai.

Ahilyabai had sent extravagant exclusive gifts. Now the treasury had no strength to bear this burden. She sent for the lawyer and directed him to draft a reply saying… 'The taxes were not being paid at Maheshwar. They were being collected directly by Tukoji at Vaafgaon. So, when the payee was in Pune and the Payer in Vaafgaon, how had the letter come to Maheshwar? Shreemant Peshwa should exact an explanation from Tukoji!'

The lawyer stood with folded hands …looking down…

"True...but what do I write in the reply...?"

"Exactly what I said!" The lawyer was taken aback. This would be deemed as non compliance...and could evoke a backlash..."It would only be proper for you to not say this and wiser for me to not write so..."

Ahilyabai too knew she could not refuse the payment. 2 lakhs was not a large sum. She could without doubt send it from her personal financial credits. But she knew...Tukoji wanted exactly that! Her personal wealth was being used for welfare...He now had designs on that...She was not about to let that happen...she picked up the ink pot and the nib pen...

Harkuaai thought... 'Only she can do this...'

****

Few more months went by...No word from Tukoji still. The summer tasks were concluding...Grain storage...drying of the crispies...pickles, chilli powder, turmeric, spices and masalas...activities pounding away the terraces and courtyards...

The farmers received their rightful share. High quality seed distribution and water irrigation plans were put in place. The waters of the Narmada had dried up a little in the summer but the banks of the river, were overflowing with people...visiting temples, reciting devotional songs and chants...but the loudest notes that reverbrated through Maheshwar were about Ahilyabai's philanthropic work...her charity...No one ever exhausted of praising her and acknowledging her dedication to the welfare of her people..

That day, everyone in Maheshwar was tapering down their chores for the day. They all had to attend a special darbar in the afternoon. Shreemant Peshwa had honored Ahilyabai by bequeathing a souvenir for the wedding...as an appreciation of her loyal services. Everyone wanted to see their beloved benefactor being honored...

In the afternoon, bugles were playing and drums were

beating…people crowded the darbar… On a large round silver ornamental platter, the gifts and souvenirs were displayed.

Ahilyabai was seated in the center…medium built…white sari, dusky radiant skin…long eyelashes…a string of pearls in the neck, two plain gold bangles, a glow on her face…and even at that age hardly any trace of grey hair…

As soon as the lawyer from Pune presented the gifts, a spontaneous flourish, of a thunderous applause resonated through the crowds! Nathoba, Balabai, Muktabai …all were clapping… but Harkuaai clapped the longest…even after the others had stopped…she had tears in her eyes… Ahilyabai's entire life flashed across her blurry eyes…as she commended and celebrated a well-deserved honor…

Ahilyabai was presented a white silk Paithani …a string of big, natural, rare pearls with a pendant and a dexterously crafted shawl…

Everyone was shouting slogans for Ahilyabai! The lawyer picked up the red velvet scroll …a note from the Peshwa…

' Respected Matoshri Ahilyabai…Kindly honor and humble us by accepting these souvenirs of honor presented to yourself. Your services and the loyalty to the throne of Pune is immeasurable …your good wishes immense… your philanthropy unmatched…your statesmanship, unparalleled… Please continue to shower your blessings on us always!'

Another deafening applause tore through the darbar! Ahilyabai waited for the applause to recede before she began to speak…

"Respected members of the darbar and my beloved people…The Sun is finally shining brightly in Pune. We must express our gratitude to Nanasaheb and Haripant Tatya , who with tremendous dedication and loyalty ensured that we all witness this day…the wedding of the young Peshwa…Let us all pray to Lord Shankar for the health, safety ,success and long life of Sawai Madhavrao Peshwa!"

Many people stepped forward to narrate stories of the splendor at the wedding. One such junior officer described the wedding so vividly that Ahilyabai gifted him a pearl string and offered him free education saying that he had a way with words…and that he should study further! She was certain, he would go on to become a great orator or a writer…The darbar was dismissed on this cheerful note.

Ahilyabai reached her room. Harkuaai was waiting there for her with red chillies and salt to drive away the evil eye! Harkuaai did not rest before she relentlessly performed all the rituals to ward off evil…Ahilyabai was aghast! "Harkuaai, I am 58! Evil eye???!!!"

****

The next day Ahilyabai got news of another gain by the British…Bidanoor. But fortunately, Tipu regained it and the British caved in. Ahilyabai thought to herself… 'All the sardars need to be united. They need to sift these odd-even stories they hear, before they believe anyone…else, the British who have entered the country on the pretext of commerce will very soon swallow the entire country …along with its trade and commerce…with their 'divide and rule policy'. Coming here for trade, I say, and then what business do they have setting up platoons?!We have to give up infighting…'

****

Some people from Mahitpur were waiting to meet Ahilyabai. They had complaints about the sardars who were demanding 200% and at times more in taxes…and if the people did not pay up, they had to repay in kind by their rigorous labor …or then…providing them the women from their homes…be it wives, daughters or sisters…

Ahilyabai was enraged! She shot out an order for her palanquin to be readied…and headed straight to Mahitpur. She called a meeting of the villagers in the square. After enquiring and investigating, she sent for the sardars. She issued a stern threat to them against harassing the people...and warned them against intimidating the people who have complained! She cautioned them about having her informers and spies in Mahitpur. She directed them to refund all taxes collected unduly, within 48 hours. Saying so, she started towards her palanquin. The sardars brought fruits and milk for her and invited her for a meal, considering she had travelled a distance. She stopped ...stared at them... "I will return for this once you confirm that the orders have been implemented." She pulled the curtains of her palanquin. As soon as the palanquin was on its way the people shouted out aloud... 'Mata Ahilyadevi ki jai!'

****

She barely reached Maheshwar and she had a few brahmins waiting for her...They looked harassed and emaciated. They folded their hands , "Matoshri, getting our daughters married is becoming ever so tough..."

"...and why should that be? You belong to educated families..."enquired Ahilyabai.

"Every groom's family demands gold, money, jewellery in exchange for our daughter's hand in marriage."

Ahilyabai requested them to take their seats and sent for Mukund Hari. Ahilyabai ordered him to write out a proclamation. 'Henceforth, demanding money, in any caste or creed, by anyone, at the time of marriage or later, from the bride's family will be treated as an offence. The administration will recover twice the amount demanded from the receiver and an equivalent amount from the giver, as well as, the matchmaker. This administration also reserves the right of pronouncing additional fines or punishment as deemed fit in such cases of extreme aggravation.'

Ahilyabai directed Mukund Hari to make 50 copies and

send it to all provinces. Ahilyabai also ordered that the Brahmins be paid two rupees each, as their conveyance expenses…

****

Ahilyabai and Harkuaai were enjoying a rare relaxed evening, sipping their warm saffron milk, when Ahilyabai mentioned to her that she had sent seven lakhs as assistance to Mhadji Patil, who had been fighting Hastings for over a year now…

Harkuuaai was stunned. "How could you send assistance to those who had indeed plotted to usurp you four years ago? It was a good lesson to them when the soldiers refused to participate in the planned attack! Served them right! The soldiers had said… 'tell us to fight the Shindes or even the Peshwas…we will do that…but if you tell us to fight Matoshri Ahilyabai , we lay down our arms here and now!' Have you forgotten this or forgiven?"

"Neither …Harkuaai! This is politics…Right now we need to be united against the British!"

"….only you can do this…!" said Harkuaai and Ahilyabai together! Ahilyabai knew her customary , signature remark! Both women laughed heartily!

Their laughter was interrupted by a message dated 11th December 1783 informing Ahilyabai of the death of Raghunathrao. Both women merely exchanged glances. 'Raghunathrao was a curse to our political landscape. His ill placed ambitions helped the British make inroads into our land…his, is a story of misplaced valor. He was not a man of his words and in fact susceptible to temptations. This rot should have been wiped out earlier…better late…'

"I am going in to bathe …" said Ahilyabai. "An eclipse has passed over" A traitor was no more.

****

Yashwantrao Phanse arrived with a silver bowl of sweets announcing the recapture of the Gwalior fort which was under siege. Ahilyabai's happiness knew no bounds. She immediately announced a salute of three cannon ball firings in honor of Mhadji Patil. She also distributed sweets and offered her prayers at the feet of Lord Shiva.

She looked at Yashwantrao , "I wish Tukoji had involved himself in this historic mission rather than travel to the South all the time…"

" Well," hesitated Yashwantrao, "It is said that Nanasaheb and Haripant Tatya themselves keep him away from the North to avoid clashes with yourself. But Naro Ganesh is his bane. People in Indore talk about the relations between Naro Ganesh and Rukhmabai…Even her own son, Malhar, does not speak with her. After all he is not a child anymore…he understands…"

"If only Tukoji had a better grip on Naro Ganesh and his own greed for money…fame, victories and immeasurable wealth would have been his, for the asking…" rued Ahilyabai.

****

The last few days had been extremely exhausting for Ahilyabai. She still could not get over the death of her brother Mahadji. She had to be a source of emotional support for his family. On the political front she had been engulfed by stormy events…She had to arrange a backing of 25,000 soldiers to be dispatched to Pune… Tukoji needed some reinforcements too…Some villages reported attacks by thugs and dacoits…She had sent security forces to bring those under control…She was fatigued now… and simply lay in bed…

Harkuaai entered her room…Ahilyabai was drained. She propped herself up as she asked Harkuaai, "Will you please take care of the palace for a few days …I am feeling very restless…I wish to go to Jaamb near Indore…" Harkuaai agreed, that Ahilyabai needed some rest and change of weather, and assured her she would look after the palace…

****

Ahilyabai's palanquin left Maheswar , along with some soldiers, Renu, Anjana, Mukund Hari, Bharmal dada, Ambadas and their families. As Indore drew closer, Ahilyabai's mind started drifting on a sojourn back into the past...

'That's the road to Depalpura...the horse riding school...the cannonball factory...The first home where she witnessed receiving the Subhedari papers as a nine year old...That ceremony was still vivid in her memory...

The palanquin stopped in front of the palace. Sub consciously Ahilyabai looked up at Khanderao's palace...her first night...her last night, when she was in a white sari...and Khanderao had said that it flatters her...and then...that day on the battle ground...after which she wore nothing but white...

Ahilyabai's gaze was frozen...she stood motionless... staring at the windows on the first floor...

"Baisaheb...", Ahilyabai could faintly hear Renu's voice but nothing seemed to register... "Baisaheb...." Renu called out again...Ahilyabai nodded and entered the palace. For a few moments she stood in front of Baiji's room...her hands on the closed doors...But she did not seem to have the might to push open the doors...She took a deep breath, cleared the lump in her throat...and slowly pushed open the doors of the room...Baiji's empty room. Ahilyabai dragged her feet heavily to Baiji's bed...and collapsed on it...Tears were streaming down relentlessly...

Ahilyabai could not remember how long she sat there...Malerao's questions...Khanderao's answers...all flashing through her mind...After what seemed like an eon gone by, she pulled herself together...and went towards the temple...where Baiji taught her good values and Malharrao, valuable lessons in politics...Her father-in-law had given her his pearl necklace in appreciation of her superior efforts.

She remembered women gathering in this very palace to disapprove of her for breaking the tradition of Sati...and then the death ceremonies of her husband's mistresses who probably experienced that love, her mother had told her about…the union of Shiv and Shakti .Those blistering memories soothed by Baiji's love and Mamanji's protection…

Ahilyabai had a few jobs to attend to…Some complainants needed justice...some orders awaited her signature and approvals… But Ahilyabai felt heavy all over again. She pushed herself back into Baiji's room…and lay there for hours after that…staring at the ceiling…tears flowing down the sides of her ears, drenching the sheets under…

The next day there was a Puja arranged at the pond of Jaamb. Kirtans, mantras, shlokas …Ahilyabai returned to Indore at night. She declared she could not go into the palace that night but would stay at the outhouse instead…her head resting on Baiji's statuette in the garden.

"You showed me the way Baiji…" she thought… "I walked and walked…and now I am tired. Call me to meet you soon now..."She could see Malerao's room from there. She thought… 'Malerao…my son…you deceived me the most. I was so busy being an unforgiving mentor that I could never be the forgiving mother…Had I known you were going to leave me and go away so early in life…I would have probably chosen to be the forgiving mother…I was so busy preparing you to be an heir that I lost a son…"

Ahilyabai sat motionless for long…Renu and Anjana went to her. Ahilyabai was unconscious. She was running high fever…

****

Ahilyabai returned to Maheshwar a little before the monsoons started sprinkling their greenery on wet ground…Of late, she did not keep good health yet conducted her work from her chair. She still knew exactly who owed her and how much …regions where the tax collection was slack. It gave her great anguish when Hundis of her contribution to Pune were delayed.

These days Ahilyabai would lose her cool easily and break down even more easily. Losing the grip on her emotions made her feel very uneasy. In all this she suffered a severe attack of gastric infection…which left her dehydrated and drained.

"Harkuaai…looks like my time is getting over…" Harkuaai reprimanded Ahilyabai for saying that…"Really? Do not worry! You are going nowhere! You have to work another ten years at least. Get well soon…there is a lot of official communication pending…updates to be taken…Mhadaji Patil has borne a son. A meeting is being arranged between him and Anderson…you can't be laid up in bed like this…and after all you have to send me on my final journey first!

The two ladies smiled… a smile that was hiding pain more than announcing happiness…

Harkuaai 's voice softened… "Come, sit up for a while…Santaji is here to meet you…"

****

Ahilyabai regained her health slowly and was back to her punishing routine…On Makar Sankranti, Ahilyabai distributed 'Tilgul', the traditional sweets of roasted sesame seeds rolled in jaggery …But this year she felt the sweets seemed to crumble…the jaggery could not bind the sesame seeds firm and stiff…Maybe more jaggery was necessary to bring in the sweetness and the bind…

Just as Keso Bhikaji left, Ambadas Shashtri, the family pundit entered. He wanted to take a few days off to go visit his daughter who was married into the Dehadroy family of the Puntambe town. He had to perform the thread ceremony of her son.

Ahilyabai's mood lifted up a trifle… "Of course! Do give my blessings to your daughter and grandson…and also a small gift for the occasion…I would like to bestow the 'sanad papers' [deed of rights] of 'Pathrai' near the town of Nandurbar , which indeed means that your grandson becomes the Jahagirdar of that region! This is for your daughter…I have seen her grow up before my eyes…I remember her coming to the palace as a little girl…"

Ambadas thanked her deeply for her generosity and with great gratitude accepted the gift.

"Ambadas, I am more than certain that your grandson will trace your steps in education, loyalty and commitment. I want good families with noble values to be at the helm in all regions. Please ask Mukund Hari to prepare the papers and have them sent to me for signature and seal."

****

One day, Harkuaai, without revealing the details, showed Ahilyabai an old letter, intercepted by her sources …saying she must read it and be assured that Shreemant Peshwa and Nanasheb had indeed warned Tukoji that he could never garner their support to bypass Ahilyabai…Ahilyabai smiled…and handed over a letter that she was reading by Mhadji Shinde Patil informing her that Tukoji had demanded his share from Mhadji. But since army expenses had come from Ahilyabai he would deny him anything… unless of course Ahilyabai were to direct him to the contrary… Harkuaai smiled…

Ahilyabai wrote back saying, Tukoji has not contributed anything so he gets nothing.

****

Ahilyabai was about to start her work at the court of justice when a widow arrived from the Siroj region.

"Why would you have to come this far, lady? We have our courts run by Panchayats in the smaller villages…"

The widow was quiet for a while…and then she gathered courage and informed Ahilyabai that she was a childless widow and wished to adopt a child. But the head of that village was demanding 3 lakhs as a 'fee' to allow her this adoption. Ahilyabai spent some time verifying her claims and talking to the boy to ascertain if he wanted that lady as his mother.

Ahilyabai immediately sent for Visaji and instructed him to prepare two orders. One, to summon the headman, Khemji Raghuji and two, to allow the lady the right of adoption.

After four days Khemji Raghuji arrived. Ahilyabai looked at him, "When you see a hapless but rich widow…do you see it as an opportunity to make money? Under my regime, corrupt people will not be spared... not even my own. Kindly pay 5000/- rupees as fine and you are suspended from your work. I will review suspension orders after six months!"

Khemji was furious. He asked Ahilyabai, "Do I not get a chance to present my side of the story?"

Ahilyabai nodded and merely looked at Mukund Hari. He said, " Khemji Raghuji, this is the seventh complaint against you. After the second complaint, Matoshri had sent spies to unearth some details…so be very careful before you say anything…"

Khemji Raghuji's face lost color…He bowed and left.

****

Ahilyabai returned to her chambers …She was very quiet today…Her mind was in turmoil. All around her she only saw people with money and power spending it on alcohol and women. In all this, her hope was to give Nathoba the values of Malharrao Holkar and pass on the flag of the Holkar house to him. Her only worry was his health…very delicate…with fever every now and then.

But above all she was upset with her own daughter… Muktabai…she wanted to bring in a second wife for Nathoba. "But why?!!" an anguished Ahilyabai had asked… "When a woman is expected to be with just one man all her life, why can't a man be with just one woman? Who has started this custom, that men have found it very convenient to reinforce over the decades?" Ahilyabai clearly told Muktabai that she was against this second marriage. But Muktabai as well as Yashwantrao, both wanted to oblige the parents of a girl…and get Nathoba another wife. A ten year old girl was set to enter the palace today…

Ahilyabai wondered …at our social structure where parents were willing to give away their daughters as second…third wives to grooms…

****

"Today…" stated Ahilyabai, "is a black day in the history of the Holkar's darbar. This darbar has not been summoned to felicitate any bravery or courageous act…but to conduct an enquiry on the Mamledar of Chandwad and Tularam Holkar. After careful investigations, and examining evidence, both are found guilty of corruption. Mukund Hari will oversee the confiscation of all unaccounted money and the same will be diverted towards developmental projects. We as administrators have to guard people's money not capture it…"

Ahilyabai also proposed to ban the manufacture of alcohol but in a court full of men …finding support for this was going to be tough. People discussed how it would indeed be impossible to do so, rather than suggest how they could make it possible. She knew this would take time…but one day she hoped, she would succeed in preventing thousands of families from ruin…

****

Balabai was upset. Nathoba's new wife, Gauri was getting all the attention. Balabai would ask Ahilyabai … "what does this mean…that Gauri's horoscope spelt good luck for Nathoba…marriage to her, would improve his health…" Ahilyabai would spend hours with Bala …amusing her…making her smile…Ahilyabai knew this feeling well…The only thing Ahilyabai wished for was good health for Nathoba.

She feared the dreaded Tuberculosis. She had announced rewards to encourage all medical practitioners to find a cure for it. She would shut her eyes tight hoping to drive away her worst nagging fear ...She would plead with God to take her away in exchange for a long healthy life for Nathoba.

****

14

Back home, Shahaji mama... a very unwell Shahaji mama who had walked out on her, was lonely. Ahilyabai had him brought over to the palace...so that he could be looked after in his last days. She was upset with his son ...Ranoji...yet she sent for him through Harkuaai. After all, a son must be informed ...Shahaji mama was counting his last days...Ranoji arrived and Shahaji passed away that very day.

Ahilyabai, at 62, was emotionally worn out...one by one everyone seemed to go away...some here, yet far and others very very far away...

Ahilyabai had to drag herself up...ammunition had to be sent ...Hundis of ten lakhs had to be sent to Pune for their battle against Tipu Sultan now...and Nathoba...he was losing weight with every passing day...the fever had the boy in its clutches...no medicines ...not even the chanting and mantras were helping now. Ahilyabai was willing to try any and every remedy that was suggested...She prayed hard...Nathoba today weighed a mere 41 'sher' ... (equivalent to pound)

****

Ahilyabai was engaged in her work when Bharmaldada and Bapu Holkar arrived with the glorious news of Tipu's defeat at Srirangpatana. Both of Tipu's sons were captured and taken hostage. Negotiations started and truce was signed on 7th Feb 1787. Tipu conceded 50% of his property and 3 crores!

Ahilyabai was listening to the courageous war stories intently, with tremendous pride... "Bapu, you deserve a great felicitation...From the times of the Pandavas, the region from the river Atak to the ocean in the South ...has been ours. The Greek tried their luck, after that we found a savior in Shivaji Maharaj who protected this land...This is a golden moment in History...I would like to hold a grand lunch at the darbar and felicitate you!"

"I have only done my duty, Matoshri"

"Of course! But duty ...very well done..."

****

Miraculously and by the grace of God, Nathoba's health showed signs of improvement. Ahilyabai was over the moon...He had no fever, last few days. Ahilyabai organized a Puja to thank the Lord for his mercy...

Nathoba with both his wives, beautifully dressed, looking pretty sat down around the holy fire to perform the Puja. The puja was in progress when a cloud of dust rose outside...a horserider approached the main entrance... Ahilyabai recognized him...Shivdev...her trusted spy...

Ahilyabai left the Puja to meet him in her private office. "Matoshri, the Rajput kings have joined hands and plot to challenge the Peshwas! We have to act fast. Udaipur has readied an army of 10,000. Nimbaheda, Javad ...are showing hectic activity...Chandrawat has captured Rampura already...If our forces don't block them the consequences will be catastrophic..."

Ahilyabai rushed out. The Puja was almost concluding. She told Muktabai to oversee the function, look after the guests and keep some 'Prasad'[20] for her. She left for her main office.

She ordered for all the horses from the stables, ammunition from the factories to be gathered. Ambaji pant and Ragho Ransod were put in charge. Messages were sent to all sardars...Ahilyabai assigned two more spies to send her updates every three hours...Ahilyabai too prepared to leave with the forces...

Ambaji pant stopped her saying it was important that she remained safe at Maheshwar. "Matoshri, do not be anxious...the Rajputs will be set right in no time..."

Ahilyabai, drew strength and herself gave the war beats on the drum! The soldiers were electrified with the sight and marched towards Mewad. Ahilyabai stood atop the fort ...gazing out...long after the army was out of sight. Ahilyabai spent the entire night at the watch towers. At dawn, she rushed through her morning chores and prayers and returned to the watch tower...her eyes impatient to spot the first messenger with an update...

At dusk she saw a horse rider approach. Even at that age, her pace quickened...and she came down as fast as she could to meet Shivdev...who hung his head...looking down... Ahilyabai's heart was beating fast...

"Matoshri...Ambaji pant..."

"What happened...quick...talk...captured?"

"N..no...killed"

Ahilyabai's heart sank...she sat down...her mind overwhelmed with Ambajipant's memories...but she could not dedicate even a few more moments to his condolence...She rose. The armies sent by the sardars had gathered. She organized a good meal for them...

After the meal...she addressed the army...giving one of her best speeches to inspire her men to victory...promising huge rewards and decorations...She concluded by shouting out victory slogans...energizing the entire division of soldiers...

As soon as the soldiers left, she got busy ensuring arrangements for smooth supplies of food and other necessities for her army. A day and a half that went by seemed like the longest wait...until Shivdev and Nimba arrived with the good news...

They informed her that 'as soon as the army started marching towards Rajputana, the King of Mewad immediately joined our forces. Rampura was recaptured from Chadrawat!' Ahilyabai was relieved. Shivdev said he was carrying a request from the Shindes for Ahilyabai...

The appeal was that all the women of the Shinde household wished to leave their Mahals and come to Maheshwar and feel safe and secure under Ahilyabai's protection.

Ahilyabai nodded and said... "Please tell them they are all more than welcome. This house is always open for them. But the women of the Holkar and Shinde houses are not known to panic and run for shelter. Stay put wherever you are. Be assured... in case of even a hint of danger, my security forces will reach them in time and whisk them away to safety..."

Shivdev left...Ahilybai returned to her task of accumulating soldiers and strengthening the forces...100 more were enrolled...another 50...another 500...all dispatched as reinforcements. Ahilyabai received regular updates... 'some group of our soldiers attacked the Rajputs without orders from Ransod...they were beaten back...in the meanwhile, Ranipura and Nimbkheda were captured...a lot of loot was recovered...A sleeping Bhavansingh's fort was blown away by our cannonballs...'

Ahilyabai continued to send money... food... ammunition...She had lost all appetite for food. She only awaited updates from Shivdev and Nimba...It was almost evening...no news yet...Ahilyabai was pacing up and down the watchtower...and ...and...Shivdev, Nimba came running to her...

"Victory to the Holkars!" They could barely breathe...very excited...gleaming with pride... "Matoshri...we have won! The Rajputs had spread gunpowder on the ground expecting our forces to come...and erroneously a firearm from their own camp blew the entire patch away...along with most of their soldiers...We could only capture Sobhagsingh..."

Sobhagsingh had suffered severe burns. He fell at Ahilyabai's feet...pleading pardon...

Ahilyabai said, "Pardon is for the first mistake ...even second or third mistake...but you...have raised your ugly head countless number of times. You kept even my late father-in-law engaged with your wicked ways and reprehensible activities...you have been a nuisance for years. We have lost thousands of our men...You cannot be pardoned..."

Ahilyabai left...the soldiers were shouting victory slogans...The glory of the Holkars was soaring ...and Ahilyabai's prestige, elevated...

****

Nanasaheb summoned a special darbar and saluted Ahilyabai's courage and prompt action by firing three cannonballs in the air! Nanasaheb and Haripant Tatya knew that evening that it would have been their gravest blunder ...had they sided up with Tukoji ...

They would now remain ever grateful to Mhadji Shinde who had warned them against sending an army of 5000 to Maheshwar. "Do not ever make that mistake!", he had said. "The lady is brighter, sharper and has more spunk than all of you put together...After all, she has been trained by Malharrao Holkar himself..."

They could never forget that had it not been for her, Tukoji, Naro Ganesh and Maniram would have defected to Raghunathrao and today, all the wealth of the Holkars would have been lost to them...Ahilyabai's loyalty was undoubtedly with the Peshwa throne...and she had more than once, successfully averted massive debacles...

They also had to always remember that not even one soldier would have ever been willing to pick up arms against her. She would personally look after their well being…enquire after their families and at times lend financial help from her personal wealth…

The best of rewards offered would not allure a single soldier to fight a war against her!

Today, despite Tukoji hijacking so much income from numerous regions, the lady had managed to contribute lakhs and lakhs to the Peshwa reserves! Mhadji Shinde had said, "She has strong intelligence, unmatched ability and immeasurable popularity…

Nanasaheb said…had we disregarded Shinde's advice, today the glory of the Peshwas would have been lost…We salute the lady one more time!'

Appaji Jagdev sent a detailed update from the court of Pune to Ahilyabai…

****

The day the letter from Appaji Jagdev reached Maheshwar…everyone was proud of Ahilyabai! Even Nathoba's parents-in-law who were visiting to enquire after his health were impressed…They were appreciative that Gauri was growing up under Ahilyabai's care…

Gauri's parents had now given up worldly pleasures and turned to spirituality …living in ashrams away from the snare of these worldly illusions and relations…They even refused to accept gifts from Ahilyabai.

But Ahilyabai insisted that she could not send them away empty handed …they were but free to donate those gifts to anyone they considered deserving on their way back or even later…

****

Little Gauri would often ask Ahilyabai about her childhood and it would seem so distant now… "My dear, I do not even remember the village I belonged to…or how I used to be…I only remember Mamanji… Baiji… Malerao… accounts… cannonballs…I am lost in work…Now I do not want to remember anything…I want to forget everything and go away…far far away…"

Nathoba's fever was rising again… the smile on Muktabai's face had disappeared…She too was looking pale. Balabai was old enough to know that all was not well with Nathoba's health and her prospects…

There was an awkward silence in the palace…subdued activity …hectic prayers…The Vaidyas had given up hope…saying only prayers and faith could now heal Nathoba.

On the full moon night in the month of Ashwin…sipping on some milk, was enough to give Nathoba a dreadful bout of indigestion. His stomach could hold nothing. He would bring out every bit of food ingested…The cough had spiked up accompanied by wheezing …

That day, the Vaidya brought out some medicines… Ahilyabai felt her energy draining out of her body…She had seen that concoction being made earlier once before…

Ahilyabai feebly dragged herself to her room and shut the door. She did not have the courage to open her eyes…she wanted to see nothing. The vision of that medicine being prepared haunted her…she had seen it when Baiji …'MahaMrityunjay' mantra was being chanted. Nathoba called out to his grandmother… "Come…sit here…don't go anywhere…"

A lump in the throat was choking Ahilyabai…tears in her eyes were blurring her vision…she sat next to him caressing his forehead…pressing his hands and feet … Ahilyabai did not have the courage to look up at Muktabai. Yashwantrao had never looked so dazed before…Nathoba too had no energy but he made an effort to draw himself closer to his grandmother…

Ahilyabai who had aged many years in the last few days understood…She picked up his head and placed it on her lap…the way he would sleep when she told him bedtime stories. Just then a huge bout of cough gripped Nathoba and out came a spurt of blood …on Ahilyabai's white sari…

All night various medicines were being administered simply to give Nathoba some relief and calm his cough…By the next morning people from Maheshwar crowded at the palace…Nathoba's chest was barely moving and when it did it was like a sudden surge of a single breath…

Ahilyabai put the holy water from the river Ganga in his mouth…and then…the chest did not move at all…was still for a long time.

Ahilyabai needed the strength of the entire universe to look up at Muktabai…who stood there frozen as she looked at her mother…the silence shattered by a thump… Muktabai had slumped on the floor…her eyes a mere gaze. Her only child Nathoba was no more…

By afternoon Nathoba's body was kept on the pyre. Ahilyabai knew what lay in store for Gauri and Balabai. She decided to stand up for them now. But to her utter horror and despair, both Yashwantrao and Muktabai urged Ahilyabai to let the little girls go Sati…

Ahilybai argued that they had a whole lifetime ahead of them… various questions were posed saying, 'Exactly! They had a whole life ahead of them and so … 'who will look after them'… 'what if they fall in love…no one marries widows'… 'What if they become the prey of lusty men around them….who will protect them…'

Ahilyabai insisted hysterically that she would think of a way out for them…But Muktabai told her calmly… "You had a strong father-in-law to protect you…we are not that strong and neither do we have the courage to go against the religion…"

Ahilyabai …now feeble and frail, was shaking…Muktabai asked the Vaidya to give her some medicine to calm her down…Muktabai offered her water. As soon as Ahilyabai had the water she felt better...calm...too calm...almost drowsy...losing consciousness...as people helped her lie down on the bed...Muktabai was trying to speak to her... "Matoshri...Mat..o..shri..."

****

Ahilyabai had not stepped out of her bed for how long she did not remember...She could only see flashes of those two little girls... dressed in the typical clothes for sati...white sari...green bangles...mangalsutra...kumkum smeared forehead...and Ahilyabai would shut her eyes tight to drive away those flashes...The next moment she would hear the drum beats and she would put her hands on her ears...then after a while, hesitatingly she would open her eyes...and the room would be spinning around her...

The thought of Muktabai...a lonely Muktabai with no one she could call her own, to look after her, seemed to send incessant tears streaming down the corners of her eyes as she lay still...Every time Ahilyabai would lay still she would have visions of herself running towards the tower of the fort and jumping down to death...

Muktabai was trying to wake her mother up...shaking her gently...Just then Yashwantrao whispered something in Muktabai's ears...Muktabai was shocked! She looked at Yashwantrao...

Who was going to break this news to Ahilyabai.... someone had to....

****

"Matoshri..."Ahilyabai half opened her eyes as she heard Muktabai call out to her. Muktabai helped her sit up in bed...She gave her some water...Ahilyabai barely managed to look around. She was filled with frustration and in fact, anger, at every one ...the society...the religion...her destiny...and even

Muktabai…

Ahilyabai looked away…expressionless. Muktabai patted her mother's back and turned her face towards her… "Matoshri…I know you are upset with me now…but…right now I have to convey something to you…We can discuss our differences later…Matoshri...get a hold on yourself…I have just received news that Kashirao Holkar's wife is no more. Kashirao is not here…your help is needed there and you are the eldest …you will have to go…"

Ahilyabai could hardly hear anything leave alone register…her heart felt like wood…Muktabai tried to gently push her mother up…Ahilyabai pleaded with her… "Mukta…I beg of you…do not take me there…I have no strength left in me…Why does God not take me away? Can he not see me? He seems to see everyone around me and takes them away…how does he fail to notice me each time? Muktabai…I plead again…I cannot bear these flashes of Gauri and Bala…I do not want to be awake…give me that medicine…let me sleep…"

Muktabai had tears straining down…She had never seen her mother like this…A lady who was against opium all her life today was finding solace in small doses of sedation…

"Matoshri…get up…you have to now visit Kashirao's house…On your return I will give you something for peaceful sleep…but for now, make this effort…"

Ahilyabai's palanquin reached Kashirao Holkar's house. She still felt a little drowsy…Anandibai's body was lying there. Ahilyabai stood there…looking at her… and then simply said… "Anandi, I request you to take care of my little girls in heaven… They have gone there just a little before you with Nathoba…"

Bharmaldada, Mukund Hari, Ambadas Shashtri…were all present there…each one of them fighting hard to control their tears…

The same women who were at the palace, had now gathered here…Ahilyabai could hear them whispering amongst them about remarrying Kashirao to someone's brother's daughter! Ahilyabai was filled with flaming anger…men could remarry the moment the wife died…and those little girls did not even get a chance to live? And who was perpetuating this? Women themselves! They were their own enemies…and then…again she could see Gauri and Balabai in the crowd…Ahilyabai wondered if she was awake…or drowsy…

Anandibai left on her final journey and Ahilyabai's palanquin returned to the palace. She went to her room…lay there motionless…unresponsive to everything around her…

****

Nanasheb opened a letter from Keso Bhikaji. It gave an update from Maheshwar.

'Months have somehow pushed past. Tukoji has sent letters of condolence to Ahilyabai but not called on her personally. Nothing other than spirituality seems to interest Ahilyabai these days. She spends her time looking at Nathoba's shawl…Gauri's toys and the last jug of water that the little girl had filled for Ahilyabai in her room. She looks at those things and breaks down. She does attend office but seems disconnected and far removed. It is rumored that Tukoji is scheduled to visit Ahilyabai tomorrow.'

Next day, Tukoji arrived and fell at Ahilyabai's feet…Ahilyabai was steady but cold …she gave her blessings. After some dull discussions Ahilyabai said, "You look pale and much leaner. Unfortunately you do not keep good company but hope you are keeping good health at least…" said Ahilyabai very matter of factly.

"I am aware Matoshri…I know…you are referring to Naro Ganesh… I am aware that his behavior, Rukhmabai's behavior, is less than ideal…but I am helpless. On the one hand Naro Ganesh defrauds me of money and on the other the Shindes swindle my share…"

Ahilyabai simply raised her hand and blocked Tukoji's further dialogue right there. She spoke slowly but surely, "My spies inform me Tukoji, that Naro Ganesh alone is worth 30 lakhs... Where has it come from? And then, you are his master...not the other way around! But that is your personal lookout. As far as the Shindes are concerned, consider this a solemn forewarning...As long as the Shindes and Holkars remain united the British will stay put in their place. The day cracks are apparent in this alliance, the British will undeniably exploit it without a moment's delay. Trust no one but in fact the Shindes...and as far as your share is concerned, there is no deceit there...Earnings are always proportionate to your contribution..."

Tukoji had no answers ...he asked for Ahilyabai's leave. Ahilyabai blessed Tukoji with more glory and many more victories...and Tukoji left.

Ahilyabai, gradually yet progressively, got back into her routine...Work took longer these days...and Ahilyabai liked it that way...What did she come back to? ...an empty palace...a grieving daughter...filled with the emptiness of her own loss...an ageing Harkuaai who could not pull herself together...and Ahilyabai who was herself shattered...with not just her loss but her inability to prevent the practice of Sati...

Mahadji Mama's daughter sent her little girl Anu to stay with Ahilyabai hoping to cheer her up...She knew, in the palace, Ahilyabai would find happiness in Anu and happiness would find Anu in some form...

****

Malhar had started frequenting Maheshwar ...Ahilyabai was not so old yet, that she would not realize , that it was neither the love for his grandmother nor the dislike for his mother that drew him to Maheshwar...Ahilyabai got cautious...a 13-14 year Anu and a much married Malhar... She called him to her room and before she could delicately unfurl the complications of such an alliance he stunned her by pronouncing that he would like to marry Anu! Ahilyabai's words dissolved in her mouth …she looked at him … "You are already married …secondly, your mother is not going to be happy to hear about this alliance from my maternal side…it will further enmesh the present complications…I will not…"

Malhar folded his hands as he interrupted Ahilyabai… "My first wife is in every way comparable to my mother…dressing up all day , sitting in front of the mirror, laughing, chatting with other men…"

"So what do you want, Malhar? That, women should not even laugh or talk to men…when men can even marry countless number of times?"

"Matoshri, I cannot win this argument …but I can only say that you get me married to Anu or I will end my life in the Narmada…"

"…end my life…" these words just crippled Ahilyabai now…She just sat down…death…Nathoba…Gauri…flashes just spinning around her. She drew a deep breath…shut her eyes… "Malhar, my strength is now cheating me…please get permission from your mother for this marriage…"

"I do not wish to see my mother's face …Please be kind enough to send Harkuaai to inform my mother that I am remarrying and that she need not bother to come for the wedding…"

Ahilyabai simply raised her hand and ordered Malhar to stop. She was not going to entertain any son speaking poorly of his mother. He stopped…Ahilyabai was silent…so much bitterness…

Ahilyabai was still shuddering at the thought of Malhar eloping with Anu or worse…

Ahilyabai marveled at the fact that mothers were willing to get their young daughters married to an old Kashirao who had just lost his wife, Anandibai…simply because he was a Holkar! So what were the chances, she thought, that Anu's mother would object...

The wedding date was set. Amidst all the other Holkars, Santaji , Bapu Holkar ...the wedding celebrations were underway...No sign of Rukhmabai or Malhar's first wife.

Ahilyabai asked Malhar to enquire about their arrival to which Malhar answered saying, "Women who cannot come to condole at deaths in the family should not be welcome to join in at joyous occasions either..."

Ahilyabai remained silent... Gauri... Balabai... Nathoba...she felt energy draining out of her body...she was blacking out...getting drowsy...

****

Ahilyabai's informers from Mewad sent word...Naro Ganesh and Tukoji seemed to have fallen out with each other. Conversations were far and few...in fact hardly any.

Ahilyabai sensed danger here. She immediately wrote a letter to Tukoji. 'A Subhedar and his accountant are like a needle and thread. As long as they work together, the seams of the treasury remain hemmed in. As soon as they separate, one can prick the other and the other can slit one's throat...Remember we are all in the service of the Peshwas. Shielding the wealth and augmenting it is your prime responsibility. Personal differences, leading to interference in this service, is unpardonable.'

****

The news from Delhi was demoralizing. There was so much happening in Delhi that it was hard to fathom the consequences of those events in their entirety. Ghulam Kadar, Taimurshah, the British...treachery, betrayals...No one could be trusted. The British were playing tricks, tempting the weaker kings... whipping up their greed with attractive offers.

'Why can't we...' thought Ahilyabai, 'imbibe the discipline of the British instead? We are allowing those who have a toehold in trading to get a foothold as rulers...If only we remain united, we have the force to rule the world...'

Ahilyabai would be troubled by these thoughts ...but now, did not have the fortitude to pursue a line of action for it...She would go to the temples in the evening...sit on the banks of the Narmada...listen to the stories from Ramayana...engulfed in the visions of Nathoba...Gauri...Balabai...which made her dizzy....sent her in a trance...

Malhar, these days was not willing to leave Maheshwar. An ageing Ahilyabai seemed to give him a sense of power...Her slowed walk gave pace to his dreams...The slight tremble in her voice sharpened his desire to be obeyed...The mild hunch of Ahilyabai's shoulders seemed to electrify his backbone...her tentative footsteps brought a definite spring in his walk...

Ahilyabai could perceive this change. The gentle Malhar she knew, now had a moderately high handed and stubborn streak in the way he dealt with people...Behind her back he was beginning to swing on this heady sense of power.

Ahilyabai's health was not bright...her heart felt heavy...her emotions, dull...But she would never allow the sword of the Holkars to lose its sharp edge.

She summoned Malhar. She did not beat around the bush. She simply said one thing. "I have to merely caution you that for me, the well-being of my people is second to no one. I repeat, no one and nothing...and if you wish to stay at Maheshwar, you must remember that...else it may make great sense for you to join your father at this time..."

Malhar said nothing. He simply nodded and took her leave. Harkuaai was observing this from the corner of the room. She walked up to Ahilyabai and said, "This child...worries me. You need to be alert. He seems greatly influenced by the Moghul strategies who do not hesitate to put their own kin under house arrest ..." Ahilyabai's eyes were dark...Harkuaai lightened the moment by saying... "But then, don't know how...but I know one thing… you can do it…!" Both ladies tried hard to push their smiles up to their eyes…

Ahilyabai received a scroll from Rukhmabai informing her that Malhar's first wife had attained an age where she could now commence her married life with Malhar. She would therefore like to bring her to Maheshwar…

Ahilyabai sent Bharmaldada along with another colleague, to accord all respect to Rukhmabai and Malhar's first wife and bring them to Maheshwar. They arrived on a Thursday and Malhar left the palace. He refused to meet his mother despite orders from Ahilyabai. The ceremony was to be held on Monday. But Malhar did not return. This was not something Ahilyabai was going to tolerate. She knew exactly what to do…who to hold hostage…to ensure Malhar followed her orders and returned to the palace not just meet his mother but to touch his mother's feet and seek her blessings.

****

15

One day, out of the ordinary, Ahilyabai received a letter from Rukhmabai pleading her to spare some time and visit her in Indore. 'I have a lot to share…' it said.

Ahilyabai left for Indore. Rukhmabai spilt all her woes. The enmity between Tukoji and Naro Ganesh lay bare now. Tukoji had had Naro Ganesh arrested…tortured and divested of all powers, dislodging him from all his properties. All rights of Rukhmabai too were suspended…all flow of money to her was blocked. Rukhmabai now pleaded with Ahilyabai, to help her and reinstate her rights.

Ahilyabai assured her that she would make all efforts to secure the release of Naro Ganesh…for two reasons. One, Tukoji was as much to blame for this debacle as Naro Ganesh was.

Two, using power to settle personal scores was not a Holkar tradition.

Ahilyabai told Rukhmabai that she was unable to advise her on how a wife should approach a husband for reconciliation but as far as her legitimate monetary rights were concerned she would certainly look into the matter.

Rukhmabai touched Ahilyabai's feet. Ahilyabai was ready to leave for Maheshwar. "Take care of your health", said Rukhmabai. Ahilyabai smiled. She knew where the concern was coming from.

"Well…my time is now running out. I need to consult the Peshwas and now retire…"

****

On her return to Maheshwar, Tukoji's letter awaited her… The letter with great respect beseeched her to not retire as clashes in Mewad, Jaipur, Udaipur were raising their ugly head again…and this time the Holkars and Shindes had conflicting interests, disagreeing on their affinities on backing the warring factions. At this rate, the fear was, that one day, the armies of the Shindes and Holkars would come face to face…'

Ahilyabai was losing her patience and cool as she progressed through the letter. It takes a lifetime to build allies…and Tukoji was about to devastate the strongest alliance in the country! The Shinde-Holkar unity…Ahilyabai's breathing paced up. She continued to read…Malhar was plotting to gain more power. He needed to be curbed. The letter maintained that only Ahilyabai could restrain Malhar's activities…

Ahilyabai closed her eyes…angrier than before at Tukoji's helplessness in dealing with tough situations. She was weary…but continued to read the concluding part of the letter which requested her to dismiss Mukund Hari as he was Naro Ganesh's nephew!

Ahilyabai was enraged… 'What!' she thought… 'Dismiss

Mukund Hari??' Her trusted man …simply because he was related to Naro Ganesh!!? Ahilyabai could not check her anger now…she was murmuring to herself…

' Could not take care of his own wife…and now wants to vent his frustration by torturing Naro Ganesh…by chaining him…branding him with hot iron…spraying chilli powder on him..stuffing ashes in his mouth…Shame! Only weak men use power to settle personal scores…I had cautioned him much earlier about Naro Ganesh…but does not want to take advice when it comes...and now…wants me to clean this mess! How dare he ask me to discharge Mukund Hari…'

Ahilyabai felt her palpitation rising…a bit dizzy…and sat down for a while…when her informer entered…bringing in news from Dharwad, Venglur…The army needed two cannons and hundis of 3 lakhs…She took a deep breath…She had to make all arrangements…

****

She now wanted to detach herself…maybe go away to Brahmapuri… away from the selfish games of people who cared neither for the welfare of their motherland nor the glory of the flag. But Ahilyabai was disappointed in no one but herself. She had only herself to censure, she thought…She had spent a lifetime in the service of this land but was unsuccessful in creating an able, second line of command….She had no one capable enough to hand over the reins to…

Ahilyabai rested her hand on her knee and stood up with a little support. Just as she steadied herself, Mukund Hari came rushing in…he was looking down…he folded his hands and requested Ahilyabai to release him from her service. Saying so, he put his pen down in front of Ahilyabai. He admitted that Naro Ganesh was no saint…he could be imprisoned…but not tortured. He explained to Ahilyabai that he was under pressure from two sides...His family urged him to help Naro Ganesh as he was not the only culprit…and on the other hand, the Subhedar threatened him with dire consequences if he continued in her service…

Before he could complete his sentence about the threat from Tukoji, Ahilyabai thundered… "Mukund Hari, let me see who has the courage to as much as even touch you! Pick this pen up and you will put it down only when I die…" Mukund Hari immediately picked up the pen, said, "Please do not talk about death but the physical torture of Naro Ganesh, only you can end…"

Ahilyabai nodded sharply. "You are aware of Naro Ganesh's details…Have no fear. Put your mind to work and leave the rest to me…and now, four lakhs are due from Khando Baburao…the Deshpandes of Chandwad need some arbitration…also we need to check the accounts of Raver." ...and the list of tasks seemed endless.

The next day, Rukhmabai's palanquin arrived at the palace…She went hastily to Ahilyabai, urging her… to expedite matters…free Naro Ganesh…restore her rights…She rattled on further about how Ahilyabai was in fact savoring her helplessness…how she had done nothing to prevent her son from turning against her…and now how she was doing precious little to help Naro Ganesh..

Ahilyabai waited patiently for the dramatics to fade and at the end of the histrionics, Ahilyabai calmly said, "You reap as you sow! I had cautioned you against Naro Ganesh. I tried to groom your son but failed miserably there…Not that I had any support from you on that count. So now, why cry over spilt milk…Yet, in all fairness, only Naro Ganesh cannot pay for something that you and Tukoji are equally to blame for…" Ahilyabai calmed her and sent her back to Indore.

****

Ahilyabai was restless. The allegations of Rukhmabai were

ringing in her ears...She sat in front of the deity in the temple...hoping for some peace. She lit an oil lamp, some incense sticks and sang a devotional song. But she had no idea what was about to happen ... As she put the oil lamp down Muktabai came rushing to her...

Muktabai informed her mother that all of a sudden Yashwantrao had come down with a severe stomach infection...He could keep nothing inside him...no food ...no water. ..he was bringing out... whatever he ingested ...and had a running stomach too. Ahilyabai shuffled as fast as she could to Muktabai's private quarters. Yashwantrao lay on the bed. The Vaidya was on his way. He arrived with two assistants. He very swiftly administered herbal medicines, used medicinal massages...

Yet, as soon as he swallowed anything, he would bring it all out the very next moment. All night, the sheets were being changed. By next morning Yashwantrao looked wrinkled...drained and weak. His eyes were listless, his voice barely audible. He could not even focus on Ahilyabai as she tried to speak to him. Muktabai, Ahilyabai...Harkuaai...all were around him.

He made an effort to shake his head...whispered...he put his hand on Muktabai's but before he could give it in Ahilyabai's hand ...he had a severe bout of watery motion ... The Vaidya hastily pushed down a strong dose and instantly the medicine came out, bringing out with it, the last of his life energies...

Yashwantrao lay there...motionless...Ahilyabai froze. Just this morning Yashwantrao had come to greet her. He looked pale...but after Nathoba no one looked bright...Yashwantrao Phanse...who could beat four warriors with one stroke ...who had contained the Bhils in a matter of days...a strong young man gone in a matter of hours...

Muktabai was inconsolable...but Ahilyabai could hear nothing...see nothing ...feel nothing. She sat there like a statue. She had blurred visions...of Muktabai's marriage...Nathoba's birth...Nathoba's death...Yashwantrao's valor...and now...he lay motionless...

It was only when Muktabai started talking of not leaving her husband's hand...going with him...Sati...Ahilyabai was knocked back to her senses...She never ever contemplated, even in her wildest reflections that Mukta would speak the language that she had struggled to disallow, in fact, forbid all her life..

Ahilyabai stood up...she was pacing up and down...prohibiting Muktabai from even attempting to think what she indeed was...and then...in a blink Ahilyabai started pacing towards the water tank...she did not want to live this life anymore...Harkuaai and some other people held her back...Ahilyabai was distraught...she could not bear to see her Mukta dressed in a white sari...preparing to end her life with her husband on his funeral pyre...

Ahilyabai fell at Muktabai's feet...folded her hands.. "Stay back...I beg...Do not leave me alone and go away..." Ahilyabai could barely see...her tears were flowing incessantly. Muktabai was calm. She hugged her mother. "Let me go, mother...I cannot live without him...and who do I live for...my son, gone...daughters-in-law, gone...you are almost 66-67...our togetherness is only for a few years more...after that what? I will have a void that scares me..." Ahilyabai was now sobbing... "Spend your life for the people of Maheshwar..."

"I am not like you Matoshri...I am not strong, I do not understand politics...Please let me go..."

Ahilyabai collapsed...as she continued to beg Mukta with her eyes to not leave her alone...Mukta's heart was in shreds. She held her mother. "The whole world sings your praises...they need you. Your people need you...your life has a goal...mine has none...let me go...now, I beg..."

The mother and daughter hugged and hugged...sobbed and sobbed...inseparable...tears flowing down, drenching each other's saris...wiping them ...talking with their eyes

…arguing…begging…convincing…hoping and finally… accepting fate as Muktabai turned around to walk towards the pyre…to go away on a journey with her husband…never never to return into Ahilyabai's arms…

Ahilyabai stood there… helpless… broken… devastated…defeated and lonely. Muktabai turned once…looked at her mother and waved, smiling mildly…

Ahilyabai was unconscious.

****

For days now Ahilyabai had not stepped out of her room. Her physical strength had waned…she had no drive to wake up or eat…The books of accounts lay untouched, the correspondence unopened. She wanted to meet no one. The twelfth and thirteenth day ceremonies were over…charity, Puja…Ahilyabai went through those on cue…doing but not feeling…numbed by fate…

****

One day, Mhadji Shinde's letter arrived, articulating her achievement, praising her, telling her how strong she was …most importantly reminding her that she too had a few years of life left, just like him. He urged her to continue doing her good work as long as she lived. She had crusaded all her life… "Do not give up now…let us leave this world fighting and protecting what we created…not crestfallen and crushed. You have the strength. Destiny has been cruel to you…let nothing but death overwhelm you…"

Ahilyabai read the letter again and again. She remembered the 8-9 year old girl…protecting her creation…she shut her eyes, took a deep breath…just a couple of years more she thought…

The next day, she woke up early and reached the treasury before everyone else…

****

Ahilyabai was further pained that ,the strategies of two British officers, had achieved some success in sowing the seeds of enmity between the Shindes and Holkars. She was further ashamed to discern that it was Tukoji who was the target of these strategies. Mhadji Shinde still stood strong by the Holkar-Shinde unity…struggling hard to protect it. Mhadji had said, "When two stalwarts begin to construct themselves against each other, destruction is certain."

Ahilyabai was barely beginning to grasp the gravity of this situation when she received news that completely dislodged her…Tukoji had killed Naro Ganesh. Ahilyabai was furious. She was after all accountable till her last breath…She had to push herself to act. Act now.

****

Mukund Hari arrived with Naro Ganesh's son and daughter-in-law. He folded his hands, "Matoshri, I am in turmoil. I do not wish to resign from your services, but I am unable to overlook the fact that Tukoji has killed Naro Ganesh. I would therefore find solace if I handed over my work to his son, Ganapat Narayan. This way, I will salvage my position among my relatives too…I will train him into an able accountant in about four months…"

Ahilyabai nodded. She needed to think. "This will need approval from Pune. But in the meanwhile let them live in the palace as my guests."

Ahilyabai sent a message to Tukoji, insisting that he come and see her immediately, in fact, the very next day.

A few days went by. There was no definite news of Tukoji's visit. Ahilyabai realized her word was losing weight…In the meantime, Ahilyabai's spies informed her that Tukoji was loading 25 cannon carts. Ahilyabai immediately recognized that this was aimed at the Shindes with distinct provocation from the British. Ahilyabai stood up firmly now. She sent an official order to the Subhedar to not bother coming to Maheshwar at all but instead proceed straight to Pune.

The very next day Tukoji arrived at Maheshwar and touched Ahilyabai's feet. He spoke about how he was heartbroken with Mukta's news…Yashwantrao's death…and did not have the courage to enter the palace and face Ahilyabai…

"It's two years now since we have met. I sent you seven letters, one everyday…after Mukta's death. Spare a thought…I am living in this palace even after Muktabai has gone…Life has to be lived…and faced…you cannot run away…But that is not why I called you. You may freshen up and then meet me in a while…"

****

Ahilyabai had a lot to say to Tukoji. They met in her study. She had to discuss Naro Ganesh's killing, status of the Shinde alliance, Malhar's behavior…

"The Shindes seem to have impressed you. Do you not see my achievements or you choose to ignore them?" asked an agitated Tukoji. "No doubt you have achieved a lot…but you are capable of achieving a lot more… so much that your glory and praises should have been reverberating throughout the country. You do not seem to have the vision, moreover you remain embroiled in your household tangles and tales of vendetta… The Shindes have grown from strength to strength…They have served the Peshwas better today…and regrettably, the Shinde-Holkar unity seems to be undermined…"

"This brotherhood is a mere eyewash, Matoshri…" Ahilyabai blocked Tukoji's speech by a simple sway of her hand. "Tukoji, I can give you at least a hundred citations of their noble intent…Ali Bahadur episode, Fatehsingh, Battle of Lakheri …" Ahilyabai's voice was now rising… "Not for a moment must you forget that Mhadji Shinde could have finished you in one stroke…but he did not"

Tukoji was visibly upset at this statement. Tukoji had nothing to offer in his defence so he chose the offensive route… "Looks like I have nothing creditable to my account…"

"Yes indeed you have! You have killed Naro Ganesh…you have been too busy to pay a condolence visit to Maheshwar after Mukta and Yashwantrao passed away…" Ahilyabai now was losing her grip on her emotions, getting sarcastic…

"I am engaged in battle most of the time…where is the time for…"

"If you are occupied so successfully, then you should have been the jewel in the Peshwa's crown!'

"Armed battles need money but you never allowed…"

'Not one word! Quiet! I have never failed to send you reinforcements for battles…what I have rejected, is sanctions for your personal expenses…never again even attempt leveling this charge…"

Tukoji was quiet. He said, "With my poor health I do not wish to go to Pune."

"Neither am I getting any younger, Tukoji…If you do not wish to go, I will have to go myself to Pune."

Tukoji stood up. "I will go, Matoshri. But after this I will be unable to carry this burden of Subhedari."

Ahilyabai stood up too…I have already invited everyone to the palace. Bapu Holkar, Malhar, Kashirao Holkar…

"Then please be kind enough and make the announcement of who will inherit this Subhedari…"

"In my view" said a resolute Ahilyabai, "I have known your son to be immature and impatient…and he has shown no hints to the contrary which could compel me to alter my view…"

"But he is intelligent and educated…" protested Tukoji…

"To rule what you need is good intent and integrity above all. His intelligence will be used merely to empty the coffers. Kashirao may be physically weak due to his deformity but is a man of good integrity. Bapu Holkar is courageous. So Kashi, will be the Subhedar and Bapu Holkar, the commander-in-chief of the army."

"Matoshri , Bapu is not my son …nor my heir…" objected Tukoji further.

"You were not my son either…" Ahilyabai reminded him! Tukoji single-mindedly disputed this saying, "What if today your own son was alive…?"

Ahilyabai was prompt in responding. "If he was found incapable, the Subhedari would have still come to you!" Tukoji had no more arguments left…

Ahilyabai came out of her study…made the announcement to the other people who were invited…urged everyone to stay back for lunch and left for her private quarters. She was mentally spent now…

As soon as she exited, the initial muffled murmurs grew louder …gradually rising into a crescendo of comments… discussions…celebrations…anger…disappointments…

It was a lavish meal of traditional delicacies of Basoondi, Puran Poli, Karanji, Chirote, Sheera…Rose water sprays in use after a long time…incense sticks sending wafts of mild aroma across the six feet tall oil lamps …flowers …rangoli…with drums and bugles playing gently in the background.

Ahilyabai had barely settled in her room when an angry Malhar rushed in. With extreme impoliteness he questioned Ahilyabai on her decision…How could the next Subhedar be announced when Tukoji was still alive…how did she sidestep his right… How could she treat him this way? He was also her son-in-law, by his marriage to Anu. His eyes were like embers…spewing fire…his demeanor, threatening…

Ahillyabai was calm…almost like she had anticipated this. "It gives me no pleasure to sidestep you. But raiding people …looting them, are the traits of dacoits, not rulers. Also do not be under any illusion that being married to my Anu may bring you any special privileges or concessions…"

"Well...do not forget then...I am a full blooded Holkar...fearless...with strength in my wrist, not a weakling! I will undoubtedly obtain my rightful share of the wealth ...here and now!" Tukoji too had come in close behind the heels of his son sensing peril. Ahilyabai shot a glance at Tukoji and said, "Give me one reason...here and now...why I should not order the arrest of this boy?"

As soon as Ahilyabai uttered these words...Malhar dashed out of the room, bumped into Anu on his way out...He stopped for a moment ...wiped off the kumkum on her forehead, pushed her aside ...got astride a horse and darted down the slope of the fort and disappeared, leaving behind a humungous cloud of dust...and a crying Anu.

Ahilyabai and the others, who stood equipped to respond in case of any untoward event, were astounded. "These are not the qualities of a leader, Tukoji...you need to control your son...I am now on the last chapter of my life..."

That afternoon, two letters arrived from Pune. One from the Peshwa himself, and the other from Appaji Jagdev.

'Respected Matoshri Ahilyadevi...Manaji Gaikwad of Baroda passed away ...Had requested Tukoji to proceed to Baroda for a ceremony to be held on 3rd December 1793.But he consistently cites poor health to turn down such missions...but never misses to demand his share which many a times is out of turn...he cannot advance the glory of the Holkar empire at this rate...Kindly ensure that he reaches Pune at the earliest. There is an urgent need for discussions to chart the future course of action...'

Signed and sealed: Shrimant Sawai Madhavrao

The other letter from Appaji Jagdev alerted Ahilyabai of the growing influence of the Shindes at the court of Pune...Ahilyabai thrust both the letters in front of Tukoji. His face lost color and he left the room...

****

It was unanimously decided…On the auspicious day of Akshay Tritiya, Kashirao, Bapu Holkar and Tukoji would leave for Pune for final approvals. Ahilyabai even dispatched a letter to Pune announcing and assuring their arrival and hoping that this meeting would also herald a new beginning of a glorious Shinde- Holkar era.

But destiny had something else on the cards…

Mhadji Shinde died in Pune of a brief, severe, illness…Ahilyabai was crestfallen. Once again fate had skirted Ahilyabai's hopes… One of the two pillars of the Peshwa administration had crumbled…She was grieving for a man whose heroism and fearlessness had successfully kept many enemies of the state, at bay. It would be generations before people could come to witness a man of his stature again…

Tukoji did not seem sad…In fact, destiny provided him with a brilliant excuse to evade this expedition… "All does not look good at Pune…How can a strong, healthy man die all of a sudden…I think, I need to exercise caution about going to Pune, Matoshri…"

****

Akshay Tritiya had come and gone by…Tukoji did not leave for Pune. There was also news of Malhar…he was assembling armies! Ahilyabai sent for Kashirao and Bapu Holkar to go after Malhar and bring him to Maheshwar by using a good word …if not, by force.

Ahilyabai said only one thing to Tukoji… "Is it not amusing, that Malhar times his rebellion exactly at the time you had to go to Pune…?" and left the room.

****

Harkuaai had been away for some work. She returned to the palace after a long time. She was pained to know about Malhar's rebellion and his eventual arrest. Tukoji made fervent appeals to free Malhar. But Harkuaai too agreed that Tukoji did not have the force to control Malhar. After the killing of Naro Ganesh, Rukhmabai too was keeping very poor health. Tukoji himself could not stay away from alcohol despite repeated promises to Ahilyabai… and in fact, even after imposing a ban on alcohol in some cities…

The two women spent a long time conferring…Ahilyabai felt much stronger now with Harkuaai's return…

****

Finally, once again, Ahilyabai set a date … an auspicious moment for Tukoji's departure to Pune. Tukoji looked rather disinclined as he left unenthusiastically. Soon enough, Ahilyabai received news that Tukoji had not crossed the Narmada and had, in fact, turned back citing bad omens! Ahilyabai was exasperated…but she kept her patience …once again found another auspicious time…performed many rituals for his well being…and managed to set Tukoji asail! She kept gazing at the boat carrying Tukoji…wondering if she had enough time left …to ever see Tukoji again…Harkuaai touched Ahilyabai…snapping her out of her stupor…Ahilyabai did not feel like going home…she wanted the Narmada to now engulf her…bring peace…

****

Soon after returning home Ahilybai received news of Rukhmabai's demise. Tukoji was away…Ahilyabai was in a dilemma…But before she could fix on a course of action…a letter from Tukoji pulled the rug from under her feet. The letter was one final request to Ahilyabai… 'Free my son, Malhar, else I will abort my mission to Pune…and slash my throat here and now!' The letter also assured Ahilyabai that Tukoji would ensure that Malhar would never be a menace…

Ahilyabai read and re-read the letter. So this was a deal.

Malhar's release, in exchange of Tukoji's life and the Holkar pride. The honor of Ahilyabai's word that Tukoji would indeed arrive in Pune and inheritance issues would be discussed. Ahilyabai was closing in on 70 now. She simply wanted to rest the kingdom, at the feet of the Peshwas ...with its glory intact…without bloodshed within the family or internal feuds. Ahilyabai freed Malhar but warned him not to come to Maheshwar when he requested for a visit. "Go straight to your father on his way to Pune", was her reply.

The only final mission for Ahilyabai now, was an uneventful handover of the Holkar kingdom. It was under her trust…given to her by her father-in-law. She had protected it…developed the land…promoted education…Now she wanted to retire…retire at a time when she knew her reflexes were failing…strength depleting…she was no longer fit to be at the helm. She wanted to step down gracefully and more importantly not bring any disgrace to the Holkars.

The next day, Ahilyabai had some tasks set. She knew she did not have much time left…Harkuaai saw Ahilyabai going towards her private treasury.

Ahilyabai came out with sacks full of gold coins…and a letter addressed to Tukoji stating very clearly that she was using her private wealth, to repay the debt incurred by Tukoji in the name of the State. The accounts stood cleared…and thenceforth she was to distance herself from any and every transaction made by him under the Holkar seal. She sent a final word of caution to Tukoji …about his alcohol addiction and his son. She emphasized that both spelt ruin.

Harkuaai nodded her approval ...giving Ahilyabai a look brimming with admiration and respect. The two women were once again engrossed in discussions…

"I will have, just one regret …" lamented Ahilyabai… "I could not mentor a competent heir for the Holkars…and that is a leadership failure…not creating a second line of command with vision, commitment and a sense of propriety."

"That was due to the fact..." Harkuaai dared to point out softly... "that you looked for a 'Holkar'..."

Ahilyabai agreed. I should have looked for but a valiant sardar ...not a Holkar sardar. I tried my best Harkuaai...gave my life here...but am leaving behind a legacy of uncertainty. Had I started even a few years ago, I could have still fostered a second command line..."

"...and got killed by Malhar?" reacted Harkuaai impatiently!

"If it meant the rise of the Holkar flag...it would have been every bit worth the sacrifice..." contested Ahilyabai.

"Even today, your sacrifice is every bit worth its while..."beamed Harkuaai...

The two women...almost the same age...were more friends than a mother-in-law and a daughter-in-law...

Ahilyabai was tired. She lay down on the bed. Harkuaai got her some fruit juice...but by then Ahilyabai's eyes were red and watering...fever had set in and her eyes looked glazy...

****

It was Makar Sankrant ...the sesame-jaggery sweets arrived from Pune. Ahilyabai had no appetite. She was just relieved that Tukoji had reached Pune. Harkuaai sat next to Ahilyabai. The fever was hardening its grip on Ahilyabai. In the last four months she was reduced to half her size...

Ahilyabai was restless without work...She would push work as long as she could in the day...By evening she would have no energy...she simply awaited news from Pune.

Ahilyabai made arrangements to financially secure all her trusted people...Renu, Anjana, Raghoji, Bhagoji, Bharmal dada, Appaji ...her informers...She sent huge chunks in charity to her native town and many places in 'Maharashtra'...Pandharpur, Jejuri, Kolhapur, Rajapur, Chaundi, Puntambe...

All papers were signed and sealed. Ahilyabai sat down for

meditation…and a scroll arrived from Pune.

****

Some guests from Pune were on a pilgrimage to Kashi. Ahilyabai was requested to make arrangements. A tired Ahilyabai was energized …She sent for Bharmaldada, Ganpat Narayan and others. She could visualize the route… Verul..Ghrushneshwar…Burhanpur…then Nemad…our Maheshwar…further towards Ujjain following Bundel up to the Yamuna…the Prayag…then Kashi and finally Gaya. She made sure all posts were informed…security was arranged with horse riders lining the route…emergency arrangements, escape routes in an eventuality…everything was detailed. She wrote nine letters…It was past midnight as she retired…

****

Every day, news of the Nizam, gaining strength was doing the rounds. Forces were gathering at Pune. A clash with the Nizam seemed inevitable. Every single day Ahilyabai hoped that the Holkar flag would fly high and lead the Peshwa's forces valiantly … regain and establish their supremacy at Pune. Harkuaai would sit next to Ahilyabai…assuring her…diverting her mind… pushing her to eat…

Ahilyabai's health was failing…energy barely breathing now in her frail frame. The fever was rising by the day and the sparkle in the eyes had dulled…

…and one day, the news of the victory of the Peshwas arrived with a letter from Bapu Holkar giving her the details of the victory…the courage shown by the Holkars…the Shinde-Holkar unity had spelt doom for the Nizam… supported ably by the Bhonsales and the Patwardhans… Complex tactics and impregnable maze by our soldiers brought them to a truce…5 crores to be received in 3 years…territories worth 30 lakhs…fort of Daulatabad…and more!

Ahilyabai was ecstatic! She seemed to have a burst of energy! For someone who could barely speak a few sentences…she was now smiling wide…the smile reigniting a bleak twinkle deep inside her eyes. She managed to get up and sit…announced distribution of sweets to every household…expressed her desire to sit in the palanquin atop an elephant and go to the temple of Lord Shiva…showering hampers of sugar and sweetmeats on her subjects…

Harkuaai was worried…so much exertion…She tried to calm an excited Ahilyabai who was almost trying to get up and walk towards the palace temple…Harkuaai and others supported her as she went to offer her gratitude at the feet of the Lord…showered flowers on the Holkar throne and their flag…and then everything around her began to spin…a blur…she was losing consciousness…disoriented. Ahilyabai was smiling and talking incoherently… Peshwas…. Holkars…remembering her father-in-law…the promise…The Vaidya rubbed some concoction on her tongue and Ahilyabai calmed down…

****

The month of Jyeshtha[*] had passed by…the last two months had been the same…every time medicines were administered, Ahilyabai would sleep peacefully…then as the effect wore off she would discuss the past with Harkuaai in a drowsy state…muttering incoherent incidents from her childhood. The month of Aashaadh[*] saw some slight improvement. Ahilyabai would go the temple on the banks of the Narmada, with the support of Renu and Anjana…sit on a white square rug…listen to devotional songs and kirtans…as and when the fever rose, she would rest her back on the bolster…her head resting on her shoulder…eyes shut…drowsy. The people of Maheshwar could not bear to see the once energetic …sharp…brilliant lady sitting in this weak frame…

That week, Trimbak Hardas, a renowned Pundit had a lecture

on Ramayana. Ahilyabai would attend it every evening... The last day of the lecture series...Ahilyabai returned home and that night developed very high fever...accompanied by shivering and chills. The Vaidya was trying all medicines...her fever could not be controlled...people began to congregate at the palace...Bharmaldada would not allow anyone in...When Ahilyabai got to know...she spoke softly to Harkuaai... "Let people come in to see me...they are like my children...do not stop them..."

Even lying on the bed Ahilyabai would instruct on how taxes on food for the common man should be minimized...Maulavis would come with blessings...Pundits with prayers...her energies were depleting with every passing day... Ahilyabai had stopped intake of food from 'Ekaadashi'[**]... she could barely move her lips now ... she was drowsy...

...and then a letter arrived from Pune. Harkuaai opened it and she knew Ahilyabai had to hear this. She sent for the Vaidya. He had to pull Ahilyabai back into consciousness for this letter...somehow...

The Vaidya said he would try but he had to wait until the evening till the ambient temperatures dropped and it was cool for the medicine to take effect... Oil massages and the 'Mahamaatra'[21] was administered..There was some movement. Harkuaai called out to Bharmaldada. He read out the letter hurriedly.

' Respected Matoshri... I hear you are not keeping good health. You are the strongest stalwart of this regime...a woman who can achieve the impossible. You safeguarded the Shinde-Holkar unity...brought us glory and protected the honor of the Peshwas, every moment of your life...The Peshwa regime is eternally indebted to you and needs you...Please take care of yourself...'

Signed and sealed by the Peshwa.

Ahilyabai smiled...a smile of peace... relief... fulfillment...a smile that faded away into drowsiness ...lost to unconsciousness.

But Bharmaldada and Harkuaai showered the Vaidya with gifts...this was a debt they could never repay... restoring Ahilyabai's consciousness so that she could hear the words of the Peshwas...The last words she heard, validated and encapsulated the purpose of her life...her promise stood fulfilled.

The night moved very slowly...The rays of the early morning sun gradually defining something fateful ...the silhouette of an extraordinary era receding...Ahilyabai had passed away peacefully ... It is known, that her beloved cow in the shed at the palace too breathed her last along with Ahilyabai....

Ahilyabai's palanquin left the palace. All the flowers of Maheshwar lined her final journey. The skies, drizzling grief...the river waters of the Narmada, overwhelmed...An extraordinary lady...Karmayogini's last journey with the Holkar flag flying high...

A grieving crowd feeling orphaned...as they followed the palanquin to the banks of the Narmada...where Lokmata Ahilyadevi was to rest forever in her embrace...The city of Maheshwar resonated ...as people extolled... ' Lokmata Karmayogini Ahilyadevi Amar rahe! Amar rahe! Longlive Lokmata, Karmayogini...Ahilyadevi!

****

References

1. Rangoli : Designs created by a coarse white powder on the ground as decoration

2. Vahini saheb : Vahini is a way of addressing the brother's wife. 'Saheb' is a reckoning of respect.

3. Tai saheb : A way of addressing the older sister or a sister-in –law.

4. Subhedar: Chieftain; Subhedari: Rights conferred upon a Subhedar

5. Mamanji : A way to reckon the father-in-law.

6. Aai : means mother.

7. Dada: A way to address the older brother

8. Paithani: A silk sari woven at a place called Paithan. The signature border designs used real gold and silver threads for weaving intricate patterns

9. Goddess Lakshmi: Goddess of wealth.

10. Mangalsutra: A neckpiece of black beads normally strung in a gold chain with a pendant worn by women as a mark of being married.

11. : Navratra is a festival celebrated for nine days . Pujas and dance mark the nine days and nine nights. The tenth day is celebrated as Dussehra.

12. : Gurudakshina :A tradition where after the guru or the teacher completes imparting knowledge to the pupil can ask for

an offering from the pupil as fees, or otherwise.

13. : Dharamshala : A place where travelers could stay at nominal charges or at places free of cost.

14. Prasad : A bite size offering (morsel) of sweetmeat or fruit or any other food item which held the blessings of the deity to whom the entire offering was made during a Puja.

15. Dandpatta: A native form of combat using long free flowing, sharp and flat metal belts .

16. Daasi : A female servant

17. Dharma : religion

18. Khaandaarani: a lady who becomes the wife by virtue of her marriage to the person's sword

19. Navratna : Nine precious gems

20. Prasad : A part of the offering made to the deity, said to carry the blessings of God , to be shared by all devotees after the Puja.

21. Mahaamatra : a special mega dose of medicine.

22. Mahals : Palaces

*. : Months of the Hindu Calender : Chaitra, Vaishakh, Jyeshtha, Aashaadh, Shraavan, Bhadrapad, Ashwin, Kaartik, Maargasheersh, Paush, Maagh, Falgun coinciding with March and ending around February

**. : Ekadashi : Means the 11th day of each half of the month in the Vedic Lunar Calender.

Chronology of Events

It must be noted that historians differ in their beliefs regarding the occurrence of certain incidents, dates, time and their places. For eg: According to respected Shri M.S Dikshit, Malerao became the Subhedar on 3-6-1766 ; whereas respected Shri Hiralal Sharma maintains that it was on 23-8-1766.

16-3-1693	:	Malharrao Holkar was born
1720	:	Malharrao proved his valor against the Nizam
Around 1721	:	Mama Bhojraj Baargal offered his daughter Gautama to Malharrao Holkar in marriage. Malharrao married Gautamabai
Around 1725	:	Ahilyabai was born at Chaundi
Around 1725	:	Dayabahadur's defeat
25-2-1728	:	Palkhed Mission
Around 1729	:	Defeat of Mohamadshah Bangash
1734	:	Battle of Boondi
20-1-1734	:	Malharrao receives Subhedari and private territory worth 3 lakhs in the name of Gautamabai

22-2-1735	:	Truce between Mir Baksh and Malharrao Holkar
1736	:	Malharrao accompanies Bajirao on missions to the North
1737	:	Battle of Bhopal
1739	:	Malharrao and Bajirao engage with Nadirshah from Iran
28-4-1740	:	Bajirao Peshwa's death
25-6-1740	:	Nanasaheb becomes the next Peshwa
1742-1743	:	Malharrao's missions at Prayag, Malva,Bengal
1745	:	Birth of Ahilyabai's son Malerao
1746-1748	:	Malharrao on missions to Karnataka, Rajmahal,Nevai
1748	:	Birth of Ahilyabai's daughter Mukta
15-12-1749	:	Death of Shahu Maharaj
14-12-1750	:	Suicide of Ishwarsingh
17-3-1754	:	Death of Ahilyabai's husband Khanderao
July 1755	:	Jayappa Shinde murdered
September 1755	:	Madhosingh poisoned to death
12-3-1756	:	Battle of Saavnur
Around 1756	:	Marriage of Ahilyabai's son Malerao
22-1-1757	:	Mayhem by Abdally in Delhi
10-1-1760	:	Killing of Dattaji Shinde
1-8-1760	:	Delhi captured by the Marathas